BLACK LIGHT: ROCKED

LIVIA GRANT

BLACK COLLAR PRESS

Published by Black Collar Press

Editing by Paul Von Karmann

Cover Artist - Eris Adderly

Ebook ISBN: 978-0-9982191-2-7

Print ISBN: 978-0-9982191-6-5

Author's Note: Black Light: Rocked is a steamy bad-boy rocker romance with an HEA. It is meant for mature audiences only. It has explicit sexual situations as well as BDSM power exchange elements that may not be suitable for all readers.

First Electronic Edition: December, 2016

First Print Edition: August, 2017

❋ Created with Vellum

BLACK LIGHT SERIES

Infamous Love, **A Black Light Prequel** by Livia Grant

Black Light: Rocked by Livia Grant ✓

Black Light: Exposed by Jennifer Bene

Black Light: Valentine Roulette by Eight USA Today and Bestselling Authors

Black Light: Suspended by Maggie Ryan

Black Light: Cuffed by Measha Stone

Black Light: Rescued by Livia Grant (coming summer 2017) ✓

Writing stories is my passion. Being an author is my dream. It's only made possible because of the love and support of my dear husband and kids. With a more than full-time day job and writing into the wee hours each night and every weekend, it doesn't leave much time for 'normal.' Thank you for the hundreds of meals you've prepared, dozens of loads of laundry you've washed and thousands of hours you've let me put on my headphones and slip away into my own little world rather than being present in yours.

I adore you for your understanding and support.

BLACK LIGHT: ROCKED

They had unfinished business.
She went there for closure, but he deserved his revenge.
They both learned to be careful what you wish for.

When Samantha Stone hears the popular rock band Crushing
Stones created by her childhood sweetheart is headlining at a new
dance club nearby, she considers it fate. She's waited seven years
to get answers. Why had he deserted her without even saying
good-bye?

Jonah "Cash" Carter has scanned the throngs of fans for years
looking for her. Waiting. When he spots Sami in the crowd, he
freezes mid-song. He'd named his band for a reason, and tonight
would be the night he finally got to crush a Stone.

Too many secrets. Too much history. Can they find their way
to the truth without destroying each other?

CHAPTER 1

"*I* give up. You win. I'm gonna leave your boring ass here alone, sitting on this couch in your raggedy old robe surrounded by your boring law books. I'm meeting the girls at Mickey's Pub and we're gonna have fun without you." Samantha's friend Megan paused to pin her with a pitying smile before delivering her parting shot. "It's Friday night! You're supposed to take a break. The saddest part is you'll probably be parked here studying all night."

God, she hated to lie. She sucked at it. For the briefest of moments Sam considered letting Megan in on her little secret, but just in the nick of time, Megan leaned in to give her a peck on the cheek good-bye and spun to head out of her apartment.

Samantha called after her friend just before the door slammed, "Have fun!"

The second the door closed, Samantha sprang to her feet, throwing her terry cloth robe to the back of the chair to reveal the black mini-skirt and fitted gold blouse she'd been hiding. She caught her reflection in the long decorative mirror next to the entertainment center and stopped dead in her tracks.

Who was that woman and what the hell was she thinking? Her

heart thumped hard against her ribs as Samantha allowed renewed doubt to wash over her like a tidal wave. The litany of fear had been running on a continuous loop in her brain for the last two weeks. Eleven days to be exact. Since the minute she found out Cash Carter would be in town. She considered it divine fate that his band, Crushing Stones, was headlining at the new Runway club less than three blocks from her apartment.

He's never going to remember me.

Even if he does, he probably hates me.

He has a girlfriend.

No, he has many girlfriends.

I've wasted enough of my life regretting losing something I never really had.

Rinse. Repeat.

She glanced at the designer watch her father had given her as a graduation gift. The show would start in just over an hour. She needed to get moving if she was going.

Guilt crashed in on her as she contemplated defying the direct orders of her overprotective parent. There had been nothing ambiguous in her father's instructions. Jonah "Cash" Carter was no good for his little girl, which meant he was off-limits to Samantha. Hadn't she been hurt enough by his desertion seven years before?

But she was twenty-three years old now. And daddy was a thousand miles away. And the VIP ticket to the grand opening night's show she'd spent $1,425 on was burning a hole in her backpack. She'd be a fool to throw away that kind of money.

Talking to the empty room, Sam launched into a monologue as she rushed towards her small bedroom. "Hell, even if I don't go in, I can at least go down and see if I can just catch a glimpse of him from afar while I pawn the ticket to try to get my money back."

Even as she said it, she knew that was a lie, too. She was weak. There was no way she'd be this close to Jonah and not watch the show. She started a fresh litany as she rushed to get ready.

It'll be way too crowded for him to ever see me.

I'll just watch from a safe distance.

It'll be great just to hear his music in person again.

I was there when he wrote his first song. I deserve to see his success.

No, I deserve to see his new life—the one he chose over me.

She had picked her apartment for its relatively low rent, which meant she could barely fit her queen mattress set in the small bedroom, but it had been worth it to get the en suite bathroom that sported a whirlpool tub and a huge mirror. It was one of the few luxury items in the small space. She hadn't been able to put on her makeup before Megan stopped over so she rushed to throw on some mascara and lipstick, reassuring herself primping wasn't really important since he'd never see her anyway.

She threw on the high-heeled pumps she'd planned on wearing, but had second thoughts as she could see light snow coming down in her Georgetown neighborhood. She reached under the bed to pull out her black leather fashion boots. She normally wore them with her more conservative skirts, but she had to admit she looked good as she caught one last glimpse of herself in the full-length mirror.

Grabbing her black leather jacket, she threw her cross-body purse on and headed out the door before she could chicken out. She didn't bother with the elevator, taking the three stories of steps to the lobby of her apartment building just off Wisconsin Avenue.

Jamal, the building's doorman and pseudo security guard, held the door wide as she approached. She appreciated his surprised whistle. "Whoa there, Miss Stone. You're looking mighty fine tonight. Do you have a big date?" The cheeky man, old enough to be her father, flashed a broad smile.

"Nope. No date. Just going to..." She stalled. If she really did scalp the ticket she'd be back in fifteen minutes.

Say it. Tell him you'll be right back.

"I'm going to a concert." She needed to stop kidding herself.

There was absolutely nothing, save her father blocking entrance to the new club, she could think of that would stop her from being in the same room as Jonah. Just knowing she'd be breathing the same air as him, if only from afar, had her heart thumping hard again.

Jamal was rambling on, unaware of her internal struggle. "... new club sure is going to bring a lot of traffic to our neighborhood. I just hope I get to see some of the famous people they keep showing on the TV. I heard the owners are that threesome that made the news last year when they went public at the political fundraiser."

She didn't have time to chitchat. She was running late already. "Yep, that's the club I'm headed to. You're talking about Jaxson Davidson and Chase Cartwright and their girlfriend. I think her name is Ella or Emma or something like that."

"She looks like one happy lady."

Sam thought so too, but hell, who wouldn't be happy with not one, but two, super-hot, rich boyfriends.

"I'll catch you later. I've gotta run."

With each step she took away from her apartment, her anxiety grew. It had been seven years since the disastrous last time she'd seen her longtime friend and short-time boyfriend, Jonah Carter. Looking back, she'd been such a foolish teenager full of dreams of happily-ever-afters when clearly all Jonah had dreamed of was making music. He'd never hidden his goals of fame and fortune from her. She just never thought that he wouldn't want to take her along for the ride, considering they'd been a big part of each other's lives since second grade.

Sam pushed the painful memories of Jonah's desertion of their friendship back down into the neat little lockbox she hid in her heart. Those sad memories hung out there, along with the pain of losing her mother to breast cancer when she was seven, and having to put her beloved dog, Rocky, to sleep just before she left for law school the year before.

She was still a block away when she caught up with a line of limousines waiting to round the corner to drop off their VIP guests. She was walking through the dusting of snow faster than they could creep forward through the slush-covered street.

Samantha pulled the collar of her jacket up to block out the biting wind, suddenly aware that it was a real possibility that Jonah was inside one of those very vehicles. Chances are he'd be partying with Ryan and the rest of the band as they headed to another sold-out show. That was easier for Sam to imagine than Jonah alone in the private luxury with one, or more, of the gorgeous women he was regularly photographed with. It was impossible to see a story about the lead singer of Crushing Stones without noticing the throngs of women always surrounding him. She tried to take comfort that she rarely saw the same woman more than a few times before she'd be replaced by someone with bigger breasts or a thinner waist.

The sidewalk was growing crowded as couples dressed in tuxedos and evening gowns seemed to come from all directions. Sam had to stop to let a couple cross in front of her to enter the new psychic shop. It had just opened the week before and from the looks of things, the paranormal shop was doing bang-up business.

I should have saved enough time to stop in and have my fortune read. Maybe they could tell me if I'm about to make an ass of myself or not.

By the time she rounded the corner to see the three-story grand entrance to the newest attraction in the nation's capital, it took all of her courage to keep putting one foot in front of the other. She caught a glimpse of herself in the window of the Apple store and felt self-conscious. She'd dressed for a rock concert, not a grand ball. She was close enough now to see couples exiting their limousines ahead as she came up on the VIP entrance to the club. There were stanchions setup to keep the photographers, paparazzi and nosy gawkers at bay. She dreaded having to thread through the throngs to get to the main entrance.

She pressed forward as far as she could before coming to a halt. Bodies pressed in around her, swallowing her up in the crush of shouting women, currently calling out to the A-list celebrities posing for photos in the middle of the wide red carpet. Samantha recognized two stars who'd been nominated for Oscars just the season before.

She was trapped long enough to see the next limousine pull up to deposit the newly elected Vice-President of the USA. She shouldn't be surprised to see the politician there considering the owners of the new club had very publicly endorsed the moderate ticket over Jaxson Davidson's own conservative father. Still, she had to push down the urge to turn around and flee home to the safety of her apartment.

"Excuse me, miss. This is the VIP entrance. Unless you have media credentials, I'm afraid I'm going to have to ask you to leave this area." The security guard that pressed next to her was a full foot taller than her, even in her high-heeled boots. But it was his broad chest threatening to burst out of his skin-tight black long-sleeve shirt that drew her attention. The guy was built like a brick wall—a very serious brick wall.

When she failed to answer, he reached to clamp his hand on her bicep and began to pull her out of the crowd.

Sam struggled to dig in her heels, hoping to pull loose. She might as well have saved her energy.

She tried something different. "Wait! I have a ticket."

Paying her no attention, he didn't stop until he'd pulled her all the way to the back of the crush of reporters. She finally had enough space to reach into her small purse and pull out the coveted VIP ticket she'd spent so much money on. She pushed it forward, waving it in front of the security guard's face until he had no choice but to acknowledge her again.

The guard snapped the invitation out of her hand.

"Hey! That's mine!"

He threw her a dirty look as he examined the thick piece of paper. She'd thought it curious as she'd examined it at home to find several holographic emblems embedded in the fancy paper. Only now was she understanding that tonight was by invitation only and that they might prevent her entering as she was not the initial owner of the invite.

The guard pressed the small button on the earpiece in his left ear. She saw a small microphone clipped to the collar of his shirt.

"Need a ticket check. Over." She couldn't hear the other side of the conversation, but the guard held the invitation closer to squint at the small coding along the bottom of the piece of paper. "Tango, Henry, One-forty nine."

Thirty seconds slid by as Mr. Muscles gaze dissected her. His voice was gruff when he finally addressed her."

"I need to see your ID."

"Why?"

"Please, don't argue with me, miss. Tonight's event is by invitation only and I'm quite certain you are not the original owner of this ticket."

Samantha fought down the urge to call the jerk a dumbass. She didn't appreciate being treated like a criminal, especially after dumping so much of her savings on the paper he held in his hand.

"I'm sure you're right. I look nothing like Thomas Horton."

Muscle's eyes widening was the only hint she'd surprised him. She pressed forward. "I bought this invitation off Mr. Horton, my law professor, for $1,425. Instead of using the ticket or gifting it to one of his students, the jerk decided to hold a bidding war after class last week trying to get the most cash out of the ticket as he could."

The smallest of smiles played at Muscle's lips. "Sounds like a typical lawyer to me."

Sam couldn't hide her own smile. "Hey, watch it. I'm studying to be a lawyer too."

"I'm sorry to hear that."

So typical. How she hated the idea of joining the ranks of a profession that the vast majority of the public loathed. God, she wished she had the balls to defy her father and uncle. She held tight to her pledge to use her education to defend those who didn't have a voice of their own.

Now wasn't the time to wallow about her total lack of assertiveness where her only remaining parent was concerned. She'd have plenty of time to wallow about that after the concert.

Instead of leading her farther away, Muscles turned and started pulling her by his vice grip on her elbow through the throng of onlookers. When they arrived at the red velvet swag attached to the golden waist-high pole, he reached out to unbuckle the hook, holding the swag aside to allow her to pass.

"Thanks," was all Samantha could muster as she moved forward slowly, reaching to snap up her ticket from his outstretched hand as she stepped onto the red carpet. Flashes of cameras immediately pointed in her direction, temporarily blinding her.

Wouldn't the journalists be disappointed when they tried to figure out what her connection was to the famous owners of the new club and came up empty handed? Unlike the dozens of VIP couples to walk the carpet before her, Samantha didn't bother to stop and pose for the cameras. On the contrary, she rushed towards the wide double doors being held open by two doormen.

The sound of a pounding dance beat grew louder as she approached the building. The two-story windows that formed the circular main entrance to Runway were lightly tinted in the area surrounding the door marked VIP Entrance. She could barely make out bodies moving through the smoky glass.

The second she entered the three-story club she knew she was in trouble. While the club was huge by club standards, it was much more intimate than she'd expected for a concert venue. Rather than the rows of anonymous chairs that would fade into a dark crowd, the main dance floor surrounding the rounded stage was filled with small round tables covered with linen tablecloths. Neon lights lit the space in a modern, classy hue helping the glittering bows wrapped around each covered chair twinkle in the light.

A high see-through railing barricaded the VIP entrance off from the main door to the club. In a city like Washington DC, there promised to be no shortage of VIPs and the club was certainly setup to protect their privacy.

Directly across from her stood a two-story high oval bar surrounded by high-backed glass stools where patrons congregated, ordering top-end booze from well-dressed bartenders. What looked like thousands of bottles of every liquor imaginable were stocked so high, there were rolling ladders bartenders could use to reach top-shelf liquors.

Everything about the space screamed high-class money. Samantha should know. She'd been raised in one of the wealthiest families in her hometown in Texas. Her family were very big fish, but she was reminded often since coming to the nation's capital that she'd grown up in a very small pond. This kind of opulence was over the top. Suddenly cognizant of the fact that she had shown up looking like the girl-next-door at a royal coronation made her want to spin around and rush back out the way she'd come, but people were pressing in behind her.

She was being urged forward towards what looked like a receiving line and as she got closer to the front, she recognized the threesome she had just talked about with her doorman.

Holy shit. They were welcoming all of the guests. They were going to boot her out.

Sam's heart pounded hard as she tried to come up with something to say to the owners of the club. Somehow she didn't think admitting to them that she was there because she was in love with Cash Carter would help her case since literally every warm-blooded woman in the world could say the same. They'd boot her out as a crazed stalker fan.

A beautiful Asian woman with a pixie haircut was checking invitations just before the threesome stood shaking hands. When it was her turn, Samantha held the sought-after paper out with a trembling hand.

"Welcome to Runway," the woman smiled warmly, putting Sam at ease the tiniest bit. Her smile didn't waver as she checked the bottom coding on the invitation before looking up into Sam's eyes.

"Ah, so you're the lucky recipient of Mr. Horton's invitation. He almost didn't make the final invitation cut. Seeing how he decided to profit from the invitation sent by his old friend Roberta instead of coming to the show tells me we should have cut him after all."

Surely they wouldn't turn her away. Oh God, please, don't turn her away.

An older woman with hair dyed a bit too red leaned across to hold her hand out to Samantha.

"Nice to meet you, my dear. I should have known Thomas would ditch out at the last second. The least he could have done is come by to say hi, the bastard."

Samantha didn't know how to respond to that. She agreed with red's assessment of her professor too much to try to defend him.

Red pressed her. "Let me guess. He sold you the ticket?"

"Afraid so."

"So how much cash did he make avoiding me?" At least she was smiling, good-naturedly.

"He auctioned it off. I paid $1,425 for the ticket."

The older red-head whistled a surprised whistle, "Well, at least that's something. I'd be depressed if he'd sold it on eBay for $50." Her laughter caught the attention of the handsome, tall man standing next to her.

Sam now stood face to face with the one and only Jaxson Davidson. He was even more handsome in person than in magazines. He stood over six-feet tall, looking sharp in his tuxedo. His closely trimmed beard was the only hint of his reputed dangerous side.

"Welcome to Runway." He reached to shake her hand.

"Thank you, Mr. Davidson," she managed to say calmly.

"Jaxson. And you are? I don't think we've had the pleasure of meeting."

"Oh, I'm nobody. I bought the ticket from my law professor."

He frowned as he stopped shaking her hand, gripping her a bit harder rather than releasing her.

"You don't look like a *nobody,* young lady. You should ask my Emma here how I feel about beautiful young women putting themselves down."

Samantha's heart was in her throat as surprise warred with anger that he'd chastise her so publicly. Who the hell did this guy think he was, anyway?

His girlfriend, Emma, leaned against him slipping her arm in his intimately to talk softly. It was hard to hear her over the pounding dance music wafting through the open space.

"Don't mind Jaxson. He's just had a lot of practice trying to convince me not to put myself down. It looks like he forgot that he only has the right to do that with me, not every guest here tonight."

Sam didn't miss the cautioning look Jaxson threw at his beautiful girlfriend who dared to cross him in public. The third lover to the trio, at least if you believed the tabloids, leaned in to hug Emma's back to his chest.

"You're flirting with danger, Emma. I'd let this pretty lady pass if I were you before Jax decides to remind you who's in charge tonight." Chase Cartwright was as drop-dead gorgeous as Jaxson, even if he was light to Jaxson's dark. As the men loosely sandwiched Emma, Samantha felt an uncharacteristic surge of jealousy as she realized how lucky this young woman was who looked so much like her.

Jaxson recovered, prodding Sam again. "I promise, I won't bite. What's your name, if you don't mind me asking?"

She kept it simple. "I'm Samantha."

To her relief, they handed her invitation back. She'd add the paper to her scrapbook as the last tiny link to her childhood friend and crush, Jonah Carter.

"Well, I hope you have fun tonight, Samantha. Please enjoy the cocktails and hors d'oeuvres. They're on the house for our grand opening. You're welcome to head to the bar or find a table on the main floor. We're gonna have Cash and the boys start their show in just about an hour."

Sam tucked the invitation back into her small purse as she said her goodbyes to the celebrities she'd never see again. As she meandered down the two steps to the main floor, she marveled at how accurate Jonah's dreams had been.

From the time they became friends, her in the second grade, him in the fourth, he'd known with laser focus that he would be a famous singer and songwriter. She'd always been a bit jealous of the clarity with which he saw his future. Yet if she were honest with herself, she'd loved his dream because she had always planned on being beside him every step of the way.

A familiar sadness settled into her gut. It was the melancholy of abandonment. She'd always suspected a long-term romance with a man larger than life like Jonah was a long shot, but never in a million years had she expected him to walk out on their friendship. Sure, her father had been a bit of an obstacle for them by not approving of his daughter's choice in friends, but Jonah hadn't even stayed in town after high school long enough to give their budding romance a fighting chance.

She was forced to give up on her walk down memory lane in order to plot out where the best place would be to watch Jonah from afar—undetected, yet close enough to experience the show.

As the club name suggested, a six-foot wide expanse of stage jutted out at least ten yards into the center of the dance floor, creating a runway for shows and concerts. She moved off to the far right side of the room, next to one of the circular pillars that supported the second-story balcony.

Samantha grabbed a high-back barstool as she passed a tall-top table and dragged it into the shadows next to the farthest pillar. She wasn't far from the hallway that led to the restrooms. She'd have a perfect side view of the entire runway and could still see the majority of the main stage.

The pounding beat of dance music was just loud enough to make it difficult to carry on conversations, which suited her just fine. There was no one she wanted to converse with.

The heavy techno vibe set an upbeat mood for the opening extravaganza. She craned her neck to get a good look around. On the second floor was the DJ's balcony, lit up with a spotlight on Elixxir, the big name DJ that Runway had famously nabbed from a club in L.A.

"Care for some calamari, miss?" The waiter in a white suit jacket and black pants, bow tie and cummerbund, held out the tray and a stack of napkins. She turned him away—the thought of putting food in her stomach made her nauseous.

With each passing minute, she became more nervous, questioning why she'd come. The last time she'd seen Jonah had been the fateful night of his senior prom almost seven years before. It was to have been such a special night, but it had ended in disaster instead.

In many ways, at least romantically, she'd been stuck in limbo since that pivotal night, pitifully waiting for Jonah to come back for her, which she knew intellectually was utterly ridiculous. There was no question that he'd moved on. Her hope for tonight was to get closure for her heart so she could finally move on herself.

The wait for the show to start was messing with her confidence and had her questioning if she'd done the right thing in coming. The litany of self-doubt was on auto-loop in her head again.

He won't even remember me if he sees me.

Even if he does, he probably hates me.

He has a girlfriend.

No, he has many girlfriends.

You've wasted enough of your life regretting losing something you never really had.

This time she didn't rinse and repeat. This time she flagged a waiter down to grab a flute of bubbling champagne. She held up the glass in a silent toast to her long-lost best friend.

Her pulse raced as she recognized that while she may not be able to see him, he was currently less than a few hundred feet away. It was the closest they'd been in almost seven years.

Tonight was about ending her insane obsession with her teenage dreams. Tonight, she'd see with her own eyes that Jonah had moved on. She could celebrate his magnificent success from afar and when she left this building, she vowed she'd be moving on as well.

She guzzled the flute of champagne with her final toast.

To closure.

* * *

"FIFTEEN MINUTES, MR. CARTER." It was the fifth countdown warning in the last hour. Someone seriously needed to tell the clueless stage manager to take a chill pill. She'd been running around like a crazy lady and it was giving him a headache. He was already nearing exhaustion. He didn't need a migraine on top of it. He'd learned long ago—pounding music and pounding headaches didn't mix well.

"I hope Jax and Chase know how fucking huge this favor is you're doing for them." Just what Jonah needed. Frank, the band's manager and lawyer, bitching for the umpteenth time about having to divert the whole crew to D.C. for what he thought was a pro-bono concert. "This is costing us a small fortune, not to mention, we've pissed off the entire crew by canceling part of their one week hiatus."

Jonah "Cash" Carter sighed, catching the eye of his personal stylist in the mirror who was putting the finishing touches on his 'show face.'

"Give us five, will ya, Sasha?"

"You got it, boss." The talented artist put the eyeliner and brushes down and stepped over towards the buffet table filled with opulent food and drink.

Only when the two men had a modicum of privacy did Cash lean over to set his manager straight. Frank may carry the title "manager," but Cash needed to remind him every so often just who was in charge and it sure as fuck wasn't Frank.

"For the last time, I told you to take the week off. I don't need a babysitter here in D.C. Hell, I don't need a babysitter. Period."

Jonah wasn't in the mood for Frank's signature snarky bark of laughter. "The hell you don't...."

"I'd shut the fuck up if I were you. I'm not in the mood," Jonah warned.

His manager wasn't afraid to go head to head with him, which was the only reason Jonah kept him around. He'd found that the more popular his music became, the harder it was to find people strong enough to stand up to him when he needed it. The only problem with his relationship with Frank was that they didn't always see eye-to-eye on when Jonah needed it.

"You're not in the mood because you're exhausted, too. You needed this week off. You've been balls-to-the-wall busy for six months between recording and touring. I know you're a damn workaholic, but even you have to get some downtime sooner or later."

"I'll rest when I die."

"Keep it up, and that won't be so far away," Frank warned.

Damn if he didn't regret letting his manager in on his dark little family secret he should have kept buried. Just because Jonah's father and grandfather had both died before the age of forty of heart attacks didn't mean he would suffer the same fate. They'd both been lushes, which had to play a major role in their health.

"Are you two butting heads again? Cash promises to keep his dick in his pants tonight, don't you Cash? At least until Mr. Lawyer here gets the groupie's signature on the NDA."

Jonah appreciated his best friend and keyboard extraordinaire, Ryan "River" Trubach, coming to his aid, but tonight his friend had guessed wrong on what the men had been discussing. It had been a good conjecture though, since sleeping with unnamed women without a nondisclosure agreement was the men's normal pre-show dispute.

"Stick around. We haven't even got to that argument yet tonight. We're still on the 'you're gonna run yourself into the ground' debate," Cash groused.

River grinned. "Shit. You guys are running behind. Time to wrap up the foreplay. We have a show to do in exactly…." he paused dramatically.

"Ten minutes to showtime," the nervous stage manager hollered.

"Just like clockwork. You think someone should tell her we know how to tell time?" River teased. His normal jovial grin was plastered on his face and it eased some of Jonah's tension.

The two musicians had known each other for over ten years— growing up together and forming the band together. The music industry may attribute all of Crushing Stone's success to the writing, producing and distinctive voice of Cash Carter, but Jonah knew there would be no band if it weren't for River. His friend's humor and devoted friendship through the worst times in his life were the only thing that helped pick Jonah up after he'd fallen apart almost seven years before.

"Let's just wrap this up, shall we?" Jonah pinned Frank with his best dominant stare. The glower that made lesser men shrink back and made submissive women he enjoyed playing with cream themselves hoping for a few minutes of his attention. "I owe Jaxson and Chase. You weren't around back then, but they were the first celebrities that got into my music. They gave a shit enough to talk about it publicly. You, me, River, and everyone else on tour with us owe them, and I pay off my debts. Got it?"

Frank leaned in closer so only the three men could hear his next words. "Fuck you, Cash. Don't think I don't know the real reason you're opening Runway. Could it have something to do with a lifetime membership to a private club just under our feet?"

Fuck. No one was supposed to know about Black Light. No one but Cash and River. This complicated things.

"Have you been hacking my private laptop again? No one, and that includes you, are supposed to know the club even exists."

"I didn't hack shit." Sensing Jonah was about to call his bluff, he admitted, "Next time you have a tattoo artist come and tattoo your wrist, you'd better have him setup in a more private location."

Shit. He knew they should have waited to do the tattoo back at the hotel. Still, that didn't explain how Frank had put it together.

"Since when do you have invisible tattoos that can only be seen under a blacklight? He had the barcode displaying on the monitor next to him. It didn't take a genius to figure out you were being given access to a secret location in the building. Knowing a bit about the proclivities you and Jaxson Davidson share, it didn't take long to sort it out."

"Well, you need to unsort it. It's none of your damn business."

"The hell it's not. Every time you *play* too rough with a new sub is a lawsuit waiting to happen. Do I need to remind you of the two subs I've already had to pay off to quietly go away?"

Both men sprang to their feet, bumping chests as anger flared. Cash did not need this kind of bullshit just before a show. He could feel his blood pressure rising, pumping through his body as he fought to control his temper. Some days the thousands of dollars in anger management therapy just didn't feel like enough to keep him from pounding his fist through something. Right now, that something was Frank's face.

River instinctively stepped between the two angry men, facing his friend and pressing against his leather-covered chest. "Don't do it, Cash. You'll fuck up your hand and then it will hurt like a sonofabitch plucking strings tonight. Save up some of that anger for downstairs later. I'm sure there'll be a nice little subby who'll be more than happy to be on the receiving end of some of that hostility."

Frank injected, "That's exactly what I'm afraid of. I'll start prepping for lawsuit number three."

Jonah forced himself to take a deep, cleansing breath. "Screw you, Frank. That was years ago. The NDA and written consent forms you insist on having sure as shit kill the mood, but I agree, they also stopped all the legal problems. I'll be sure to get you consent signatures."

"You see that you do, because one of these days, you're gonna run into the wrong kind of woman who could take everything. And I'm not just talking about money."

The men had been so distracted, they'd missed their host's arrival. "Am I interrupting something?" Jaxson had taken up a defensive stance close to Frank. Jonah hid his grin as Frank took a step back. If he didn't know better, he'd swear his manager was afraid of the tall model turned entrepreneur.

"Five minutes. Please, Mr. Carter. I'm begging you. Finish getting ready." The petite Latina stage manager pleaded, looking as if she were about to hyperventilate.

Cash tried to smile. "You really need to chill out, sweetheart. Nobody is going anywhere if we're a few minutes late."

The nervous woman looked like she was about to puke. Jaxson answered for her. "It's okay, Ariana. I'll make sure Maxine knows it isn't your fault Mr. Carter is dragging his feet."

Jonah shot his friend his best *fuck off* glance only making Jaxson's grin widen.

"You'd do that? Really?" The young woman looked ready to faint.

"Yes, but only if you take a deep breath and go check on something else. I need a word with Cash."

"Yes, sir." The young woman scrambled off.

"Now, to the really important question. Did you get your ink today?"

"Yeah, but I should have waited until after the show. It's bugging me and I can't very well go out there with my inner wrist bandaged looking like I tried to off myself before the show."

"You know the rules. We're doing this club right, so don't bother complaining because the same rules you hate for yourself are going to keep your private life private."

Cash knew his friend was right. Success came with a price. There was almost nowhere in the world Jonah could go where he wasn't eventually recognized by someone. He'd become a magnet for crazies who saw either dollar signs or blackmail material by trapping the musician with a bad-boy reputation in situations he'd rather keep private.

"Save the lecture. I agreed to the rules. I even appreciate them because I know they'll keep my sex life from being the center of a front-page exposé. It doesn't mean I couldn't have waited to get inked until after the show."

Jaxson teased him. "Considering you have at least a quarter of your body covered in ink, I didn't think you'd be such a pussy about it."

"Fuck you," Cash shot back, sitting back down and waving Sasha to come back over to finish his pre-show prep.

"No thanks. Chase and Emma are taking good care of me in that department."

A pang of something close to jealously flitted through Jonah's sub-conscious. Not quite a full-blown thought. More like a buried memory of something lost, which was ridiculous since he didn't let any woman close enough to hurt him. Not anymore.

I'm done getting kicked in the balls.

He told himself he was perfectly happy being the one doing the hurting these days–both physically with like-minded play partners and emotionally with women who made the mistake of not believing him when he told them he didn't do relationships.

One by one, anyone he let spend more than a few days around him had learned he truly meant it when he promised no one would ever get close enough to hurt him. He'd made the mistake of letting one woman in. Once. Even years later he could still taste the blood from the figurative ripping out of his heart. Nothing and no one would ever get close enough to fucking do that to him again.

"I can see you're getting in the zone. I'll let you do your thing. We have a few special VIPs I'll be bringing backstage after the show. Until then... break a leg," Jaxson ended their conversation with a good-natured slap on his back.

Frank said his good-byes next. "I'll see you backstage. I'll have an NDA ready in case you see your next lawsuit in the crowd tonight." He turned and left before Jonah could get a parting shot.

Sasha, the petite woman who liked to wear more makeup than the whole rock band combined, was back to applying dark eye liner around Jonah's emerald green eyes. River had wandered back to the exit where the rest of their band congregated, completing their pre-show rituals—working off nervous energy by pacing, stretching and warming up.

Despite how exhausted he was, Jonah was always relieved to feel the nugget of nerves take hold in his gut just before going on stage. He and the boys normally played to sold out auditoriums holding thousands of screaming fans. It wasn't the volume of patrons that had him nervous tonight. Quite the contrary. There was safety in numbers. Standing on stage, looking out into the sea of adoring rock junkies felt like home to him. He belonged there.

Tonight would be different. The club was huge by dance club standards, but damn-near intimate for the popular rock band. The style of stage with the jutting runway into the crowd would bring him just feet from the crowd. Too close for comfort. The fact that the venue was full of D.C. VIPs who may not even like his hard-hitting style of music was like the bad-tasting frosting on top of a shitty cake.

Still, he'd made a promise and he kept his promises.

"Good enough, Sasha. Time to get this show over." Jonah reached into the front pocket of his signature skin-tight black leather pants as soon as he was on his feet. He pulled out the thick wad of hundred dollar bills he never left his room without, pulled several crisp bills from the clip and held them out to Sasha.

"You do know I'm paid a salary through the management company, right, Mr. Carter?" The young woman always tried to decline his cash tip. He always insisted. It was part of their pre-show routine.

"Yep. And you know I got my nickname honestly. Take the cash. Buy yourself a new pair of shoes."

She grinned. "You know all my secrets."

He chuckled. "Naw. I just pay attention. I've never seen you in the same pair of shoes twice and considering I see you at least five days a week, that is a shit ton of shoes."

The young woman blushed nicely, stirring something he didn't like to admit.

Christ, I need to get laid.

For all the shit Frank gave him, Jonah found it ironic that he'd been celibate for close to a month since the last disastrous hook-up in Toronto ended up with half-naked pictures of him passed out in a post-concert party had ended up as the front story on

Entertainment Tonight and the center of a skit of SNL the following week.

The second story dressing room was almost empty now. The stage manager was back, tears in her eyes. "Please, Mr. Carter. We are ten minutes late starting the show."

He peeled a couple more hundreds off the stack of bills, holding them out to the stressed-out newbie as his way of apologizing. When she stood frozen, Cash reached out and slid the bills in the center of her deep v-line blouse, leaving cash sticking out between her pert boobs as if she were a whore dancing on a pole.

"You need to lighten up, baby. This job'll kill you in a month if you don't. I'm one of the easy ones."

He moved towards the elevator that would take him down to stage level where he'd join the rest of the band. He shoved the still thick wad of cash back into his pocket, patting it self-consciously as he did dozens of times a day. The wad represented so many things to him. Freedom. Security. Success. But mostly vengeance.

Fuck you Judge Stone.

Comforting words he muttered to himself more times than he liked to admit. Cursing his nemesis had become as much a part of his pre-show tradition as completing a sound check. Sometimes, like tonight, when he was exhausted, his vengeance kept him going.

The elevator doors opened to the sight of his band mates already gathered in their traditional pre-show huddle. As tight as they all were, he was always aware he wasn't quite one of the guys. Not really. They let him in, physically, but he never let himself relax enough to let their relationship feel easy. He'd learned the hard way how that would bite him in the ass when the friendship ended.

Nico and Juice, his bass player and drummer, separated enough to let him into their circle. Like the athletes they had never been, they each reached an arm into the center of their pack. They were connected as one unit by the hands that would be making amazing music in just a few minutes.

They stood silent, each gathering their thoughts, focusing on the coming show. They waited for him. Cash alone decided when they were ready. Tonight, an odd uneasy feeling had settled into his gut. For a split second, the thought of calling the whole damn show off crossed his mind. He pushed the urge down, determined to see his obligation through.

"Ready?" He looked from man to man, looking for their unspoken commitment to him and his music. Every note. Every syllable. Everything they played had come from inside him. He was lucky to find men who appreciated that instead of resenting it.

Milo, lead guitarist nodded first. Nico, his bass guitar slung over his shoulder, nodded next. His closest friend, River followed.

Juice was always last. All eyes turned to him, waiting for their wiry drummer to be mentally ready to take the stage. Juice was one emotional dude. The drugs he insisted on living off of made him unpredictable. They all put up with his shit because he was one helluva drummer. His eventual grin finally came.

"Let's go crush it, boys." Five hands flew in unison to the ceiling with his bandmates moving to take their place on stage behind the drawn curtain that would hide them until ready.

This. Right here. It was what he lived for. What he'd dreamed of since he could remember dreaming. He'd willed himself to success through sheer determination. As he heard Jaxson speaking, welcoming the crowd to their grand opening, Cash tried to focus on the music he loved so much. The songs that were like his children. He'd birthed them as sure as any woman birthed a child. He'd put his own blood, sweat and tears into them. He'd sacrificed for his music, giving up a little bit of himself to each line of lyrics.

The pounding beat of their opening song roared through the space. He was close, just off-stage, letting the music seep into his veins, filling him with an energy he only got from the rush of performing. The riffs and beats to the long intro to their most popular song, *Prove You Wrong*, were the perfect intro for the larger-than-life rock star.

He'd been concerned the conservative crowd would be a downer of an audience, but was reassured by the roaring applause changing into a rhythmic chant. Cash... Cash... Cash... Over and over they cried out for him.

He clutched the wireless microphone and swept onto the stage to the welcoming roar of adoring fans. Grinding his hips to the heavy beat as he took his spot center stage, a familiar fury reared its head, until he poured it out it in the opening lyrics.

Look at me now, asshole. Guess I proved you wrong after all.

CHAPTER 2

The familiar strain of the Crushing Stone's number one hit, *Proving You Wrong*, filled the crowded venue. The rather stuffy crowd that had just minutes before been sipping champagne in their evening wear seemed to shed their restraint. They pushed to their feet as the curtain opened, exposing the band to the cheering crowd.

Samantha had to resist the urge to follow several groups of scantily clad women who pressed past her to rush the runway jutting out into the dance floor. Within minutes the stage was surrounded, several layers deep, with raging fans jumping and shouting for the missing lead singer who had yet to grace the stage.

Her heart raced, anxious for her first glimpse of Jonah and dreading it at the same time. The second he burst out from backstage the spotlight shone on him, making him the center of attention. She had thought she was prepared, but in that moment Sam found herself fighting down the urge to cry.

What a fool she'd been. She'd come to get a glimpse of her old friend, Jonah, but one glance at the man center stage and Samantha knew she was too late. Jonah was gone, swallowed wholly and completely by his larger-than-life persona, Cash Carter.

And he was devastatingly perfect.

While the room clapped and sang along with the Grammy-Award-winning band, Samantha sat frozen in the shadows on her tall stool. She couldn't take her eyes off the six-foot tall celebrity currently working the crowd with his sexy dance moves.

She struggled to reconcile the current version of the popular musician with the young man she'd felt so close to most of her life. His signature gravelly voice was deeper than she remembered. God, he'd filled out so much and in all the right places, flexing his muscular arms as he fist pumped to the beat of the angry song. His perfect body was encased in body-hugging black leather pants and a sleeveless shirt. Tattoos rippled across his biceps and his shoulder-length dark hair swayed as he moved with the beat of the song. It was when he moved out onto the long runway, getting closer and closer, that Samantha decided she'd got what she came for after all.

Closure.

Her Jonah was gone.

The reality almost crushed her. It was hard to catch her breath and it was in that moment she had to admit the ugly truth to herself. She'd really come with the hope of feeling a spark of their old connection. That invisible thread that had always bonded them together. Even as young kids, she'd felt connected to Jonah in a way that felt a bit like magic. She'd felt his presence before he became visible. He'd been able to read her mind, understanding her at times better than she understood herself.

The urge to cry was almost too much. Sam swallowed hard, trying to press down the lump in her throat. As the rest of the huge club pressed in around her, she'd never felt as alone as she did watching Jonah reaching down to accept flowers and small gifts from his adoring fans, making tangible connections with strangers he now cared about more than he did her.

He was so close.

An irrational thought took hold. What might he do if she approached the runway? What could she offer him as her gift? She'd already given him her heart and he'd trampled it.

Her fingers flew to the golden heart locket she'd worn around her neck every day since the day he'd given it to her. It had been the day he'd asked her to his senior prom. The day he'd literally swept her off her feet, kissing her until she'd been out of breath. He'd told her it was to be their promise charm to each other. How many nights had she fallen asleep holding that small locket, filled with a lock of his thick hair, feeling closer, if just for a minute, to her lost friend?

He won't remember me. He's moved on. And even if he does recognize me, he couldn't care less.

Insanity. Unwanted tears finally fell as she sat frozen to her spot, unable to move. She should leave, but instead she felt trapped, there to witness Jonah in all of his perfection as he gyrated his sexy hips like the consummate showman he'd become. She could barely make out the lyrics to the next song, *Betrayal*, for all the screaming fans. It didn't matter. She had every note, every syllable, every melody memorized.

By the time the song was winding down, Samantha knew she had to leave. Instead of feeling better, being so close to Jonah had her on the verge of a full-out panic attack, something she hadn't suffered for years. She was glad now that she hadn't gone too far into the club. She pushed her wobbly feet, anxious to get outside to the frigid December air in hopes it would revive her.

She crossed in front of several tables of VIPs and patrons sporting press passes. She'd have to weave through a screaming crowd of fans to make it to the exit. The pounding music started to be drowned out by the pounding in her ears as she grew more and more light-headed. Panic and the compressed space were closing in faster than she could escape.

The music grew softer, almost subdued. Sam glanced back

towards the stage as the band began to play their one and only number one ballad from the year before. The lights that had been trained only on Jonah and the band were now scanning the crowd in a haphazard way as the first chords of *Forever* began, only bringing her tears harder. She'd always hoped he'd been thinking of her as he'd penned the lyrics, so now, seeing him walking out onto the runway to touch the dozens of screaming women as the love poured out of him—well it made her feel foolish.

So foolish she was paralyzed as she stood grounded at the end of the runway as Jonah made his way closer with each step he took. Twenty feet. Ten feet.

What she'd give to touch him again, just once. She was as bad as the screaming fans, desperate for any scrap of the famous musician's attention and it made her sick to her stomach to admit how much she'd let his desertion hurt her. He'd never hidden his dreams of being a star from her. She had no right to feel the red-hot anger bubbling up. A true friend would be happy for his success. The fact that she resented having lost Jonah to his Cash Carter guise only made her feel guilty.

He was a mere half-dozen feet away from her now as she stood frozen. Unable to go to him. Unable to leave.

She'd never know if it was fate or weird luck that trained the spotlight from above directly on her. It lasted only for a second, but in that moment he turned her way and their eyes met. His eyes widened slightly as his brow furrowed with recognition. Her brain shouted at her to turn and run away before he shunned her publicly, completing her heartbreaking humiliation, but her feet stood planted in her fashion boots.

How much time passed, she'd never know. What she did know was that the crowd was yelling and the musicians were playing the accompaniment to the song Jonah had stopped singing. Groupies pressed closer to the frozen singer, reaching up to the stage to touch his stationary boots while his glare penetrated her to her core.

He sees me. Really sees me.

The thought thrilled and frightened her. She held her breath until she was light-headed. She was in uncharted territory, unsure if she should turn and retreat or advance on the stage. The roving spotlight was back on her, throwing her into the middle of the show whether she liked it or not. She felt all eyes in the three-story club on her as everyone in the room collectively tried to figure out why the lead singer had suddenly stopped singing one of his most popular songs as if he'd forgotten the lyrics he'd written.

She never took her eyes off his, waiting for his expression to give her a hint of what he was thinking, hopeful she'd see her old Jonah crawl out from behind Cash's polished exterior. She might have been able to handle a nonchalant brush off, but with each second that passed, an angry hatred changed the handsome musician into a frightening adversary.

That's when she realized there had been one outcome she hadn't even considered.

He sees me... and he cares, alright.

He hates me.

* * *

SHE'D FINALLY COME.

The sudden appearance of the only woman he'd ever allowed to hurt him rocked Jonah to the core. For the first few years of Crushing Stone concerts, he'd scanned the crowds endlessly, waiting for the day she'd realize she'd screwed up and come back to him. As each year had passed, he'd looked less and less until her absence had become his new normal.

Christ, she looked good. Amazing even. She'd somehow maintained her innocent girl-next-door look while still maturing into the gorgeous woman he'd always known she'd be. Her long, thick brunette hair accented her caramel brown eyes.

The same eyes that were staring back at him now with uncertainty.

He'd stopped singing mid-sentence. He vaguely realized the band was still playing the accompaniment, doing their best to cover up his gaff as if this were all a planned part of the show, which was utter bullshit.

Snapshots from a different time in his life crowded his brain as the nearby media jumped up to snap photos of the frozen singer. The light flashes acted as a wake-up call that he was in a very public place, the center stage attraction, as a room full of fans witnessed his astonishment. He shook his head, trying to shake the rushing memories out and willing the lyrics to a song he'd sung a thousand times or more to come back to him.

But instead of lyrics, he thought about school bus rides and elementary lunch rooms. Flashes from Friday night football games and late night band rehearsals in Ryan's family garage— always his best fan, Sami, never more than a few feet away as she looked at him as if he were the center of her universe.

It was when memories of their last night together crashed in on him that his surprise turned to anger. This was the woman who had turned on him—throwing away everything good without a backward glance. He'd thought he'd come to grips with her betrayal through therapy. Seeing her here being surrounded by security made him know he'd been a fool to think he was over her deception.

Jonah stood frozen until the security guards started pulling Samantha away from the runway. She kept craning her neck, fighting to stay behind. Fighting to maintain their visual connection.

Fuck if I'm going to let her get away again. She owes me answers, goddammit.

Without a plan, Jonah closed the last few feet at the end of the runway and jumped out into the crowd turning his confused fans into an impromptu mosh pit. He struggled to get his boots on the floor as dozens of hands clutched at him, happy just to touch their idol. He never took his eyes off the burly security guy currently manhandling Sami towards the exit of the club.

She was getting away.

His forward progress was halted by a concerned Jaxson who had stepped into his path.

"What the fuck, Cash? You're in the middle of a show here, dude."

Jonah reached out to his friend, pulling him close to talk into his ear in order to be heard over the chaos erupting in the club.

"I need to stop that woman from leaving." He pointed at Samantha, giving the nearby press a confirmation on exactly what, or rather who, had grabbed his attention.

"Seriously, your booty call is gonna need to…"

Jaxson never got the chance to finish his sentence. His anger spilling over, Jonah grabbed the front of his friend's tuxedo, pulling him chest to chest.

"Fuck you, Jax. This isn't a booty call, dammit. I have to talk to her."

The men had known each other long enough that Jonah recognized Jaxson's acceptance of his odd request.

Chase had joined them and all three men swung to watch Samantha fighting security in an attempt to break free.

Chase questioned, "You mean Samantha?"

Hearing her name out loud rocked him. He had so many questions. Why was she here? How did Jaxson and Chase know her?

To their credit, his friends formed a human plow in front of him and began pressing through the crowd with Jonah on their heels. Security almost had her shuffled to the revolving door marked VIP entrance when Jaxson waved and started shouting at them to stop.

"Blake! Hold up!" The security detail must have heard through the din because they stopped a few feet before the door, just next to the VIP coat check counter. The crowd was thinning the farther back in the club they got until Jonah could finally walk freely without being groped by passing fans.

Sensing their friend's need to reach the frightened Samantha, Jax and Chase separated, allowing Jonah to take long strides, closing the final distance between them quickly. It took all his effort to stop himself from grabbing her up—to kiss her or to squeeze the life out of her, he wasn't sure which.

The band's instrumental rendition of the ballad Jonah had written for the very woman now standing only an inch from him felt like the soundtrack for the dramatic scene playing out. The club lights had been dimmed for the show making it difficult for him to read her despite their proximity. Long seconds passed with neither speaking.

As his eyes became accustomed to the dim lighting, he could see the fear bordering on panic flitting in her eyes. He should have felt vindicated by her fear, but her vulnerability instead awoke a protective persona he'd abandoned years before.

"You came." He choked the words out.

Her eyes widened before she answered with a simple, "I came."

His left hand reached out and squeezed her right bicep on its own accord. "Why?" The venom in the single word matched the strength of his bruising grasp. He was grateful she had on long sleeves. It would be too dangerous to touch her skin.

When she stood frozen, a deer-in-the-headlights look on her face, he reached out with his right hand, grabbing her other arm and shook her. "Why are you here, dammit? Why now?"

Her panic was taking over. He recognized her starting to gasp for her next breath, and old memories crashed in, spurring him into action.

"Where's your inhaler?" he questioned as he released her to grab for her cross-body purse, scrambling to find her medicine.

She was shaking her head, trying to answer through her breathy gasps. "…Didn't bring it. Don't need it… anymore."

"Like hell, you don't," he shouted, angry at her for endangering herself and then even more angry at himself for giving a shit.

Jaxson pressed closer, "Listen to me, Cash. We have first-aid supplies on every floor. I have an EMT on my staff. You need to get back to the show and let me handle this for you."

Jonah hated his options. He wanted no part of climbing back onto that stage and going on with the show as if he hadn't just been figuratively kicked in the balls. He could see her turning pale. His indecision was delaying getting her the help she needed.

He tore his gaze away from Samantha to stare into his friend's eyes. "You swear to me you'll help her?"

"You have my word," Jaxson promised.

"She's not to leave until the show is over and I can talk to her, got it?"

"Got it." He saw the promise in Jaxson's eyes and knew he really did have a good friend who was jumping in to help even though he had no clue what was really going on.

Samantha objected, "It's too late, Jonah. Why not just let me leave?"

He grabbed her arms again, pulling her fully against his body until their faces were so close he could feel the warmth of her breath on his cheek. He fought the urge to kiss her.

"You and me… we have unfinished business, Miss Stone."

She flinched at his use of her surname.

He forced himself to release her, letting her fall back against the coat-check counter as he turned to his friends.

"Keep her backstage." Jaxson nodded just as he added on, "And we'll need someplace private as soon as the show is over."

Jaxson grinned, "I have just the place."

With a final glare at the woman he never thought he'd see again, Jonah stepped back, getting in a final shot before returning to the stage. "That's great. Let's hope it's sound proofed or the press may get an earful, eh Samantha?"

CHAPTER 3

"*R*eally. I'm feeling better. Please, take this off. I need to leave." Samantha's voice was muffled by the oxygen mask affixed over her mouth and nose. Embarrassment mingled with regret, serving up a dangerous cocktail of emotions. She tried to lift the mask off her face so she could make an escape before Jonah finished the concert, but the medic was having none of it. She could hear the pounding beat of the heavy rock music in the distance and was still unaccustomed to the thrill of knowing Jonah was under the same roof as her.

The tattooed man who looked more like he belonged in a motorcycle gang than working at an upscale dance club reached to place the blood pressure cuff on her upper arm. He then put a stethoscope on the inside of her elbow, pumping the cuff up, and slowly letting the air out while listening. Once he was done, he removed the cuff, then put his fingers on the inside of her wrist to count her pulse.

A minute later, he took the pressure cuff off first and then finally the oxygen mask. "Looks like the medication helped. Your pulse is normal and your blood pressure is back in a normal range at one-twenty-five over eighty-five. Still a bit high, but it's coming down."

Sam was anxious to leave before Jonah could arrive and destroy the last shred of their friendship by taking out the anger she'd seen in his eyes on her. She pushed to her feet as the guy whose name she thought was Travis turned his back to pick up the medical supplies he used from the brand-new first-aid kit laying on the desk in front of them.

Only when she turned to head towards the door did she see the tall Jaxson Davidson standing in front of the closed door, blocking her escape. He leaned back against the six-panel door, his arms crossed in front of him and legs crossed at the ankles as if he were trying to relax, but she wasn't fooled. His penetrating glare scanned her, looking for answers to questions he hadn't even asked yet.

Sam pulled to a quick stop, locked in a visual showdown with the famous model.

He spoke first. "Thanks, Travis. I'm glad we hired you. I suspected we might need an EMT one day, but I never dreamed it would be on opening night."

The burly medic stood several inches taller than his boss. "Yeah, I'm happy to help, but I'm sure Maxine is ready to kick my ass for being gone so long. Time for me to get back behind the bar."

Jaxson pushed upright, stepping aside to let the medic out, but careful to close the door quickly, making it clear Samantha was not allowed to leave. At least not yet.

The wall surrounding the door Jaxson stood in front of was one long wall of windows. She could make out people walking past the smoky glass, not paying any attention to what was happening in the large, opulent office.

"It's one-way glass. Don't worry, the press can't get any more pictures while you're in here. In fact, they aren't allowed on the third floor. Period."

35

It hadn't even crossed her mind to worry about the press. A new panic set in realizing with Cash Carter's fame, there was more than a small chance that her father might see an article or two on his daughter's previous friend and crush. It wasn't every day a star jumped off the stage in the middle of a show to chase after someone in the audience.

There was nothing she could think of to say, so she held her tongue as she looked around the office, taking in the large, open seating area, the three desks that formed a U-shape, and the wall of bookshelves. A long conference table took up the center of the room, giving the space a bit of a boardroom feel. A single door opened to a small bathroom. She was surprised to be in their private office.

Jaxson was advancing on her. He walked slowly, as if afraid to frighten her. She glanced up at him to see a small smile light up his handsome face. Being so close to a celebrity made her jumpy... well more jumpy that she already was.

"I don't want to pry, but I confess. I'm curious. I've known Cash for a few years now and I've never seen him jump off any stages to chase after a woman before."

Flashes of the dozens if not hundreds of stories flitted through her memory—always with pictures of Jonah with a beautiful woman on his arm, or in the case of last month's National Enquirer, on his lap.

Shit, I don't want to be his story of the week.

"Yeah, well maybe you just don't attend enough concerts."

"Maybe, but I don't think that's it."

She pressed again. "I'd like to go home now." She hesitated, before adding a soft plea. "Please."

For the first time since the medic had left Jaxson glanced away, looking uncomfortable. By the time he trained his eyes back on her, the look was gone and dominance had returned.

"I've agreed to hold you here until Cash can speak with you and that's what I plan to do. I can, however, at least make sure you are as comfortable as possible while you wait for him." He pulled his right arm up to crook his elbow towards her. "Would you please join me for a short walk?"

Samantha hesitated long enough she could see doubt in Jaxson's eyes. She had the feeling if she made a real stink, he would let her leave, yet there was an invisible magnetic pull holding her in place.

God, she wanted answers. Why had he left her the way he had —without saying goodbye? Without even short notes to keep in touch. I mean she understood why he'd taken the money. He'd never hid his dreams of making it big. It hurt like hell to know he'd chosen success over her. Was there really anything he could say to her to explain it away? Not really.

Jaxson gave her the time she needed to sort through her complicated feelings before she reached out with her left hand and placed it in the crook of his arm, letting him pull her into motion.

The music got much louder as soon as the door opened. They were on a balcony of sorts that jutted out into the air. Only when they got close to the railing did Sam see they were now on the third floor of the dance club. He paused long enough for her to peer over the edge to look at the stage two stories below.

She could see the drummer sitting, surrounded by his equipment. The other members of the band played and sang while stationary. All except Jonah. He was out front singing, this time a guitar over his shoulder as he played the melody of their newest release, *Revenge is Sweet*.

She'd heard the song many times, but tonight the edgy lyrics took on a new meaning as Jaxson pulled her back into motion, looping around the entire oval shaped balcony towards a door labeled PRIVATE. The last strain she heard as the heavy door closed hit her hard.

As nice as Runway was, the opulence of the private location they had just entered caught her attention. She tried not to make a fool of herself by gawking at the gold plated sconces decorating every few feet with a soft lighting. Her high-heeled boots clicked on the marble floor as they neared a single door at the end of the hallway.

She watched as Jaxson first inserted an electronic keycard and then stepped forward to let the retinal scanner take a picture of his left eye. The door popped open with a quiet snap, and he pushed it open and swept his arm out as if to welcome her to precede him.

The click of the door locking them in had her pulse spiking again. She was truly alone in a locked room with a man she knew next to nothing about, other than what was printed in magazines or on the entertainment shows. As nervous as that made her, knowing she'd be just as alone with Jonah when he finished the show was worse.

When she stalled, Jaxson moved ahead, leading them through the short hallway and into a mammoth bedroom, whitewashed in subtle shades with just a few colorful throw pillows on the bed and couches to lend a splash of color. The huge bed had to be custom made. She'd never seen a bed like it and to her embarrassment she must have stopped to stare at it long enough that Jaxson commented.

"Chase, Emma and I plan on staying over sometimes." He offered his answer matter-of-factly as if the picture of their steamy threesome piled naked he'd just painted in her mind was normal.

She knew she was blushing like an innocent and she hated it. She didn't want Jonah's friend to think she was judging them. She quickly turned away from the bed to take in the sitting area with a wall of shelves surrounding a fireplace with a flatscreen TV above the mantle.

"It's a bit chilly in here. Let me light the fire. Have a seat. I'll turn on the closed circuit coverage of the show. I'm sure you'd like to catch the end of the concert."

Samantha collapsed into the plush white leather chair, relieved to get off her feet. She watched as Jaxson used the remote to turn on the concert. When he turned to face her, the gas fire crackled in the hearth behind him. He walked towards her and handed her the remote control.

She was disappointed when he sat on the coffee table directly in front of her, blocking her view of the concert on the gigantic flat TV behind him. Sam wanted him to leave, desperate for a few minutes of privacy to try to pull herself together after all that had happened. It wasn't to be.

He'd left the volume low, all the better for the conversation he was determined to drag her into.

"How are you feeling Samantha?"

She hesitated, afraid to tell the truth that she was freaking out at the thought of being alone with Jonah in this room with the unprecedented bed. Her eyes must have darted in that direction because Jaxson picked up on it.

"Would you prefer I have you wait for Cash in a different location? Some place a bit less… " He stalled. "Private?"

It wasn't the privacy that worried her. It was his anger.

Her voice came out a bit wobbly. "The privacy is good. I think we've already made a big enough public spectacle of ourselves tonight."

Jaxson smiled kindly, "It was exciting. It's not every day Cash decides to treat his fans as a mosh pit."

She cracked a smile at that, remembering how surprised she'd been as he had flung himself off the end of the runway with complete faith he wouldn't smash into the dance floor.

"Can I at least get you a drink or something to eat?"

She answered truthfully. "I don't think it's a good idea to eat or drink right now. I'm a bit nervous and I've already had several glasses of champagne."

He hesitated, looking like he wanted to press her harder to talk with him, but then thought better of the idea. He finally stood and handed her the remote.

"I guess I'll get back down to Chase and Emma and leave you here to collect yourself. You are safe here, Samantha. No one will bother you until I return after the show with Cash. I'll be coming with him."

He pinned her with a knowing glare as if to let her know he wouldn't be leaving her alone with Cash until he knew she'd be safe. Relief swarmed her at the realization and then guilt. Guilt that she had to acknowledge she was actually afraid of the Cash Carter persona she'd met tonight. He was unknown to her and that made her feel uneasy.

"Thanks for that, Mr. Davidson. I really do appreciate your hospitality. You've made me feel so much better."

"The name's Jaxson. Mr. Davidson is my father, and believe me, I want no part of being associated with him."

With a final smile, he stopped long enough next to her to reach out and squeeze her shoulder in a sign of support.

She held her breath until she heard the door click closed behind him. Glancing around nervously, she finally felt she had some privacy. Sam raised the remote and pressed the volume button higher, filling the space with the masculine voice of her long-lost friend. The feed playing on the TV looked like it was a well-produced movie, catching the band from several angles.

Finally relaxing a bit, she lifted her boots to the matching leather ottoman directly in front of her, sinking back and trying to calm her nerves before she had to go another round with Jonah.

* * *

JONAH SOMEHOW MADE it through the rest of the show on auto-pilot. He had done something he'd never done before—phoned it in. Because he loved what he did, he lived for spending time on stage playing the music he'd poured his heart and talent into for his growing fan base.

But not tonight.

Tonight the only thing he could think about was rushing through the line-up of songs as fast as possible so he could get back to her.

The band normally did several encores, but he couldn't bring himself to spend even one more song on the stage when he knew the answers to what the fuck had happened seven years before were here in the building in the form of Samantha Stone.

Frank was the first one to greet him when he rushed back stage, adrenaline still pumping through his veins.

"What the hell was that stunt all about, Cash? You aren't happy getting women to sue you over rough sex. Now you want to get dozens of people suing because you landed on them when free-falling off the stage?"

Jonah wasn't in the mood. He tried to brush past the older man in the three-piece suit, but Frank held out his hand, stopping him from moving past. Jonah was already on the edge. He didn't need to add punching his manager to the list of shit on his plate.

"No one is gonna sue me and you know it, Frank. Now, back-off. I have somewhere to go."

"Not until you tell me who she is." Jonah's face must have shown surprise because Frank grinned an ugly smile. "Oh yeah, I saw. Every person in the club saw. I think I deserve to know the name of your next lawsuit, don't you? This was new even for you. Interrupting a show to pick out your next fuck-buddy?"

Frank's vulgar language had never bothered Jonah before, but somehow hearing Samantha referred to as a fuck-buddy didn't sit well with Jonah. "Shut the fuck up, Frank. You don't know shit about it."

"So educate me. I saw her with Jaxson. Don't lie and try to tell me she isn't hidden somewhere in the club, waiting for you. Now who the hell is she?"

"Don't worry about it."

His long-time friend River had caught up to him, pulling him around. The entire band had pressed in, sandwiching him in the narrow hallway. He wished they looked angry. He was jacked up enough that he wouldn't mind a good fight. Instead, each musician looked concerned.

Juice pressed him first. "That was some flying leap you took there, Cash. If I was a diving judge, I'd give it a 9.1." Juice was the only one to laugh at his silly joke.

Ryan pressed him, "Who was she?" The worried look on his friend's face gave Jonah a hint that Ryan knew exactly who she'd been.

"Don't worry about it. I have it under control."

Frank injected, "No you don't. Not until you get her signature on the NDA."

Jonah had had enough. These guys were keeping him from answers. He needed to go.

"Fuck the NDA. We don't need one for Sam."

Ryan pulled his arm back, keeping him from pressing down the hall towards the coming Jaxson.

"I fucking knew it. Is it *your* Samantha?"

Jonah stopped in his tracks, turning back to his friend clinging to his arm. "You of all people know damn well she isn't *my* anything. She is and always has been daddy's little girl."

"Bullshit," Ryan challenged him.

"Let it go, River."

"The hell I will. I'm not gonna scrape you up off the floor again like I did the last time this went south."

"It was seven years ago. All I'm looking for now are answers."

River looked skeptical. The friends were still in a stare down when Jaxson stepped closer. "You guys gonna hang out in the hall all night? I have some refreshments setup up in the second floor dressing room. Why don't you all head on up. I need to talk with Cash here for a few minutes."

The band reluctantly peeled off from the group one by one with Ryan the last to leave. Jax waited until the two men were left alone before he started silently walking towards the small elevator in the corner, knowing Jonah would follow.

Jonah's pulse increased with each step he took towards the lift that would take him to Samantha. It wasn't until they were in the elevator and Jaxson had inserted a keycard to make it start moving that the silence between them became awkward.

"How is she?" He finally asked the club owner.

Jaxson kept his eyes forward, refusing to look his way as he replied, "Emotional. I stayed with her until she'd calmed down."

"Thanks."

"Want to talk about it?" This time Jaxson glanced sideways and Jonah could see his curiosity.

He said the most honest thing he could in the moment. "No words, man."

Jaxson whistled, surprised, "That bad?"

Jonah nodded, refusing to let emotion take him over. "Worse."

The door opened to a small vestibule. Two large French doors were directly in front of the elevator and he knew without Jax confirming that Samantha was behind those doors. He felt her and it unsettled him. He remembered a time when he loved feeling his connection to her, but now… all these years later… that connection was supposed to be dead and buried.

I'll have to be sure to kill it before I leave here tonight. I don't need this kind of trauma in my life.

Jaxson was speaking again. "This card will get you out of the suite and call the elevator. That will get you back down behind the stage or to the dressing room, but you'll have to phone me when you're ready to go down to Black Light. You won't have access there until I escort you the first time."

Before tonight, Jonah had been so looking forward to playing after the show in the new BDSM club also opening in the base-ment of the building. Funny how Samantha showing up had knocked him on his ass so much he'd forgotten about it completely.

The doors clicked as Jaxson used the keycard and his retina to unlock the private space. Jonah was only a few steps into the suite when he saw her. She'd been standing close to the fireplace, as if she were warming herself. At the sound of the door unlocking, Sam spun around, self-consciously hugging her arms tight around her thin waist as her eyes widened.

She'd taken her jacket off and thrown it over the back of the couch, exposing the form fitting blouse that hugged her ample breasts. She'd filled out perfectly. Gone was the picture of the too-thin teenager he'd had stuck in his memory for the last seven years; replaced by this womanly version of herself.

When his gaze swept up to her face, he wasn't prepared for the panicky look in her eyes. She appeared as if she were about to jump out of her skin. He wanted her fear to make him feel vindicated.

She should be afraid of me, dammit.

Jaxson leaned in to talk softly. "I have a bad feeling about this. Maybe I should stay. I'll hang out in the kitchenette."

"No offense, but I need you to get lost, Jax."

"You'd better damn well get her safeword and live by it."

With regret, he answered truthfully, "Wrong guess. We've never played or scened together, man."

That surprised his friend. He couldn't blame Jaxson. Samantha looked like exactly the type of groupie Cash Carter usually played with. He hadn't done it consciously, but in that moment, he knew he'd been subconsciously picking out play partners who had reminded him of Sam all these years. How fucked up was that?

"Fine, if not sex, then how the hell do you know each other? And don't fuck with me."

"We went to elementary school together, okay? She was my best friend all through school."

Jaxson let another soft whistle of surprise escape before he leaned closer to make sure Sam couldn't pick up on their conversation from across the room. "If you say so, but I got news for you, buddy. Best friends aren't supposed to be afraid of each other. So let me make this clear for you. You hurt her, and I kick your ass. Got it?"

It took a second for Jonah to internalize the very real threat. He tore his gaze away from Samantha to look at his fellow Dom and friend.

"Yeah, I got it. Now get the fuck out. It's time I get some answers."

CHAPTER 4

*T*he silence was deafening. Jaxson had nodded to her just before he turned and left, pulling the door closed behind him. She'd almost panicked and yelled to him to stay behind, afraid to be alone with the angry man staring her down from across the room.

If possible, he was even more devastatingly handsome than ever before. He hadn't taken the time to shower or even change after the show. His thick hair and muscular arms glistened with sweat from the exertion of his art. It had been surreal to watch the concert on the television knowing he was performing just two stories below her.

A full minute of silence went by as the old friends sized each other up. The anger in his eyes hadn't diluted so when he took a step closer, her boot stepped back out of self-preservation. The old friends danced a silent two-step; each move Sam made was chore-ographed to keep as much distance between them as possible.

"Since when are you afraid of me?" His voice was foreign to her.

"I've never met you. You're a whole different person, Cash."

She'd said the words to shock him, hoping he'd stop scaring the shit out of her. It didn't work.

"I'm exactly who you made me into, Miss Stone."

"Stop calling me that." She wasn't sure why it bothered her, but she somehow knew he meant it as a slur.

"Why? It's your name, isn't it? Or did you already get married? Daddy get you married off to a nice stiff from the country club yet?"

"Not yet. For some odd reason I've resisted his matchmaking efforts. Maybe that was a mistake."

"Oh baby, I'm sure it was. I expected you to be living the high life, ruining people's lives at a breakneck speed by now."

Samantha felt her fear fleeing, replaced with bubbled-up anger. "What the hell is wrong with you? If anyone should be angry here, it's me. You're acting like I set out to ruin your life when instead, I'd think you could at least say you're sorry if you're not going to say thank you."

"Thank you?! What the *fuck* do I have to thank you for, Samantha?" At least he'd used her first name, even if he had said it like it was a curse.

"Oh, I don't know. Maybe the fact that you're a Grammy-Award-winning, multimillionaire musician."

He was closing the distance between them one step at a time, careful not to spook her and make her run, although she had nowhere to go. Her brain was screaming to put more distance between them, but her other body parts were being drawn into his magnetic field, just like the old days.

If anything his green eyes got darker. "Even if I do have success, why the hell would I thank you for that? I have what I have because I worked hard for it. I had to overcome all the bull-shit obstacles thrown at me by you and your fucked up family so thank you? No. More like *fuck* you."

It was worse than she ever dreamed. Not only was Jonah gone, but Cash Carter was a jerk. She decided she needed to let him know.

"You're a real asshole, you know that, Cash?"

It wasn't much, but she saw the small flinch at her use of his stage name. It gave her the courage to press on. "I never should have come here tonight. It was a mistake."

"Hell yeah, it was. Why'd you come, anyway?"

The sadness of losing the last trace of her best friend threatened to weaken her to tears. She fought to stay strong. She didn't want him to see how hurt she was.

"I was curious, I guess. I live in D.C. now and I mistakenly thought fate might have finally brought us back together when I realized you were going to be playing just a few blocks from my apartment."

She should have shut up then. She'd already said too much, but he was moving closer and she had circled around the couch and was close to being cornered by the advancing, angry man.

The words just kept falling out of her mouth, "Maybe I came because I mistakenly missed my friend. I wanted a glimpse of what your life was like. To see what you looked like having everything you ever dreamed of." Emotion had her choking to get the final words out.

His wicked laughter at her distress brought tears to her eyes as he spewed, "That's funny, Sam. What would you know about my dreams?"

Her anger was deserting her, leaving her deflated. "I used to know everything."

He was almost close enough to reach out and touch her. She was relieved when he didn't as he spewed his next angry rant. "Used to is right. You don't know shit anymore."

She tried to rally her anger again. "I can see that. At least your new name suits you. What a fool I've been. Missing you. Wishing things had turned out different for us."

"There never was an us. Your father and uncle saw to that."

It was true her father had never liked her choice in best friends. Jonah and his mom had lived on the wrong side of the tracks—figuratively and physically. She loved her father, but he really could be a judgmental jerk. Jonah had witnessed that first hand.

The memories softened her so his next attack hurt her hard. "What's the deal? Your fiancé know where you are tonight? Maybe you're here because he's no good in bed and you always wondered what good 'ole Jonah would have been like in the sex department?"

"You really shouldn't talk about things you know nothing about." She paused, unsure how much to share. "I'm not with anyone now." She bit her tongue before adding the truth, that she never had been.

"Ah, I see. So you decided to come on down and slum it with the token bad-boy in your life. Is it exciting going behind daddy's back to come see me?"

Why she felt the need to come to her father's defense she didn't know, but she did. "Well at least my father has never hurt me. He loves me."

"Oh, baby, don't I know it." He hesitated then, only inches away. He was close enough she could feel his warm breath on her as he leaned in to deliver more hateful words. "I've always wondered how close the two of you have gotten since I left."

He was trying to hurt her and it was working. His innuendo was clear and it infuriated her. She reached out to slap him, but he caught her hand easily. His grip was firm enough to hurt, but it was nothing compared to the devastation when he reached out with his other hand to grab her breast, squeezing so hard it hurt through her blouse and bra. "Does Daddy like your tits? How about your little cunt?" His hand slid lower, cupping her sex through her skirt while she fought to be free. "Did he get to finish off what I started our last night together? I always knew he was jealous of me."

Her outrage gave her the strength to yank her hand away. She wound up and slapped his left cheek as hard as she could.

It was a toss-up who was more surprised by her striking him. His eyes darkened another shade, yet a smug smile curved his lips into an ugly smirk.

Anger consumed her.

She raised her hand to slap him again, but this time he was ready. He stopped her arm mid-strike, subduing her easily by pushing her right arm up behind her back and yanking her whole body against his. It was like hitting a brick wall, he was so hard.

Their faces were just inches apart as she spat her angry rebuttal. "I didn't think it was possible, but I hate who you've become."

"That's rich, Sam, since you and your family are the ones that made it all possible."

She didn't understand his anger at all. Fame and money had corrupted him. There was no other explanation for it. Unfortunately, she'd gotten exactly what she'd come for.

Closure.

There would be no more daydreaming of what might have become of her and her best friend and high school crush. She knew now that he was dead.

She needed to get away from him so she could lick her wounds. She knew when she left him, she would grieve his loss all over again.

"Let me go. I want to leave."

"I don't think so. I told you. We have unfinished business."

"I thought so too, but I got what I needed tonight. You've shown me Jonah is dead. Thanks for helping me get that straight." Her voice quavered as she fought the urge to cry. How could her Jonah be physically so close and yet caverns away from her emotionally?

"I'm so happy for you, but I think I deserve closure too, don't you?" His grip was tightening, making her more aware than ever of his physical perfection as he ground his erection into her tummy.

Samantha pushed down her excitement at knowing she still had the power to arouse him. A long-lost thrill consumed her as memories from stolen moments past clouded her judgment.

He continued on, pinning her with a hard gaze she was helpless to avoid. "I will only get closure by finishing what we started six years, nine months and fourteen days ago."

Her heart lurched. Even she hadn't counted the days they'd been apart. That he had, was interesting enough. What really freaked her out was she knew in that moment the exact event he was referring to.

I'm in serious trouble.

His next words confirmed it. "You owe me one hard fuck, Miss Stone."

* * *

HE WAS ON THE EDGE, ready to lose control. He knew it, yet he felt helpless to stop it.

Jonah let his other arm surround her, hugging her lithe frame tight against his body as she half-heartedly tried to fight him off.

Her caramel-colored eyes were staring at him with such profound disappointment he couldn't take it. Slamming his eyes closed as tight as they would go, he struggled to recall some of the calming techniques he'd learned in his anger management classes.

When that failed, he tried to think of Frank and the damned lawsuits. He knew that to proceed with what his body was screaming for would surely end with him in deep trouble, and he wasn't talking about the legal kind.

I'm losing myself again.

Hatred for her family poured through his veins unchecked and her fake innocence was almost more than he could handle. He'd have preferred her to own up to her choices. At least then she wouldn't be reminding him of what a fool he'd been to believe her good-girl routine.

She should be a fucking actress.

His threat to fuck her had rendered her speechless. She was wiggling in his arms, fighting to be free as he shuffled them backwards the few feet until her back pressed against the bookshelf. In their struggle, they crashed into the shelf hard enough to tip over a decorative vase, shattering it with a crash.

How many times had he gone to sleep dreaming of finishing what they'd started that night so long ago. Never, not once, had it gone like this in his head. Yet, the sick bastard inside of him, desperate for revenge for all they'd put him and his mother through, wouldn't let him stop.

She finally found her voice, pleading with him as tears fell down her cheeks. "Don't do this, Jonah. Please. This isn't you."

He snapped. "You're right. It's Cash." He ground his steely cock against her as hard as he could. Only the clothes they still wore prevented his entry. "As you can see, he's very happy to meet you."

Raw fear shone from her eyes and it checked him briefly. He closed the last inch between them, going in for a kiss. But Samantha turned her head at the last second and he latched onto the tender spot where her neck met her shoulder instead.

He started with a lick and then a nibble. God, she tasted so fucking good. He caught a whiff of the same perfume she'd always worn, throwing him back seven years. They were in the backseat of his run-down Chevy, making out like the teenagers they had been. He was encouraged when he felt her body melting against his.

Only tonight felt different. She'd always made him feel more like a man when they'd been together. No. Like an *important* man in her life, even when he had only been an eighteen-year-old punk with big dreams. How ironic that standing here now as a twenty-five-year-old success, he felt like a coward forcing himself on her out of some sick need for revenge.

In his anger, he bit down, stopping just shy of breaking through her skin. He had marked her. How juvenile was it that that brought him joy? He wanted to mark her as his. No matter who else had her—past or future—there was a part of her that would always belong to him. He had had her heart first.

The urge to mark her in every way consumed him. He deserved closure too, didn't he?

He separated enough to look into her eyes. Her fear had receded and there was a spark, just a grain of desire in its place.

His hands flew to the front of her blouse and in one terrifying moment, he let the anger he'd pushed down erupt, tearing her blouse open, buttons flying in several directions as her ivory skin was exposed. Her chest heaved, with fear or excitement, he wasn't sure. She tried to cover herself with her now-free hands, but he didn't allow it. Instead, he took hold of her black lace bra and ripped it apart with his bare hands.

"Oh God, not like this." Her tears were coming harder as she struggled to free herself from his grasp. She was no match for his strength. He had her trapped against the shelves and as she pressed for freedom, he reached under her skirt and ripped her panties away as easily as he had her bra.

Jonah was helpless to stop from bringing the lace in his hand to his nose, taking a long drag of his current drug of choice —Samantha.

He was a man crazed. Starved for years from the one thing he'd really wanted and now, when it was there in front of him, laid out like a smorgasbord for the taking, he was helpless to deny himself.

He tried to convince her too. "Your body doesn't lie. Admit it. You want me to finish it too." He grasped her by the arms, shaking her lightly.

"No. Not like this." She shook her head from side to side as her eyes pleaded with him.

"What? You want roses and chocolates? I'd have thought you'd have been paying attention to the gossip columns."

"That's not you, Jonah. Not the real you."

"Are you so sure? Maybe you need a little demonstration to see the new and improved Jonah?"

He lurched forward then, determined to show her how cruel revenge really was. He captured her lips in a brutal kiss, plundering her mouth with his tongue. He could taste the remnants of the expensive champagne she'd drunk as her own tongue dueled back.

His heart was about to explode under the strain. The pressure of his hard manhood pressing for release from his leathers warred with the thumping of his heart, ready to pound of out his chest. His heart physically hurt as if he were having a heart attack. Memories—good and bad—rushed him. Confused him.

Within seconds, her body relaxed into him. The kiss had rendered her putty in his arms. His brain tried to reason now was the time for the ultimate revenge. He would toy with her affections, so that when he was done with her at the end of the night, maybe she would be as broken as he had when he'd been the one tossed aside.

Only the kiss was affecting him in ways he could not ignore. A spark of recognition of a long-lost magic crackled inside him, trying to ignite into a flame. He clung to the feeling just as he clung to his Sami.

The urge to consume her was overwhelming. It was more than sexual need. Even more than dark revenge. There were no words for the emotions washing over him. He just knew he would die if he didn't get inside her.

Their kiss had become ragged, each of them out of breath. He reached for the zipper of his leather pants, fighting to free his aching cock. Samantha felt his movement and renewed her struggles.

With great relief his erection sprang free, pressing between their bodies. Her eyes widened as vulnerable tears flowed down her cheeks. He leaned in, sticking his tongue out and licking the salty wetness just as his free hand reached back under her skirt, this time coming into direct contact with her soaking wet slit.

Victory. She wanted him as much as he wanted her. He stroked her pussy with little finesse. His need was too great. He lifted her skirt to her waist, enabling better access to her core. A kernel of reason tried to sprout. He suspected it was his conscience. It was shouting at him to stop.

Jonah listened to it as well as he listed to Frank and even Sami herself.

He closed the final distance, using his hand to guide the tip of his cock to her entrance. They were finally, all these years later, exactly where they'd been when Jonah had had his heart ripped out. He looked at her then. Really looked at her. How could she have the same innocence in her eyes she'd had back then as a sixteen-year-old virgin? The unique caramel shade with swirls of gold flecks were exactly as he remembered them.

He'd dreamed of those eyes more often than he cared to admit. Memories of Samantha admiring him adoringly had kept him going on the dark days when it seemed his dreams were out of reach. Echoes of her whispers of encouragement had spurred him on over the years. That she was here, in his arms was unreal. A mirage.

If this was a dream, he never wanted to wake up. Only this scene wasn't following any scripted vision from his past.

She whispered, one last plea, "Please, Jonah. Not like this."

"I'm sorry Sami. It's all I know."

He closed his eyes to tune out her haunting expression and then surged forward, crashing his body into hers with a velocity that shook several books off the bookshelf behind them. His cock rammed into her core with a ferocious vengeance so dark he almost missed the tearing of her thin barrier.

It took all his effort to stop, frozen buried deep inside her hot channel that was impossibly tight. With dread, Jonah opened his eyes and knew from the pain shining back at him that he'd just made the biggest mistake of his life.

Praying he was mistaken, he pulled his shaft out of her body, separating from her enough to look down. The sight of her bright red blood coating his own flesh was like a knockout blow. All thoughts of vengeance were gone, replaced with a crushing guilt.

What have I done?

"Christ, Samantha! What the fuck?" He searched her pained face for an inkling he'd been mistaken. Finding none, he choked on his next words. The tip of his cock still inside her as they clung to each other, each unsure how to recover.

"How? Why?" He waited for answers in stunned disbelief that she'd remained a virgin for the seven long years they'd been apart. Hell, he'd fucked at least a hundred women in that time.

Her tears turned to sobs before he got his answer. "No one else was you!" It was a shouted plea and he felt it in every fiber of his being. God help him, but she had pulled him back in. He may have been the one to overpower her body, but she had won this battle. She had overpowered his need for vengeance, plunging him into a dark need to finish making her his in every way.

Their lips found each other again as their bodies ground together, renewing their need. This time, it was Samantha who pulled away, a strange new expression he couldn't read on her face.

"Please, Jonah. Let's finish this. You were right. We both need closure."

"But..."

Her lips cut him off, sucking him into a different kind of kiss. Gone was the frantic frenzy meant as a prelude to a sexual act. In the space of a few minutes, it felt like all of the bullshit that had conspired to tear them apart had been blown away. What was left was such raw emotion; it scared the shit out of him.

He had to catch her weight as Sami jumped up, lifting her legs to wrap them around his body in an attempt to take control. His cock slipped a few inches deeper, dragging a pained groan from the woman in his arms.

"Are you okay?" It was a stupid question, really. For all intents and purposes, he was in the process of raping her.

The blush across the bridge of her nose and cheeks was adorable, kicking him in the gut. He'd been a fool. The look of innocence he'd picked up on earlier hadn't been a show. She really was... or at least had been... an innocent.

"I will be." He knew the look in her eyes. He saw it every night looking out into the throngs of women who came to their show. He may have forced this upon her, but now that they'd started, she'd become a willing participant.

He had to be honest with her. "I don't think I can any more. I know I hurt you."

"What you did to me physically didn't hurt me as much as what you're doing emotionally. I don't know why you hate me."

In that moment, he couldn't honestly remember either.

He gave in to her pleading eyes and his throbbing cock as he turned to carry her across the room towards the huge bed against the far wall. As they approached the bed, Jonah resumed their kiss, breaking only to lay Samantha gently beneath him.

She kept her legs wrapped around him as they ground their hips together, each thrust driving his cock a bit deeper. He pulled back, looking at her one final time and seeing the spark of his old Sami shining back at him.

They both cried out as his shaft drove home, buried deep inside the beautiful woman lying beneath him. Part of him wanted to hide from her gaze, not deserving the acceptance he saw in her eyes.

Again and again he took his pleasure, delivering as good as he got. It was too emotional to last long. When he knew he wouldn't last much longer, Jonah felt between their bodies, finding her

LIVIA GRANT

sensitive clit and pressing it hard enough to bring her eruption just as he exploded inside her.

Only as he laid gasping for his next breath, never wanting to leave her body, did it dawn on him that he'd just had unprotected sex for the first time in his life. Rather than feel upset or angry, Jonah felt vindicated. He had truly marked his Sami this time. No one had burst in to stop them.

In the post-coital haze, the final adrenalin from the concert and Sami's appearance left his body, leaving him drained. He managed to roll to his back, pulling Samantha along with him so that her head rested on his chest, using him for a pillow as she snuggled as close as possible.

He wasn't exactly sure what the future would hold now in light of this new change of events, but he suspected it was going to be interesting.

Exhaustion closed in. He fought to stay awake, not wanting to miss any time with Samantha, but sleep claimed him as powerfully as his revenge had just minutes before.

When he awoke disoriented some time later, it took him a few seconds for the memories to return. The lights were still on, making it easy to see he was alone. Jonah sat up with a groan, swiveling around, disappointed when he confirmed Samantha was no longer there.

His examination of the room did find one thing changed. At the edge of the bed, sitting on top of several smears of her virginal blood they'd spilled on the white comforter, was a folded piece of paper. His name was scrolled across the front in her distinctive handwriting.

Cash.

With dread, he reached for the sheet. He didn't need to read the note to know she was gone. He could no longer feel their magic in the room.

When he lifted the single sheet of paper a gold necklace spilled to the bed. He recognized the locket he'd given her on her

58

sixteenth birthday immediately. It had been the same day he'd asked her to his prom. He'd never had the money for real gold, but Sami hadn't cared that her gift was a knockoff.

There was a lump in his throat as he opened the tiny latch to the locket, not surprised to find the small lock of his hair she'd insisted on putting in the compartment. She'd been carrying a bit of him around with her and he could tell by the tarnished condition, she'd worn it regularly.

In an odd way, he'd been with her all these years apart.

The flip side of the sheet of paper had more of her distinctive penmanship.

Cash,

Consider us "closed." If you ever see Jonah again, tell him I used to miss him.

Samantha

CHAPTER 5

*S*amantha stumbled out of the elevator on the first floor of Runway to find herself backstage. She was grateful that with the Crushing Stone's concert over there were only a few band support personnel still there. From the aroma in the air, they'd hung around to enjoy a joint while shooting the shit.

The pounding beat of the dance music being served up by DJ Elixxir in the main club gratefully drowned out the sound of her boots on the tiled floor. Sam pulled her leather coat tighter around her, keeping her eyes on the ground, desperate to make her way out of the building without having to talk to anyone.

She'd taken a couple of minutes to wipe off the sticky blood on her legs before leaving the suite upstairs, but with each step, she could feel new wetness sliding down her inner thighs. In a trance, she forced one foot in front of the other, desperate to be alone so she could process all that had happened tonight. She took a peek around as she walked, grateful that Ryan, the only band member who knew her, wasn't there to confront her.

Sam was almost to the exit when she heard a shout behind her. "Miss! Stop! Where is Cash?" It was the voice of a man she'd never heard.

Samantha rushed to close the last six feet to the exit. Her hand was on the door before she felt someone squeeze her arm, pulling her to a grinding stop. Frustration at missing her exit combined with repressed anger from her encounter with Jonah spilling out in aggression. Balling her free hand in a fist, she spun around and connected with the man's left arm with enough velocity that he stumbled back, pulling her with him.

Their bodies bumped flush against each other as he glared at her. She struggled to be free, but he only held her tighter. "I need your signature before you leave."

In her precarious mental state, this confused her. Did he think she was a celebrity of some sort? She didn't really care. She just wanted to be alone.

Sam yanked hard and freed herself from his grasp long enough to turn back to the door. This time he tackled her, pressing her body against the hard metal door.

"You can't leave, yet," he growled into her ear.

"Like hell I can't! Let go of me!" Panic was closing in. Being manhandled by Jonah had been bad enough. She wouldn't survive another attack by a stranger.

"Let go of her, Frank." Jaxson's voice boomed loudly across the backstage area. Samantha almost wept with relief.

Her attacker's grip loosened, but didn't end until Jaxson was crowded in next to them, pressing himself between the two. He had his back to her, but she could feel the tension rolling off his body as he stepped in to protect her.

"Back off, Jaxson. This isn't your concern," the man named Frank argued.

"The hell it's not. This is my club. Get lost."

Frank pressed, "She's a problem."

"If she is, I'm making her *my* problem."

"But, you can't protect Cash like I can."

She was close enough to Jaxson to feel his growing anger as he leaned in to shout into the guy's face. "If Cash did anything he needs protection from, then he's gonna have to deal with me first, not this young woman."

She watched as the two well-dressed men stared each other down before the kinda smarmy looking guy finally took a step back and turned to walk away in a huff.

Only after she was relatively alone with Jaxson did she realize she should have tried to sneak out when the men had been busy with each other. When Jaxson turned to face her, she felt a wave of aggression rolling off him after his encounter with Frank. His expression only got darker as he raked his gaze up and down her disheveled body.

"God damn him." It was an under-his-breath curse, but she still heard it.

When he stopped to stare down at her legs, she knew the streak of wetness between her legs was now visible. By the time he wrenched his eyes up to meet hers, she saw rage and concern warring in his green eyes.

"Tell me the truth, Samantha. Did Cash hurt you?" She couldn't have formulated words to save her life. The lump in her throat was almost choking her as she fought to hold back the wave of tears building up inside her like a coming hurricane. She didn't know how much longer she could hold it off.

I need to get the hell out of here.

When she turned to leave, Jaxson reached out to hold her back. He was the third man to manhandle her in less than an hour. Unlike the two before him, he must have realized how his touch was affecting her because he released her, moving to stand in front of the door to block her departure instead.

She was so close to losing it. She was hanging on by a thread. She sensed Jaxson was an honorable man who was only trying to help her, but delaying her departure was making things worse.

"I promise you this. If he hurt you, I don't give a shit who he is. He'll be behind bars in an hour."

He spoke so passionately that she believed him. The events of the night were so jumbled. With their long history, Samantha truly didn't know how to process what had happened upstairs between her and Cash Carter. She knew she couldn't let herself be swayed by the small glimpses of her Jonah she'd seen in Cash's unguarded moments. For her sanity, she had to believe that she'd been with Cash tonight and that her Jonah was gone. The renewed pain of losing him, this time forever, struck her like a bolt of lightning, leaving only tears in its place.

Jaxson pulled her into a warm and comforting hug. The second his arms encompassed her, she felt safe for the first time that evening. The harder he embraced her, the harder her tears flowed until she was sobbing big ugly sobs against his expensive tuxedo.

"Everyone out!" She was only vaguely aware of his scooping her up and carrying her over to a plush couch along the back wall. She tucked herself into his chest, covering her face with her free hand in an attempt to hide herself from the grumbling groupies being forced to vacate their spot.

She suspected she should feel awkward being cradled by a near stranger, but for some odd reason, the handsome A-list millionaire made her feel safe—as if he were the big brother she'd never had, ready to protect her at all costs.

Like the gentleman he was, Jaxson pulled a cloth hankie from his inside tux pocket, holding it up for her to blow her nose as she slowly calmed down.

He pinned her with a concerned look. "You ready to talk about it?" he pried.

Unable to trust her voice, she settled for shaking her head.

He didn't give up so easy. "Did he force himself on you?" Several silent seconds later, he pressed again, "Samantha, did he hurt you?"

She was ashamed of how completely she'd allowed Cash to crush her in every way. Physically and emotionally. How much of it was his fault, she was still not certain of. She'd been saving her virginity for him, unable to find someone else worthy of her special gift. That he'd taken her offering and trampled it broke her heart, but she suspected she bore some burden of guilt.

Her inconsolable tears filled the silence, leading Jaxson to his own conclusions.

"I'm gonna kill the bastard." He juggled her in his lap to pull out his cell phone.

She knew he was calling the police, which was the last thing she wanted to happen next in the little soap opera playing out that evening. She reached to stop him, shaking her head until she found her words.

"Wait. No police." She could see the storm brewing in his eyes and added, "He didn't do anything I didn't agree to."

"So what's wrong?" he pressed.

"I came to see my friend Jonah, but he's gone. It makes me sad." Her grief was so much more complicated than that, but those words were true.

He urged her for more details. "I'm not buying it. I think the police should help us sort this out."

Visions of talking to police officers about what had happened merged with the fear of a medical examination followed by public outcry against Cash Carter. She shook her head to get the nightmare out of her head.

"I'm begging you. Don't call the police. Jonah and I have a long and complicated history. I made a mistake coming here tonight. He shouldn't have to pay a price for that."

Jaxson looked doubtful. He hadn't put his phone away yet.

She spoke up, "If you want to help me, can you call me a cab? I don't live far, but I just want to go home."

He had a way of looking at her that unnerved her. He knew she hadn't told him the whole story and she could see him trying to decide how hard to push her. When he dropped his eyes to scan up and down her body, she knew things would get worse.

Sam pulled her leather coat closer around her, careful to hide her ripped blouse. It didn't fool him. His right hand moved over her fist, gently but firmly pulling at her until her coat opened to reveal her ripped blouse and bra.

His voice was deceivingly soft, "I think it's time to call the police."

"Oh God, no. Just let it go. It would ruin him. He finally has everything he ever wanted."

"Fuck that. And what about you?"

Defeated, she could feel what small fight she had left in her seeping out as she answered, "I got what I needed too." She looked into his eyes, "Closure." When he didn't react, she added a final plea, "Please. I just want to go home."

She held her breath as he used his phone to make a call. She exhaled with relief when he barked an order to have his limo brought around to someone on the other end of the line. After Jax hung up the call, he put his phone in the inner pocket of his tuxedo and came out with a business card.

"My driver will be here in a few minutes. He'll take you anywhere you want to go." He looked into her teary eyes as he pressed the card into her trembling hand. "If you need anything, *ever*, you call me."

"Why?"

The handsome man softened as he answered, "You remind me of my Emma. And despite my current urge to beat him to a pulp, Cash is my friend. I don't know your history with him, but even if Cash isn't able to help you himself, I somehow know he'd want you taken care of."

Sam wasn't so sure of the validity of his assumption, but she took the card and slipped it into the side pouch of her tiny cross-body purse, certain she wouldn't be using it. In her distress, she'd nearly left without returning the security keycard she'd used to get the elevator to go down. She held it out to him sheepishly, worried he might be angry.

"I'm sorry I took this. I used it to come down," she whispered.

Jaxson took the card and reassured her. "I'm glad you did. I just wish I'd stayed behind. I should have trusted my gut and not left you alone." He spoke with such conviction, she believed him.

"It's okay. None of this is your fault." Her words did not convince him.

The next few minutes were a blur. She was grateful for Jaxson's protection as they pushed to their feet, out from backstage, through a back hallway and out onto the main floor of a rowdy Runway dance club. He sheltered her from the pressing crowd and lingering press there to cover the grand opening. She kept her head low to avoid the flashing cameras from catching her face as they pressed through the VIP circular door together to find themselves in the frigid early December night.

The snow had continued to fall while she'd been inside. The club had put down salt to hold down the ice, but the resulting slush was slippery. She clung to Jaxson as he guided her to the open door of a stretch limo waiting at the curb. The burly security guard who had tried to eject her in the middle of the show stood holding the car door open, an unreadable expression on his face.

The men helped her into the back of the car. She sunk into the rich leather with relief. Jaxson leaned in to talk softly to her. "I mean it. Call me if you need anything, even if you change your mind and need someone to go to the police with you."

When the lump in her throat at his kindness prevented words, she nodded, letting a fresh tear fall down her cheek. For a second she thought he might swoosh it away, but he didn't. He instead stood and closed the door before pounding on the roof, the signal to the driver he could take off.

She'd been trying to escape Runway for what seemed like hours, but was probably just minutes. Yet, as the limo started to pull away, a new panic consumed Samantha. She had this uncontrollable feeling that she had forgotten something—left it behind. Her brain knew it was her grief of finally cutting the last tenuous thread she'd maintained to Jonah over the years.

The ride to her apartment was only a couple of minutes, not nearly long enough for her to collect herself. When the door next to her opened, this time it was her doorman, Jamal, that greeted her.

"Well, I'll be! You sure are coming home in style, Miss Stone. You must have had a lot of fun."

As nice as Jamal was, she didn't have it in her to converse with him as if she hadn't just had her heart ripped out of her chest and trampled while she watched. She needed the privacy of her apartment where she could lick her wounds and put on a brave face that could fool the rest of the world that life was normal.

But life would never be normal again. It wasn't the sex, although that was a huge enough milestone in her life to alter her forever. No, even without the benefit of time to examine the events of the evening, she knew the last of her innocence had been trampled. Her blind trust and adoration for Jonah had been naive and tonight, she'd paid a high price for that naivety.

The doorman held her elbow as they traversed the snow-filled sidewalk before making it into the lobby of the building. When he tried to press her for details of her evening, Samantha brushed him off, letting him know she was exhausted and would be sure to tell him more some other time.

Sam held her breath when she got in the elevator that would take her up to her third floor apartment. She normally preferred the stairs, but knew tonight her wobbly legs would buckle under further exertion. She managed to get the key out of her purse, taking a few extra seconds to open her door when the key jiggled in her trembling fingers.

Once inside, she didn't bother to turn on any lights. She made sure the door was locked, bringing her immediate comfort, before she shuffled through the dark apartment, through her bedroom and into the bathroom. Her first stop was at the tub, pressing down the stopper and turning on the water as hot as she thought she could handle it. She went through the motions of preparing a bath as she had countless times in her life, moving on autopilot.

It wasn't until she was naked and caught a glimpse of herself in the full-length mirror on the back of the door that she froze, unable to look away from the disheveled reflection staring back at her.

Just like drivers couldn't resist slowing to gape at accidents they were passing, Sam found she couldn't tear her gaze away from the reflection of a woman she barely knew in the mirror. She examined the likeness from top to bottom, praying to see a spark of recognition.

Her long hair was askew, visible tangles jutting out at different angles, but it was the blotchy redness of her face that first alarmed her. She'd cried her makeup off completely. The only traces left were black lines of faded eyeliner and mascara that streaked below her eyes.

She looked away, unable to make the connection with her own eyes for fear of what she'd find in their depth. Instead, she could see several light bruises forming on her arms where Jonah and even the jerk Frank had grabbed her roughly. The brightest mark on her body, though, was the large hickey where her neck met her shoulder. She could make out teeth marks in the middle where Jonah had bit her. Memories of the physical pain of that moment were overridden by the disgraceful feelings of surrender his possession of her body had stirred in her.

By the time she lowered her gaze, her heart was racing erratically again. Without her skirt camouflaging her, the smears and streaks of her virginal blood were front and center. She tried to reason through the calendar, hoping to blame the red on an early cycle, but then got angry at herself for trying to excuse what Cash had done to her that night.

The word rape refused to be ignored.

It was such a horrible word. She had always thought rape was a black and white word. Like right or wrong. Up or down. Hot or cold.

In that moment, she accepted it was anything but. Part of her had hungered for his possession of her. She'd had many opportunities over the years to have sex, but each time she'd gotten close, memories of Jonah had resurfaced. She may not have answers to everything, but she knew this much. She'd saved herself for him and in some sick way, although the night had not gone the way she'd dreamed it would, she did get what she needed.

Closure.

Yet the thought of moving on with her life without her hidden obsession with Jonah scared the shit out of her. Letting go of her love for the man who had let her down was a bit like the child knowing they were ready to ride the bike, but still desperately afraid to take the training wheels off their bicycle.

Tomorrow.

As she contemplated stepping into the hot water to wash away the final remnants of the man she loved, she found she couldn't do it. Not yet. She'd been strong and left her locket behind. She'd no longer have it to cling to in times of weakness. Once his cum was washed from her body, he'd be gone forever.

Yep, she'd wash him away tomorrow. She turned off the water, leaving the full tub, and instead walked naked through the dark to her bed. Samantha collapsed to the softness and pulled the blankets up high to burrow in.

She was finally safe to loosen the reins on her fear and anger, so how ironic that now the wall of tears she'd been holding back wouldn't come. She suspected she was in shock, yet when exhaustion pressed in, she welcomed it. Anything to make her fall asleep and forget.

* * *

JONAH WAS STANDING at the mini-bar stocked with high-end

alcohol when he heard the ding of the elevator. He'd been waiting for it. Jaxson's arrival. He'd briefly thought about trying to sneak out, but it wouldn't really do any good. There would be no hiding from what had happened that night.

When he turned from the bar, he saw Jaxson standing at the end of the bed, looking at the bright red stains of Samantha's blood.

"I'll buy you a new comforter," he offered.

Jaxson looked up, fire ready to burn out of his eyes he was so angry. "Tell me, and it better fucking be the truth. Did you rape her?"

Had he? He suspected he should know with certainty one way or the other, but he didn't. "No, but... I did hurt her."

Jaxson took a few steps closer and then stopped short as if he was afraid he'd hit Jonah if he got any closer. "Just so you know, I offered to call the police for her, but she declined."

Jonah's heart constricted with the news. "You saw her?" Jax nodded. He didn't have the right to know, but he asked anyway. "How was she?"

Jaxson moved closer, bypassing his chance to knock out Jonah and picking up a bottle of high-end vodka instead. After he'd done a shot, he turned to Jonah to answer.

"She was a fucking mess. Crying. Trembling. I saw the blood and it even looked like you bit her neck. So you have about two minutes to explain what really happened up here before I call the police myself. She was no sub, here for rough fun."

He suspected he should be worried about the police threat, but in that moment, he was more worried about losing himself to the guilt closing in on him at the thought of really hurting Sam.

"No, she's not a sub, but she is... well was... a virgin."

"Christ! You forced yourself on her!"

"No. You don't know shit about it."

"Then explain it to me... fast."

"Fuck off, Jax. This is none of your damn business."

"The hell it's not. That's my bed and blanket her blood is on. She's in my limo on her way home. I sent her into this locked room to wait for you. I'm your accomplice."

Jonah panicked. "It wasn't rape."

"What was it then?"

"History."

"Old girlfriend?"

"More."

"More? You don't do relationships so what's more than a girl-friend to you?"

He hesitated, unsure there were words to capture his feelings. "Fuck. I guess soul mates."

He could tell by his wide eyes, he'd surprised Jaxson. Jonah pressed forward, oddly excited to share his secret story with his friend. "I met Sami when she was in second grade and I was in fourth. I was new in that school and she came to my rescue from a group of bullies making my life hell on the bus every day. She stuck her neck out for me. Stood up to them. I was only ten at the time, but no one had ever done anything like that for me before, well other than my mom."

"I'm guessing there is a bit more to the story than that."

Jonah choked out a bark of fake laughter. "You think? It's just the tip of the iceberg. And no offense, because I really do appreciate your help more than you can ever know, but I meant it when I said it isn't any of your fucking business."

Jax closed the distance between them, bumping their chests together in an aggressive move. "That young woman was in shock when she left here. You can try to spin this any way you want, but you and me, we both know the truth of what happened here tonight. Her blouse was ripped. She was bleeding. You're done here. You aren't the kind of Dom I want in Black Light. Worse, you aren't the kind of man I want around my Emma."

"Screw you, Jax!" Jonah shouted, determined to take some of his lingering aggression out on his friend.

Instead, Jaxson's cell phone started to ring. He took the call.

"Hey, Harry. Everything okay?" Jaxson listened to the report and hung up, pinning Jonah with a darker glare. "She cried all the way home. You happy?"

He should be. He'd finally got the revenge he'd hoped for, but instead, he let the wave of guilt he'd been pushing down below the surface crash in on him.

Did I force her?

He collapsed into the desk chair, putting his head in his hands, trying to make sense of it all. Only when he had it worked out in his head did he look up at his friend.

"You're right. I do need your help. I need to talk to Spencer."

* * *

"I won't do it. He's fucking drunk." The dungeon master cackled.

"Yes, and thank fuck for that." Jonah interjected.

Jaxson reasoned, "That doesn't matter. He's not a sub."

His old teacher and the Master of Black Light, Spencer Cook, looked at him with disgust. "Don't I know it. I spent weeks mentoring him to be a responsible Dom and if what you're telling me is true, he didn't learn a damn thing."

Jonah wanted to defend himself, but he bit his tongue instead.

Jaxson rebutted, "I understand your disappointment. It can't come close to mine, but it's either this or the cops. He isn't walking away without consequences. He needs to have some sense knocked into him and... well... I'd like to handle this privately if possible."

Jonah was close enough to the mini-bar that he reached for the bottle of vodka. He hadn't had nearly enough yet. He could still see the tears of disappointment on Sami's face as he'd fucked her.

Master Spencer's hand clamped down on his, stopping him. "No more painkillers, Carter. You're gonna feel every stroke if I do this."

Jonah knew he should be afraid, but he felt dead inside instead. Like something or someone he loved had died. His first thought was of Samantha herself, but realized that perhaps she'd been right. Maybe it had been the last piece of Jonah that died tonight. Only Cash was left.

For the last few years, Jonah had counted the two alpha men in the room among his inner circle of friends, at least they had been up until tonight. He felt like shit that he'd disappointed them, too.

His friends silently got up and moved towards the door. They stopped in front of the elevator in the foyer, turning back, each pinning him with a disappointed glare. He wouldn't have said their approval was so important to him, but in that minute, regret consumed him. He'd fucked up two of his too-few friendships tonight.

Three if he counted Samantha.

He pushed to his feet, feeling stiff. He risked further censor by reaching for the already poured shot glass and downing the burning liquid, letting it scorch his throat and stomach from the inside before trailing behind them to the elevator he'd take to his doom.

The ride three floors down was awkwardly silent. Spencer exited first and motioned for Jonah to follow with Jaxson bringing up the rear.

The backstage space was empty with limited lighting, but he could hear the still partying crowd not far away on the main floor of Runway. It was ironic that not too long ago he'd been in front of that same crowd, enjoying entertaining, not knowing that his life was literally about to be turned upside down by a chain reaction of events no one could have predicted.

The hallway narrowed before they stopped in front of a curtain. The men went through a doorway to the left and found themselves in a small supply closet type space. Before Jonah could ask what the hell was going on, Spencer stepped forward, grabbing the handle of an upright mop in the corner. He pulled it towards him and Jonah could hear the click of a mechanism just before Spencer pushed the handle away from them. A popping noise filled the space at the same time the edges of a secret door came into view.

The space was now glowing in a pale purple hue. The glimmer grew as they pushed through the door to find a flight of stairs leading down, lit with the same recessed neon lighting. Jonah felt his dread growing with each step he took deeper into the bowels of the building.

How ironic that he'd been looking forward to playing at D.C.'s newest and most exclusive of BDSM clubs. His friend Jaxson had called him months ago to invite him to not only become a member, but be their entertainment at the grand opening of Runway upstairs. Now, each step he took into the coveted club came with apprehension instead.

As they hit the bottom landing, there was yet another door, this one opening into a large room with a rather low ceiling, adding to the basement ambience. The entire wall to the left was filled from floor to ceiling with small numbered lockers while the wall to the right sported several signs telling patrons to leave all forms of electronics—cell phones, cameras, recording devices—in their assigned locker. The signs surrounded a window that was greyed out with tinted glass making it difficult to see if anyone was on the other side.

The main attraction of the room, however, was a security guard setup in the center of the room sitting behind a tall desk type counter where a black light lamp was setup. Jonah watched Spencer and Jaxson step up to the light and flash their wrist under the beam. Their tattoos lit up as a scanner registered their membership ID.

Jaxson greeted his employee. "How are things going so far, Danny?"

"So far so good. A bit slow, but I'm hoping things will pick up now that the show is over," Danny answered.

When it was his turn, Jonah stepped up, placing his own distinctive tattoo under the scanner until he heard a locker to his left unlatch.

"Please put all electronics in your assigned locker, Mr. Carter." Of course the guard recognized him. He'd hoped for a bit of anonymity at Black Light, but knew he'd have to settle on their extreme non-disclosure contract keeping his proclivities from making it into the mainstream media.

Everyone else who comes here has as much to lose by being outed as I do.

The club was thankfully not very full once the final door opened to allow him entry. Jonah had been in many BDSM clubs over the last several years as he'd traveled across the country. Most were little more than an open space that could be used for small get-togethers of like-minded individuals.

The better clubs had decent BDSM equipment for couples in the lifestyle who couldn't afford to dedicate a part of their home to their sexual fetish of choice where they could come to play. He'd learned the hard way that no matter what those clubs had as privacy clauses in their contracts, when you're a celebrity, it's close to impossible to maintain any privacy when socializing or playing in a normal club. He had been the subject of more than a few tabloid stories to prove it.

It was why he was thrilled his A-list friends, Jax and Chase, decided to open Black Light. And D.C. was the perfect place for the club. As he looked around the space as he followed Spencer down the few steps to the main floor, he relaxed just a bit. The pressure of always being on display for the public was beginning to take its toll. It was the price of success. The price of fame. Before he'd achieved it, it never dawned on him that he might one day miss his anonymity.

As they weaved slowly through the different scenes in progress, Jonah started to look at the club through different eyes, and it made him uncomfortable. What would Samantha think of the submissive currently wrapped completely in latex, strapped to the gurney with only two small holes for her nostrils to receive precious air? Her Dom was walking around the table she was held captive on, using his flogger to light up every inch of her body. It wouldn't hurt much through the thick latex covering, but it was still pretty serious play considering the possible breath depravation while unable to move or speak a safeword. The Dom watched intently to ensure his submissive came to no real harm.

The deeper they got into the room, the more hard-core the scenes became. Blood play... hot candle wax... severe rope suspension where the submissive was writhing in agony. All edgy. All consensual. All kinky as fuck.

And every one of them would freak out an innocent Samantha.

Up ahead, he saw their destination. Fucking great. The St. Andrew's Cross was elevated on one of the half-dozen platforms in the space that served as locations for voyeurs to gather around to witness the punishment of the day. As a sadist, Jonah usually got a thrill right before directing a scene, particularly one where a submissive would be restrained and on display while he delivered the pain that would ultimately bring them pleasure.

But today was going to be different. He was no masochist and tonight was not about pleasure. He closed his eyes, forcing himself to relive the moment when he'd taken Samantha's virginity. The minute that she'd begged him to stop and he'd ignored her—ramming into her for his own revenge. His own sexual gratification. Fuck, his own uncontrollable urges.

He was a terrible Dom. Despite how hard Spencer had trained him, it was clear he sucked at it, because regardless if she was a submissive or not, a good Dom would have stopped upstairs. Would have protected her, not just today, but everyday. He tried to remind himself that she wasn't a complete innocent in this. She'd spent years siding with her father and then had come here out of the blue and fucked with his mojo. She should have stayed away.

They were just about to the raised platform when he saw Ryan barreling towards him, a near topless sub trailing behind. He saw the fire in his friend's eyes and knew before River opened his mouth, he wasn't going to like what was coming.

"I'm glad to see you came to your senses and lost the daddy's girl. I hope you told her to fuck off," Ryan slurred.

Jaxson was nearby and stepped between them. "You need to head back to the hotel now, River."

"Screw that! We just got here. We haven't even started playing yet." He pulled his date closer as he teetered a bit.

Even in his precarious state, Jonah could tell River had had way too much to drink to be SSC - safe, sane and consensual. Jaxson leaned in and tried to handle the situation confidentially, "You signed the contract. You know we have a max drink limit of two over a six-hour period. The rule is a non-negotiable. Go back to your hotel and sleep it off. Come back tomorrow."

"I'm flying to New York tomorrow."

"Then you fucked up, didn't you?" Jaxson wasn't backing down.

Jonah was just relieved they weren't talking about him.

Spencer had been wiping down the heavy cross that formed an X before turning to him and asking him one last time for his consent.

"You're sure about this?"

He could say no. He didn't think Jaxson would call the cops on him, but in that moment, he considered going to them on his own. He was pretty sure he deserved it. Instead, he answered, "I'm sure."

"Okay, then. You know the drill." Spencer was all business with his former pupil.

As Jonah moved towards the platform, it became evident to his friend River what was about to happen. He elected to make a scene.

"What's going on here, man?" When Jonah ignored him, he

pressed in closer. "What happened upstairs?" There was a manic urgency in his voice.

Of all the people on the planet, Ryan just might be the only one who actually did deserve the truth. He'd been there through it all —the good, the bad and the utterly horrific.

He kept pressing, "Tell me you sent her packing. She doesn't deserve to lick your boots." His friends hands were squeezing his forearm, trying to get through to him.

Jonah answered truthfully. "She's gone, yes."

"But? What aren't you telling me? Did you give her what she deserved?"

Had he? At the time, he'd sure as hell thought she'd deserved what he gave her and more. After seeing the disappointment in her eyes as he hurt her—well he wasn't so sure.

"I can't talk about this now, River," he asserted.

It was Jaxson who tried to pull River away and send him on his merry way. River was having none of it. He turned on Jaxson to defend Jonah, "I don't know what the hell you and Cook here are planning to do, but trust me, no matter what happened to Sam upstairs, she deserved worse."

"Ryan, let it go, man," Jonah tried to appease him.

His friend turned on him, "Hell no, I'm not gonna let it go." He'd started so push and shove to stay free of the dungeon monitor who'd come over to keep the peace. As the monitor started to pull River away, he started shouting back to Jaxson, Jonah and Spencer. "Don't let her do this to you again, man. I'm not gonna scrape you off the floor and prop you up again like last time. You've got so much more to lose now." When his words failed to get through to Jonah, he added, "I'm not gonna keep visiting you when you're back in jail."

Could he have shouted that a bit louder? Jonah wasn't sure the press upstairs in the dance club had quite heard the news.

He felt Jaxson's glare on him as he waited. He heard his quiet question, "Jail? Anything you'd like to talk about?"

"Naw, not really. Let's get this over."

Jonah moved in slow motion, his back to the rest of the room to try to shut them out. If he could, he'd have asked Jaxson to clear the room for him to avoid the possibility of gossip, but he suspected he didn't deserve that accommodation either.

He took his leather vest off first, revealing the wife-beater tank top underneath. He pulled the damp white cloth over his head, flexing his muscles a bit in an attempt to relax, knowing from experience it was better to remain loose.

He stepped up to the platform, leaning in and pressing his chest against the center of the X. The one advantage was that at least he wouldn't have to watch the spectators who would surely line up to watch the popular musician being strapped down to the medieval style cross.

He'd expected to have his arms and legs immobilized at the ankles and wrists. The extra straps across his biceps and thighs and one final thick belt across his ass had him feeling a tad bit claustrophobic. He tested the restraints and found them completely unforgiving. In a way, it suited him.

He hadn't shown Samantha any mercy.

He sensed someone close behind him before he heard his mentor speak quietly in his ear. "What's your safeword?"

"I don't have one."

"Bullshit. Not in my dungeon. Everyone playing has a safeword."

"This isn't a game. I'm not playing."

"Safeword or we're done here," Spencer insisted.

"Fine. Samantha."

Spencer hesitated, adding, "I've never seen a woman get under your skin like this one."

Jonah let the silence stretch between them. When he sensed his mentor pulling away, he made a final request. "Hey Spencer." When he knew his friend was listening, he added, "Don't stop until I bleed."

He heard the sharp intake of breath, but that would be the only answer he got before the sound of a bullwhip snapped as Spencer warmed up. There was a new silence to the room. As he had suspected, the scenes around the club ground to a halt with everyone interested in watching the A-list celebrity about to be whipped. Most would incorrectly assume he was a closet submissive.

Time stretched out as he waited for the first lash. Even knowing it was coming, the first strike took his breath away. He'd spent hours practicing the delivery of this very punishment so he knew that the man at the other end of the whip was a true professional. It was an art using a bullwhip on human flesh. It took superior control and aim to not strike in danger zones.

The next lash came a bit lower on his back, striking fresh flesh as did the third and fourth lashes. Each stroke of the whip drew a louder involuntary grunt of pain.

Jonah was having trouble catching his breath. The strikes were coming faster than he normally delivered them when he was at the other end. He fought down the panic that threatened when the first bites of pain seared through his body. He tried to focus on the small lamp on the wall directly in front of him. It didn't offer much light, but it provided a focal point that helped him fight down the panic.

The pain was settling in deep and he welcomed it. He let it wash over him, bringing a welcome clarity. His body was awake and with the new alertness came a flood of memories he wanted to avoid. Buried memories from their past merged with newer remembrances from just a few hours ago. He fought to think about his justified vengeance, but tears of pain and shame clouded his view as memories of the pain on Samantha's face hurt his heart just as the bullwhip destroyed his flesh.

Each strike took him deeper in his anger at her family for tearing them apart. Deeper in his desire to possess her in every way. Deeper in his regret at scaring her.

It was when the strikes started criss-crossing his back, wounds compounding on top of already raw strips of skin, that the pain drew long groans. He should have known Spencer would take his job seriously. Eventually, the pain made it impossible to think of anything else but the temptation of making it stop. He didn't deserve it. He hadn't stopped when she'd asked him to.

He tasted his own blood after biting his inner cheek to keep from shouting out his safeword. The dungeon master had slowed down his delivery, but the added time only allowed him to apply harder strikes.

Jonah felt it the moment the leather broke through his punished skin. It was precisely the same second he screamed her name at the top of his lungs.

His screamed "Samantha!" hung in the air as the room remained silent, listening as Jonah broke into tears. Everyone in the dungeon assumed he was crying from the pain of his punishment, but he knew the tears were for the empty spot in his gut as he remembered the words she had left for him on her short goodbye note.

Consider us "closed." If you ever see Jonah again, tell him I used to miss him.

CHAPTER 6

*H*e didn't remember much of what happened after they'd released him from the cross. Jaxson had been there with a dungeon monitor who assisted with aftercare by applying a lotion that stung like a sonofabitch to the worst of the lashes on his back before helping him navigate the way back up to the suite on the top floor.

Jonah was emotionally and physically exhausted. When he realized where they were taking him, he wanted to argue to return to his upscale hotel room downtown. He wasn't crazy about the idea of sleeping in the very bed he'd taken Samantha's innocence, but the second his head hit the pillow, the last of his energy left him in a whoosh.

He was vaguely aware of Jaxson and Chase taking his leather pants off before rolling him to his stomach and covering his stripped back loosely with the white sheet. He was grateful that sleep took hold of him and didn't let go.

By the time he awoke, the Saturday morning sun was shining through the windows facing to the east. He had one moment before he moved that he felt normal. He was used to waking up in a different hotel room every day so today felt no different. At least not until he stretched, and the soreness seared through his back as the tightening skin pulled, triggering spikes of pain.

With the physical sting came the memories of the night before. He lay immobile, mulling over the events from beginning to end, looking at them through fresh eyes of a new day.

Jonah lifted his head, looking around to see if he could find a clock, his phone or the watch missing from his wrist. Instead, he found the letter Samantha had left him along with her locket. He leaned over to grab it, wanting to hold it.

Her words still hurt him and that pissed him off. They were no good for each other. Clearly. He was a fucked up Dom and she was anything but a sexual submissive. More like a sexual novice. Their years apart had left them strangers and it needed to end there.

He needed to piss. He needed food. He needed… fuck, he was sick of feeling needy. What he really needed was to get the fuck out of this building. When he left, he wouldn't be coming back. Ever. Not even the lure of Black Light would change his mind.

Jonah pushed to his feet and stumbled his way to the en suite bathroom to find the toilet, a toothbrush and a shower, in that order. The hot water could only perk him up so much. He needed caffeine.

Luckily, he and Jaxson were close to the same size. He raided the huge walk-in closet to find a pair of jeans, black T-shirt and other items he'd need to borrow to get back to his hotel. He'd planned on staying in D.C. until the following Tuesday when he'd need to leave for his next concert. But, it had been months since he'd been to his loft in New York City and he couldn't get there fast enough. He would use the next few days to hide away from the world and lick his wounds. No fans. No band. No Frank. No music.

No Samantha.

Shit.

When Jonah left the suite, he tried to take the elevator down, but he didn't have the keycard to make it work. He wandered down the hall to the left of the foyer until it opened up to a U-shaped balcony that overlooked the dance club below. Unlike the first floor where tall bar tables and stools were packed in to accommodate a press of a crowd, this floor had plush couches, love seats and chairs setup in intimate groupings for VIP's.

The club was empty and quiet. He looked over the railing to see a few employees still trying to clean up from the opening the night before and prepare for the coming press of patrons later today when Runway would be hosting its first daytime fashion show.

"I didn't expect to see you up this early." Jaxson startled him.

He turned to see his friend heading his way having come through a door camouflaged in the wall of mirrors.

"Once I woke up, I couldn't get back to sleep." He added, "I hope you don't mind me borrowing a few things. I'll send a messenger over to return them when I get back to my hotel."

"Don't worry about it, man."

The men stood silent, awkwardly trying to figure out what came next.

Jaxson broke the silence first. "Come on in. We were just about to eat breakfast. There's plenty."

He wanted to turn him down, but his stomach growled at the mention of food. He didn't usually eat much before a show and the events of the night before had made him skip his normal post-show feast. As a result, it had been close to twenty-four hours since he'd last eaten.

If he thought things were awkward with Jax, it went to a new level of uneasy when they entered the large office to find Chase and Emma making out on the couch, barely dressed. Jonah stopped in the doorway, ready to excuse himself when Jaxson took charge.

"All right, you two. We have company. You'll have to put that on hold for a little bit."

Chase grinned like a Cheshire cat at being caught, but Emma pulled the nearby sheet up to cover herself, looking embarrassed. He was just starting to piece things together when Jaxson confirmed his hypothesis.

"Don't worry about it. We slept in here because we didn't want to have to go home for just a few hours."

Jonah completed the thought. "And you would have normally slept in the suite I slept in if I hadn't fucked that up."

Jaxson shrugged, "We just opened. We hardly have routines yet, but yes, that is the general idea. Our loft is only a few blocks away. We could have gone home if we wanted to."

"Well, I'll be out of your hair after breakfast. I just need to track down my..."

A shirtless Chase stood next to him wearing only his lounge pants, a full reusable shopping bag held out. Jonah took a peek to find his clothes, watch, wallet and his thick wad of cash jammed in the bag.

Emma had scurried off to the bathroom, leaving the three friends to start eating. The T-shirt he wore was just loose enough that he'd forgotten for just a moment about the wounds on his back. He winced as his punished back connected with the back of the chair.

They ate in silence for a few bites until Chase couldn't hold his tongue.

"So what are you going to do to get her back?" He had the audacity to grin the sexy grin of his that Jonah knew his friend Jaxson was not immune to.

Jonah stuffed another bite of pancakes in before answering truthfully, "Not a damn thing. We're no good for each other."

Still, knowing they were wrong for each other and forgetting about her were two completely different things. Renewed worry hit him, wondering what she was doing right that minute.

It didn't surprise Jonah when Jaxson inserted, "We need to butt out, Chase. I think Cash knows what's best."

He'd never heard Chase go against Jax before, "That's a load of shit. Anyone there last night could see their chemistry."

"I flunked chemistry in high school. I'm no good at it now, either," Jonah countered before taking his next bite.

Jaxson pressed, "Ryan stopped in this morning already looking for you. He's pretty upset."

That didn't surprise him at all. What did surprise him was Jaxson refusing to let the subject drop. "He asked me to call him when you got up today. I think he's planning some kind of an intervention."

Jonah pinned his friend with a glare. "You didn't call him, did you?"

"No. Should I?"

"Not unless you want to really piss me off."

"I couldn't give a shit if I piss you off. What I care about is making sure you've got your head on straight before you do something stupid today like you did last night." Jaxson looked up as a now dressed Emma joined them from the connected private bathroom. She looked a lot like Samantha, which gave him pause.

What was she wearing right now? It hurt to think of her.

Jaxson had patted the chair next to him for Emma to take her seat. He had already piled her plate full with food and handed her a tall glass of milk first. Jonah noticed her annoyed look until her Dom raised his eyebrow. Jaxson never said a word. He didn't need to. His submissive took the milk, taking a swig before starting in on her pancakes.

He'd forgotten for a second that Chase was there until he was caught watching their submissive red handed. "We've caught our Emma skipping more than a few meals lately. She's lost the right to fill her own plate, haven't you, sweetheart?" Chase leaned over to spear her next bite with her fork as she blushed, embarrassed at being called out.

"Unfortunately." When Jaxson cleared his throat, she rushed to add her, "Sir."

Jaxson chuckled as Chase scooped her next bite into her mouth. Despite her pink blush, their submissive's lips curved into a wan smile.

"Ryan wasn't the only one who's called looking for you." Jonah looked back at Jaxson when he paused. "Frank paid me a visit demanding I give him Samantha's full name and address. Gave some bullshit story about you asking him to check on her."

Jonah's pulse increased. He shouldn't really care what happened to her, but dammit if he didn't. "I sure as hell hope you didn't give it to him."

"I didn't."

He let his breath go. "Good."

Jaxson pinned him with a stare. "I told him you'd be checking in on her yourself and that he didn't need to bother." His friend's eyes bore into him, filling him with a renewed wave of guilt. He might be able to run away from what had happened with the world, but Jaxson was the only person, besides Samantha herself, that knew exactly what had happened the night before.

Jonah answered reluctantly, "It'd only make things worse if I went to check on her. We said our goodbyes. There is nothing left for us to talk about."

Chase wouldn't give up. "So don't talk. Body language is more powerful anyway."

"Yeah, well we tried that last night. Nothing good will come from us seeing each other again."

Chase pressed him, "What makes you think that?"

Jonah was losing his patience. "I appreciate you trying to help. I do, but we have way too much bad history between us. And even if we didn't, I'm way too fucked up and dark for Samantha. She is an... was an... innocent. I'm into way too many kinky things for us to ever have a chance, even if her family would let it happen, which of course they won't. Trust me. She never wants to see me again."

The friends let an awkward silence fall over the office as the occupants focused on eating to avoid further discussion. Jonah gobbled a few more bites before pushing to his feet. He had an urgent need to get the hell out of this office. Away from the only people to really know how bad he'd fucked up the night before. Back to his hotel where there would be a waiting throng of fans who would fan his ego and help him forget he wasn't really worthy of their adoration.

He was halfway to the door, ready to bolt out when he hesitated long enough to stop and issue a short statement. "Thanks, Jax. For... well... you know." He was on the move again, anxious to get away.

He was stopped in his tracks by Emma calling out to him. "I never thought you were a coward!"

Jonah spun around. Certain he had to hear her wrong. The fire in her eyes as she glared at him shocked him. Gone was the submissive young woman who'd been eating breakfast with them just minutes before.

"Excuse me?" Jonah prodded her, glancing at her Dom for support when she didn't back down. The proud smile on Jaxson's mug pissed him off worse than Emma's words.

"You heard me. You are acting like a coward. I don't know everything that happened to you two in your history, but I know what I saw last night. That woman loves you."

"I see thousands of women look like that at every concert. It's called lust, not love."

"That's crap and you know it," she countered.

Jonah looked back at Jaxson again, expecting his friend to get his submissive under control. Instead of support, Jaxson encouraged Emma. "I think you should tell Cash what you told me, sweetheart."

She glanced at her Dom for confirmation of his support before she continued to address Jonah. "You have no idea how hard it is for a woman like Samantha to get up the courage to come here to talk to you. Having to cut through the crowd of paparazzi, the press, and crush of screaming fans. But she did it. For you. Don't you think you could take the time to at least go check up on her for a few minutes?"

"She doesn't want to see me," Jonah argued.

"Why is that?"

Memories of waking up to find her gone, the locket and letter the only thing left of Sam hurt. He hated to say the words. "I hurt her."

"Then go there and apologize. Make sure she's okay."

"It's better this way. We couldn't have a future. She'd never understand the whole D/s lifestyle I'm used to living."

"And you know this? You've discussed it with her?" Emma was almost shouting again she was so animated.

Jonah prodded her Dom. "Are you going to let her talk to me that way?"

Jaxson stared him down. "Yes. She's right."

Jonah's annoyance grew. "You have no idea what it's like…"

Emma countered back. "No. You have no idea. I was where she is. Completely naive, in the dark about our whole lifestyle. Jaxson and Chase didn't assume I'd hate it. They took their time. Introduced me to it slowly. Helped me understand how much I loved being their submissive. If you walk away now, just know you never even gave her a chance to find out if the lifestyle was for her or not. You're making that decision for her."

Jonah wanted to argue back. Had it been anyone other than Emma saying these words to him, he would argue back. But he realized she was the one person in the building who might really understand what Samantha was going through right now. Still, he just couldn't go to her.

"I'd like to ask you for a favor," Jonah surprised Emma.

For the first time in their conversation, she looked uncertain, glancing at her Dom. Jaxson nodded his approval to her before she answered, "Okay."

"I just can't go to her, but you're right. We should check up on her and see how she's doing. You seem to understand what she is going through. Would you please go to her and make sure she is gonna be okay? Let me know if she needs anything?"

"I really think you should…"

He cut her off. "I'm not going. Please. Check on her for me."

"Okay," Emma relented.

He did feel better knowing Emma would be checking in on Sam. It helped him feel better about leaving. He had his hand on the doorknob, ready to depart when he stopped in his tracks. He had one final request of Emma.

He didn't bother turning to look at her. He knew she was still listening since the room was still silent.

"Tell her… well…" He wasn't sure what he wanted to say. He settled for, "Tell her I'm sorry."

* * *

THE POUNDING on the door got Sam's heart thumping. She'd been avoiding calls from her friend, Megan all day. She should have known to pick up and at least get rid of her, knowing she'd eventually show up on her doorstep. A quick glance at the alarm clock next to her bed confirmed she'd been leaving her apartment to go to the concert exactly twenty-four hours before.

One day. That's all it had been? She had wallowed in her grief at losing Jonah, slipping in and out of sleep all day. If anything, she felt worse now than she had when she'd left the club the night before. In fact, it felt worse now than when she'd lost Jonah when she was sixteen. At least back then, she'd had hope he'd come back for her one day.

Now, I know Jonah is gone. Lost to me forever.

A dangerous urge she hadn't felt in a couple of years tickled her subconscious. She was flirting with the kind of emotional pain that she'd found seductive years before. She shook her head, trying to focus on her calming techniques.

The knocking was back. Louder. More persistent.

"Fine. I'm coming. Stop pounding!" She grabbed up her ratty robe, thankful it was at least long and thick enough to cover herself completely. She didn't need Megan learning more than she was ready to share about the disastrous night before.

When she got to her front door, she realized in her stupor the night before she hadn't put the safety chain on. Odd. Megan usually just let herself in with her backup key if the chain wasn't on.

With dread, Samantha peeked through the peephole. For the briefest of seconds, she let herself hope Jonah had followed her. What a foolish hope that was, but she was equally surprised to find Emma Fischer, Jaxson's girlfriend, on the other side of the barrier.

"Hello? Are you there, Samantha? Can I please come in? It's Emma."

She briefly considered just staying silent, knowing she would eventually leave assuming she wasn't home.

"I know you probably don't want company right now, but I'd like to talk for just a few minutes." Thirty long seconds dragged by and Sam thought she might leave. Instead, a quiet plea met her ears. "Please."

Shit.

Sam turned the deadbolt, turning the doorknob and pulling the wood open just a crack.

"I'm sorry, Emma, but I'm not really up for company right now."

"I understand, but I was hoping you'd let me in for just a few minutes." Emma looked different than she had the night before. Gone was the glamorous gown and makeup. She wore a pair of worn jeans and a University of Wisconsin hoodie with a pair of cute snow boots. Her long, dark hair was pulled back in a pony-tail. She looked like any other grad student on the campus of Georgetown University as she held up the paper bag in her left hand. "I brought you some mac and cheese from Henry's down the street. If you're like me, you'll love it."

Samantha gave in, unwilling to be rude to someone who was going so out of their way to be nice to her. She stepped back, pulling the door open wide enough to allow Emma to enter, before she closed and locked the door again. By the time she turned, she was in time to see Emma scanning the barren room. No one had been to her apartment except Megan, who understood. She had a sudden need to explain.

"Sorry I don't have a lot of furniture. You can put the food down on the table in the kitchen. Do you want anything to drink?" It took all of Sam's energy to be a polite hostess.

"Don't worry about it. Until a year ago I was a grad student living just off campus just like you. Only I lived in a rundown house with four other roommates. My room was in the attic where I only had one tiny window and the side walls were so angled I banged my head on the ceiling at least once a week." Emma's easy smile put Samantha at ease.

When Emma started to unbox the dinner she'd brought, Sam stopped her. "I'm not really hungry right now. You can just leave it there on the table and maybe I'll eat it later."

"No offense, but you look like you could use some nourishment. Have you eaten at all since…" Her voice trailed off.

Sam wondered how much her visitor knew about what had happened between her and Cash Carter the night before. Since Jaxson had pretty much put the details together, she assumed Emma must know as well. Why else would she be here?

"Why did you come here?" She expected to hear that Jaxson had sent his lover.

Emma hesitated, making Sam wonder if she was preparing a lie. "Cash is worried about you."

Hearing his name hurt. "Right. You mean he's worried about a lawsuit."

"No," Emma quickly answered. "He's worried about you."

When Sam eyed her skeptically, Emma continued on in a rush. "I'll be honest. I don't know him well, but I could see he was upset."

"Well, that makes two of us then. I don't know Cash well either." Samantha finally shuffled to the kitchen table and took a seat in one of her two chairs, nodding at Emma to take a seat in the other.

After she'd taken a seat, Emma continued on. "That's not what he said."

"He actually talked about me?" The news surprised her.

Emma shifted in her seat looking a bit uncomfortable. "He didn't really have a choice. Jaxson can be pretty persuasive."

Emma's face glowed at the mention of her lover. Sam felt an unwelcome pang of jealously towards the very nice woman sitting at her kitchen table.

I wonder if she knows how lucky she is to have not one, but two, men like Jaxson and Chase.

"So how are you? Really," Emma pried.

"Just great."

"No offense, but you don't look so great."

"Gee, thanks."

"Is there anything I can get you?"

"No."

"Would you like to talk about it?"

"No."

Emma tried to keep the uncomfortable conversation going by changing tactics. "I'm guessing Cash has changed a lot since you knew him as a kid."

The game of fifty questions was starting to annoy Sam so her response was snotty. "I never knew Cash. I only met him last night." When Emma looked confused, she added. "My friend was Jonah. Cash killed him off."

Emma nodded her understanding. "Actually, I think I got to meet Jonah this morning at breakfast."

LIVIA GRANT

She refused to allow there to be hope. It was the only way she could reconcile what the man she'd once known as Jonah had done to her the night before. What had happened was bad enough at the hands of Cash Carter. To think it had been Jonah only made it hurt worse.

"You're mistaken. Jonah is gone. Cash swallowed him."

"Maybe. Maybe not. I just know he is worried about you."

"You can tell him I'm fine and dandy. I got his message loud and clear." The lump in Sam's throat was getting harder to ignore as she struggled not to break down into tears in front of her guest.

"What message is that?" Emma questioned.

"That he hates me. And my family."

Emma reached her hand across the small table to squeeze her hand. "The man I saw today does not hate you."

The first tear fell down her cheek and it pissed her off. She swished it away as she answered too aggressively. "You don't know him like I do and no offense, but I don't really give a shit anymore what he thinks... or feels... or does... He can go to hell. Can you give him that message for me if you see him again?"

Emma looked sad. "If that's how you really feel, sure." When the lump in her throat prevented her from answering, Emma continued on. "I know it's none of my business, but I'm a romantic at heart. I saw how you two looked at each other when he jumped off the stage to chase after you. You can't deny. There was something there."

"Yeah, there was, but he made sure to kill it last night when..." She stopped. She'd almost finished the sentence with the confession of his raping her.

Did he rape me?

She was as confused as ever now twenty-four hours later.

"I know he feels really guilty about something."

"Good. He should."

"You're sure..."

Sam cut her off, pushing to her feet and started walking

94

towards the door. "Thanks for stopping by, Emma. Please tell Jaxson thanks again for his help last night. He is a wonderful man." She opened the door, holding it open and turning back to address Emma as she made it clear she wanted to be alone. "You are a very lucky woman."

Emma stopped next to her. She looked like she wanted to say something more. Instead, she pulled a business card out of her hoodie pocket and pressed it into Sam's hand. "I know you have Jaxson's contact info and he will always be there for you, but I want to give you my contact info as well. Call me. Anytime. I know what it's like to be in love with a celebrity. It isn't easy."

The women's eyes met. "I'm not in love with Cash."

She was certain Emma knew she was lying, but to her credit, she didn't call her on her lie.

"I hope you eat the mac and cheese before it gets too cold."

She was persistent. "Thanks for stopping by, Emma."

With her final goodbye, Sam closed the door in the face of her visitor and shuffled back to the bedroom, bypassing the food. Her stomach would churn if she tried to eat anything.

When her head hit the pillow, she went to work using her calming techniques, meditating in order to stop herself from giving in to the negative self-talk playing on a loop in her head.

Why the hell did I have to go to that fucking concert?

CHAPTER 7

"*H*ey. Are you sick? It's after noon and you're still in bed."

Megan had managed to let herself into the apartment and was poking her. Samantha rolled to her stomach, pulling her pillow over her head and burrowing in to block out the bright sunlight coming in through her bedroom window. She felt disoriented, unsure how much time had passed while she wallowed in grief and self-pity.

Her friend Megan was talking louder in her attempt to be heard through the pillow. "I've been trying to phone you since yesterday. I've been worried, silly. Why didn't you answer and tell me you were sick? I'd have brought over some chicken soup yesterday."

Sam didn't know how to tell her friend that chicken soup wasn't going to cure what ailed her.

"Let me run down to the diner. I'll pick you up something."

She didn't want her friend wasting money on food she had no intention of eating. She had a nightstand full of that already. Cheese and crackers... the untouched mac and cheese Emma had brought the day before… even a PBJ sandwich she'd managed to get one bite out of before her stomach had revolted.

"I'm not hungry. Really. I just need more rest," Samantha reasoned, her voice muffled by the bedding.

Megan's sassy response was close to an insult that Sam didn't have the energy to care about. "I'm pretty sure a shower should be on your list of things you need too." When Sam shifted to give her friend the evil eye, Megan raised her eyebrow. "Sorry. I just tell it like it is."

"Well, that's great. No offense taken."

"I can't believe you aren't freaking out. I thought you had that huge exam tomorrow. Have you studied at all?"

A fresh wave of panic rolled in on Samantha. It wasn't bad enough to have to deal with the emotional upheaval of being crushed by Jonah. Now she needed to add the real possibility of flunking one of her most important classes to her worry list. She needed to get her head out of her ass and pull it together.

Maybe she's right. I do need a shower to snap out of this funk.

Still, the thought of resuming her normal routine after having her heart shredded two days before seemed ridiculous. She'd tried her best to rally her anger at Jonah, but so far, she'd failed miserably. Her heart physically hurt with longing for something she knew she could never have. She wished she could get some quality rest, but every time she closed her eyes she was back in that room at Runway… in Jonah's arms.

He'd taken her virginity. It had been a gift she'd always intended for him, so regardless of how bad it had gone wrong, she couldn't help but feel that the sex had been destined. The thing that bothered her the most was that it had been so very different than what she'd dreamed. It hadn't been "I love you" sex. Not "I've missed you" sex, or even "make-up" sex.

It had been "good-bye" sex.

Luckily her friend was too busy zipping around trying to straighten up to notice the tears coming to Samantha's eyes.

"Okay, well if I can't get you to come out to study with me, I'll leave you here to study. Text me if you need me to bring you anything, will ya?"

Megan was a good friend, but Sam was relieved she was leaving.

"Thanks. I'm sure I'll be fine by tomorrow," Sam lied.

I'll never be fine again.

Megan floated out of the room and Sam relaxed a bit. She should get up and put the security chain on to prevent another unwanted intrusion.

As Sam contemplated moving, she heard a quiet knock from the next room. She assumed Megan had just knocked over something until she heard a high-pitched squeal. Sam was too lethargic to follow what was happening until it was too late. She vaguely heard soft voices coming from the living room, but before she could get up to close her bedroom door, he was there. Standing in the doorway to her barren bedroom. Looking every inch like the larger-than-life persona he was.

Jonah.

No, Cash.

Was she awake or had she fallen back to sleep? If so, she never wanted to wake up.

He spoke from the doorway after several long seconds of awkward silence. "Can I come in?"

She said the only words she could form in the moment. "Why are you here?"

He stuffed his hands into the front pockets of his perfectly snug designer jeans, rocking self-consciously until finally admitting, "I was worried about you."

Only after Megan pressed into the room to stand between the two old friends did Sam realize she might have a problem keeping the disaster that was Cash Carter a secret from her tight-knit group of friends.

He took a step closer and it panicked her. "Stop! I didn't say you could come in, Cash."

Jonah stopped cold in his tracks. Her use of his stage name surprised him.

He confirmed it by acknowledging, "I deserved that."

Megan finally found her voice. "You know Cash Carter and never told me? No wonder you'll never go out with any of the guys I've tried to set you up with. I can't believe you kept Cash a secret!"

Christ, she needed Megan to shut up, but then she realized how bad of an idea it was to be left alone with the rock star who'd hurt her.

She was still trying to figure out what to say when Cash turned and held his hand out to greet Megan. "Actually, I'm Jonah Carter. Nice to meet you."

Her friend's eyes widened with the same level of surprise as if she'd just seen an alien walk into the room. Samantha started shaking her head frantically, praying Megan would keep her big mouth shut. Sam sent her most pitiful plea, but her silent bid for confidentiality was ignored.

"Wait. Jonah. As in *her* Jonah?" Megan's head tilted towards the bed while Jonah shook her hand in an unending greeting.

Sam rushed to salvage a scrap of her dignity. "Good-bye, Megan. Thanks again for checking on me. I'll see you tomorrow."

Megan refused to let go of the hand of the celebrity in the room. In fact, she refused to take her eyes off him as she started putting the pieces of their complicated puzzle together. "You bitch. At no point in your Jonah stories did you think it was important to tell me that *your* Jonah was actually Cash Carter?"

Cash's growing grin pissed Samantha off.

Sam threw her ratty old stuffed bear from the bed and hit Megan upside the head, but her efforts still failed to get her friend to stop staring at the grinning musician.

"I didn't tell you because Jonah is dead. Like I said. This is Cash."

That wiped the smile off his face. He extricated his hand finally from Megan's so he could lean down and pick up the wayward bear. Only as he looked at the ratty old toy did she realize it had been a mistake to throw it.

His smile was back. "You still have it? Hell, I won this for you at the county fair over ten years ago."

She wasn't sure why, but she lied through her teeth. "It's a different bear. I got it after you left."

The censoring glare he sent told her he knew damn well she'd just lied to him.

Megan put her hands on her hips, still angry at her friend for keeping such a big secret. Her reaction was exactly why Sam hadn't told her. She knew her friend wouldn't let this topic drop. Sam felt foolish enough already for holding on to some childish, romantic dream that could never be.

"OMG! You're the woman. From the newspaper. You went to his concert! Without me!" Her friend was shouting.

"Keep it down. I'm not sure Jamal heard you."

"Screw you. I can't believe you kept something this big a secret from me. Why would you do that?"

Emotions were boiling inside her. They started to erupt. "Oh, I don't know. Maybe because I knew you'd overreact. Maybe because I don't feel like I know Cash at all. But mostly because I went there never intending to even talk to him."

"For what it's worth, I'm glad I saw you in the crowd."

Damn him. Why was he being so nice? So empathetic. So... *Jonah.*

"I wish I could say the same," she countered. Seconds stretched on as she watched him struggle to find his next words.

In the silence, Megan injected. "Well I'm glad you're here. Maybe you can figure out what's wrong with her. She hasn't left her bed in two days and..."

"That's enough, Megan." Sam cut her friend off, sending her a death stare to try to shut her up.

She got the message. "Fine, I can take the hint. I'll leave, but…"

"NO! Don't leave!" The only thing worse than Megan talking too much was Megan leaving her alone with Cash. "Cash was just leaving. Megan stay."

Megan looked between the two other occupants in the room, trying to decide what to do when Jonah had the nerve to stick his hand out to her, risking another long handshake. "It was nice to meet you, Megan. I can take it from here."

Her friend gave her one last glance before she turned and left her alone with the very dangerous man in the room. Sam fought the urge to call out to her girlfriend up until she heard the front door close, ensuring the old friends were finally alone.

"Does everyone always do what you tell them to do?" Sam quipped.

"Everyone but you, apparently."

"Funny. I don't remember you asking me anything."

He repeated his first question of the day. "Sam, can I come in?"

"You're already in," she retorted breathlessly.

"I liked what she said," he said too softly as he took one step closer before stopping.

"Which part? Her excitement of being a Crushing Stones fan?"

He shook his head as he braved another step closer. "I like being *your* Jonah."

Samantha was stunned—truly speechless at this new and improved version of Cash Carter. She was struggling to reconcile him with the man who'd so clearly hated her just two nights before.

Sensing she wasn't going to respond, Cash glanced around for the first time. "What's all this?"

She followed his gaze to her nightstand covered in full plates, bowls and glasses. Two days worth of untouched food and drink.

"I'm not hungry." His green eyes narrowed as if he were unhappy with her answer.

He let it go, instead moving towards the window and pulling the curtain aside to let in additional sunlight from the brisk December day. He looked out the window briefly before turning around and stopping at the sole chair in the room. From her vantage point she couldn't see what had grabbed his attention until he lifted the ripped blouse and bra she'd been wearing two nights before during their fateful meeting.

His eyes met hers and she saw what looked like genuine regret mirrored at her. "I'm so very sorry, Sami. I didn't mean to…" He trailed off. Unable to say the ugly word that was the true label for what had happened between them.

"Don't worry about it." Why she was letting him off the hook, she wasn't sure.

"I do worry. I wouldn't blame you if you…"

"Hate you?" she finished his sentence.

"I was going to say called the cops."

She wanted to scream at him that she'd spent the last two days praying to feel hate towards him, but God hadn't answered that prayer yet.

"Like I said. Don't worry about it. I got what I went there for."

That surprised him. "What was that?"

The lump in her throat threatened to ruin her resolve. She had to get through the next good-bye with her dignity intact. "Like I told you in my note. Closure." The next words refused to be silenced. "I've been such a fool. Waiting around as if you'd just show up one day."

"Like today?" he offered.

"Nothing like today. I've been waiting for Jonah. Like you said. *My* Jonah. You showed me he is dead."

The larger than life persona in the room moved closer. "Honestly, I thought so too, until you showed up. You breathed life back into him."

He was getting too close. Saying things that confused her. Feeling vulnerable, Sam pulled the covers up higher to hide her naked body from his eyes, suddenly self-conscious of not only the fragile state of her heart, but of her body at the moment. When he took another step, she reacted. "Cash, stop!"

He listened, stopping just a few feet away, directly next to her desk. In a panic, her eyes darted quickly to the corkboard full of Crushing Stones pictures, all of them featuring her favorite lead singer. She could feel the heat creeping up her neck and across her face at the embarrassment of being caught acting like a silly groupie.

Jonah reached out to pull down one of the smaller pictures on the board. His face lit up into a smile that was so bright, it could surely power a city block. It was a good thing she was laying down because the joy on his face was a glimpse of the Jonah she loved. The Jonah who was her best friend and who, at one time, had been her entire world. It made her head swim.

"This is from the night of the talent show, isn't it?"

It was her absolute favorite picture of the two of them together. The small, candid photo he held was among her prized possessions. She could only nod a reply.

Their eyes met. "It feels like a lifetime ago," he answered solemnly.

She managed to choke out an emotional reply. "It *was* a life-time ago."

Their words stalled, but his eyes pinned her with a heated gaze. Another step closer. He was close enough to touch her now so she was surprised when he turned his attention back to her nightstand.

"What have you eaten in the last two days?" When she failed to answer, he turned towards her and startled her with a sharp command, "Samantha, answer me."

She stumbled over her words. "Wasn't hungry. I had some crackers and... other stuff."

He picked up a few of the dishes to examine them, easily seeing the crusty film covering the lot of it, the result of her neglect. He started picking up dish after bowl.

"Wait a minute. What are you doing?"

He ignored her and started walking towards the bedroom door, his arms full of dirty dishes.

She called after him. "Jonah!"

He'd only been out of the room for a few seconds, but he startled her when he leaned back in, the sunshine-inducing smile back on his adorable face as he gloated. "I told you Jonah wasn't dead."

She groaned at being caught in his trap. The second he was back out the door, she threw back the covers and bolted to her feet. She swayed a bit, light headed from standing too quickly.

She rushed towards the bathroom, grateful the second she was safely inside and could turn the lock that would keep her separated from the dangerous man in the next room.

Just the exertion of running to bathroom left her out of breath. She had barely eaten in the last two days. She hadn't even been drinking water. As she approached the full-length mirror, she didn't recognize herself. She allowed the thin blanket she'd carried with her to fall to the floor, exposing her too-thin body to her scrutiny. As usual, her gaze was drawn to her biggest and most shameful secret of all.

The tug of a familiar desire licked at her subconscious; calling to her like a siren.

Life was out of control again. Completely and wholly out of control. She needed Jonah to leave. He didn't deserve to know how far she'd gone in her failed attempt to maintain control in her life after he'd left her years before with no explanation.

* * *

HE'D DONE this to her. Broke her. Crushed her.

He should be happy. He'd named his band Crushing Stones for a reason. Only now that he'd picked one of them off, all he felt was regret. As sure as he hated hurting Sam, he was equally sure he'd never feel the same regret had it been her father or uncle who'd been crushed.

Something wasn't right. He just couldn't put his finger on it. Jonah took a few minutes to dump the leftover food from Sam's room into the garbage bin, scraping off the plates and bowls and then doing something he hadn't done in years—washed the dishes.

The more time he spent in Samantha's kitchen, the clearer his unease became.

Why is she living in poverty?

The apartment was practically barren. Exactly enough furniture and food to sustain life, with no frills whatsoever. Literally every dish Sam owned was presently dirty as he began cleaning up. The refrigerator was near empty with only half-used condiments, a couple yogurts and a few cups of milk left in the carton.

The cupboards weren't much better. Ramen noodles, peanut butter, crackers, a few cans of soup. He hit the jackpot on the next cabinet coming out with a relatively new box of Lucky Charms.

Memories he'd repressed roared back with a vengeance. The cereal had been his favorite, something his mom could usually afford. How many times had he and Sam eaten the colorful, sugary cereal as their after school snack together? He'd forgotten the simple pleasure having graduated to five-star restaurants and his personal chef's cuisine.

He grabbed two of the bowls he'd just rinsed out and poured a healthy portion for each of them. The remaining milk was just the right amount.

By the time he returned to the bedroom with their gourmet dinner, the bed was empty. There was no way she'd left the small apartment without him knowing which told him she had to be behind the closed door which he assumed was the bathroom.

After he set the bowls down, he took a minute to look around the room. Like the living room and kitchen, this room too was devoid of what he assumed would be the normal trappings of a college grad student. While the piles of books, papers and her computer on the desk seemed right, the open closet wasn't even half full. A quick check of the sole dresser found the bottom drawers empty.

An uneasy feeling settled in his gut. Samantha's family was part of the upper echelon of the Plano, Texas elite. Her father had been mayor for over fifteen years now. They were founding members of the exclusive country club in the upscale suburb of Dallas. And most importantly to their history, were intimately tied to the state legal system, serving as district judges while running the premier legal firm in the entire Dallas-Fort Worth metroplex.

Samantha should be living in the lap of luxury.

He was halfway to the bathroom door to see what was keeping her when he heard a muffled cell phone ring. His own cell was in his back pocket. It must be Sam's.

Jonah sifted through the messed bed, coming out with her smartphone just as it stopped ringing. Instant hatred consumed him at the picture of her father filling her screen. He hated the anxiety he felt just seeing the photo of a man that was likely hundreds of miles away. As successful as Jonah had become in the music industry, it bothered him that he could be mentally knocked back to a vulnerable teenager in the space of a few minutes.

Reality was creeping in. What the fuck was he doing here? There was no way this visit could end happily. He'd come out of guilt for what he'd done to Sam. Out of curiosity, looking for answers to questions he should have long ago stopped asking. He should leave, before he got pulled in further, yet his feet refused to budge as he let the sliver of magic he felt when in Samantha's presence hold him hostage.

He listened for movement, but he only heard silence from beyond the bathroom door. Sam's phone, still in his hand, started to ring, once again displaying the smug picture of his nemesis. His finger hovered over the answer button, tempted to answer and then... what? There were no words that could fix the past between the men.

He needed to leave. He would collect her, make sure she ate something and then he'd leave. Their worlds were caverns apart. She'd do better to start taking Daddy's advice and hook up with a country club elite and become the Texas royalty she was destined to be.

His feet finally moved, taking him to the bathroom door. "Samantha! Your father has called twice. You need to come out and deal with this." Jonah pounded on the hollow door when she didn't answer. "Come on! It's taking all my self-control to keep from answering and telling him to fuck off."

Nothing.

He tried the knob. She'd locked the door.

"Samantha! This isn't funny. Open the door."

How long had it been since he'd cared about another person? Really cared. As he stood outside that shitty door, pounding to no answer, a foreign kind of anxiety took hold. He wasn't sure how he knew, but something was wrong.

"Sam, open the door right now or I'm going to kick it in." He silently counted to five. "Fuck."

Jonah stepped back and in one fluid motion, connected his boot near the lock of the door, shattering the pressed wood and creating a boot-sized hole through the thin door.

He stooped down to peek through the hole. "Dammit! Sam!"

His vision was obscured, but he could see Sam's bare legs as she was sprawled on the tiled floor. He jammed his right hand through the hole to unlock the door from the inside and rushed through the door.

Christ. She was naked. Her body laid at an odd angle as if she'd collapsed. Her matted hair obscured her face, but nothing could hide the bruises on her arms, the sharp hip bones protruding from her too thin body and... what the fuck?

Scars. Dozens, no, hundreds, of neatly spaced scars. On her arms, wrists, inner thighs, stomach.

"Oh Sami, what have you done to yourself, baby?"

Jonah kneeled and with dread felt her wrist for a pulse. He was grateful to feel her thumping heartbeat. As he continued to assess what was wrong with her, he scanned her body again. It broke his heart to find streaks of dried blood and what he assumed was his spent cum on her inner thighs.

Two days. She hadn't showered?

Two days. He could see how chapped her lips were. She hadn't drank?

Two days. All that food had gone uneaten. She was starving herself.

With trembling hands, he pushed her hair away from her face. She was so pale. Goosebumps were covering her flesh from the chill in the room. Jonah moved into action, standing and rushing to the bathtub to turn on the faucet, thankful for a steady stream of hot water. He rushed to pull his T-shirt and jeans off, stripping completely before kneeling next to Sam and scooping her into his arms.

Her small groan encouraged him. He pulled the curtain and stepped into the hot stream of water, holding Samantha close, trying to share his body heat with her. The water was awakening her and she began to struggle in his arms, disoriented.

"Shhh, Sami. Let me take care of you, baby."

Jonah crouched down, sitting at the end of the tub and cradling Samantha on his lap as the hot stream of water fell on them like a waterfall from above. He held her until he felt her shivering stop. He held her until she curled against him, self-consciously wrapping her arms around his neck and snuggling closer. He held her until the water began to cool and he knew he needed to get her washed up before they ran out of hot water.

He reached for the bar of soap on the built-in shelf of the tub and took the time to run his soapy hands across every inch of her body he could touch, trying his best to wash away the evidence of their disastrous reunion two nights before.

It was when he was washing her face that she finally opened her caramel brown eyes, pinning him with the most heart-wrenching look of longing he'd ever seen in their depths. In that moment, he knew he was projecting the exact same sentiment back to her. As fucked up as the situation was, he couldn't shake the feeling that he was exactly where he was supposed to be... doing exactly what he was supposed to be doing.

He finally broke the silence when the water was getting down-right cold. "We should get out."

It was a struggle to reach the faucet. Jonah finally had to leave Sam to grab several towels from the cabinet above the toilet. He dried her first, trying his best to keep her from getting chilled again. Despite his efforts, her teeth began to chatter.

"You keep it too cold in here. Where is the thermostat?" he inquired.

"Living room. Don't like big bills."

There it was again. Why was she acting so frugal?

"Stay here." He left only long enough to bump the heat up to seventy-five degrees before returning to finish drying her off. Sam tried to pull away from him when he moved to dry her legs. She struggled to hide herself from him.

He grabbed both her wrists, stopping her struggles easily and pinning her with a glare. "When did you do this to yourself?" When she didn't answer, he added, "Why? Why the fuck did you do this to yourself?"

He could see defiance sparking in her eyes. She wanted to argue with him and he welcomed it. He'd rather see the fire in her eyes than the defeat he'd put there before.

When she failed to answer him, he did the only thing that made sense to him in that moment. He leaned over her and pressed his lips to her inner right thigh where the worst of the scaring stood out. Jonah placed tiny kisses as he inched his way across her damaged body, wishing he had the power to erase the scars as well as the pain that had put them there.

"Jonah." Her voice was but a whisper.

When he'd finished, he kneeled up so she could see his eyes. He wrapped his fingers through her wet hair and held her head stationary to ensure she would not look away as he leaned in. They were so close he could feel her ragged breath on his cheek.

"Are you listening to me?"

"Yes," she whispered.

"You will never again hurt yourself. Is that understood?"

Her eyes widened and he could see her pupils dilate at his command. She'd yet to reply.

"I mean it, Sam. Never again. Say it," he pressed.

It took a few seconds, but she finally acquiesced with a quiet, "Never again."

Satisfied, he scooped her still damp body into his arms and stood, carrying her into the bedroom and placing her gently in the middle of the bed. He propped several pillows behind her back and sensing she was self-conscious from her nakedness, pulled the remaining sheet up to cover her.

He reached for the tall glass of water he'd left on the nightstand and pressed it into her hand. "Drink this. All of it."

She didn't argue. It took awhile, but she eventually did drink it all.

He then grabbed one bowl of Lucky Charms and moved to begin feeding her. This, Sam resisted.

"I'm not feeling great. I don't think I should eat."

"You don't feel good because you haven't eaten. Open."

He wasn't going to stop shoveling bites into her mouth until she'd finished the entire bowl. They ate in an amicable silence. By the time their bowls were empty, Samantha's eyes were drooping. He could tell she was fighting to stay awake.

Jonah stood and leaned in to help Sam get more comfortable. "You need to get some rest."

The strength of her death grip on his arm surprised him. "I don't want to go to sleep."

"You're exhausted, baby. You can barely keep your eyes open."

Sami opened her mouth several times, but couldn't seem to say what she wanted to. She finally begged him, "Will you be here when I wake up?"

He detected the tears in her eyes. She was fighting not to cry. "Do you want me to be?"

"Yes. Please." The vulnerability in her eyes made it impossible to deny her.

"Then I'll be here."

Jonah crossed to the closet, happy to find a folded blanket on the upper shelf. He brought it back to her bed, pulling back the sheet and sliding into the bed next to her. He spread the blanket over them and then laid on his back, pulling Samantha into his arms so she could use his chest as her pillow.

She released a sigh as she snuggled closer, throwing her left leg over his body as if to trap him. He didn't say it out loud, but it would have taken wild horses to drag him away from her. She was such an innocent and he was so wrong for her in so many ways. But tonight, he needed to watch over her. Needed to ensure she got her rest and took the time to eat and drink. Tonight he'd play the role of her protector.

Tomorrow, he'd go back to his glamorous life and try to pretend he hadn't just left half his heart in D.C.

CHAPTER 8

*R*eality was better than any dream she'd had in the last seven years. Samantha had stirred awake fifteen minutes before, feeling overheated. It took a few seconds to realize the warmth was courtesy of the body heat of her oldest friend whose muscular chest was presently serving as her human pillow.

The sun had gone down leaving her bedroom in dark shadows. It didn't matter that she couldn't see him. Samantha's body craved his proximity as she clung to him like two locked puzzle pieces.

Jonah was there. In her apartment. In her bed. His rhythmic breaths in slumber comforted her. His mere presence calmed her in a way she'd forgotten was possible. He'd been gone so long she'd begun to think she'd imagined how close their friendship had once been. He had been her safe haven.

She wished she could go to sleep in his arms like this every night for the rest of her life. There'd been a time when she was sure that was her future, but that time had long ago past.

Lost in her memories, she missed Jonah's waking until his arm hugged her tighter. She clung to him, grateful he'd stayed with her like he'd promised.

"Thank you," she whispered softly into the quiet room.

"For what?"

"Staying."

"I said I would."

She didn't have to say the words on her tongue. They both knew he'd promised to stay before and hadn't done it.

She didn't know for sure how much time they had before Jonah disappeared again so she wanted to say the most important things first.

"I'm so sorry about your mom."

She felt him tense up at the mention of his late parent. "Thanks."

"I wish I'd known she'd been sick. I would have liked to visit her."

Enough time passed she thought he was going to ignore her comment. "She would have liked that. She loved you."

Sam heard the emotion in his voice and it brought tears to her eyes. "I loved her too."

"She told me, you know."

"What's that?"

"That you used to visit her after I left."

"She was the only one who understood. She missed you as much as I did. I hated to leave for college. When I came home for Christmas my freshman year, she'd moved away."

"Yeah, that fall I convinced her to move back to the east coast to be closer to where I was playing."

"I'm glad. I'm sure it made her happy."

Several quiet minutes passed as she twirled her finger across his hard chest, playing with the patch of masculine, dark hair that reminded her he was no longer the wiry eighteen year old he'd been before he'd left her. He was all man.

He broke the silence. "I can't believe I slept that good. I was out."

"Me too. I'd have thought you would sleep great with all of the success you're enjoying. Your music... well, it was always good, but... you deserve all of the fame and fortune you've achieved. I know how hard you've worked for it since you were a kid."

She didn't know what to make of his silence.

He finally admitted, "It's starting to feel like a job... and I hate it. We've been on the road too long. I'm exhausted."

"So why not take some time off?" She tried not to sound too hopeful that he might want to spend some of that time with her.

"I can't. I've tried, but even when we're off, I can't relax. It always feels like someone is chasing me, ready to take it all away."

She didn't know how she knew, but she suspected the people chasing him in his nightmares looked a lot like her father and uncle. Renewed curiosity gnawed at her, desperate to find out more about why they'd hated each other so much.

"Let's move on to the next awkward topic. I don't suppose you're on birth control pills by chance, are you?" he asked hopefully.

She snort laughed. "Ah, that would be a no."

"I'm a dumbass. I should have got you the morning after pill. I'm guessing it's too late now. I'm sure everything will be okay, but just in case, I'll be sure to leave you my card so you can get in touch with me if... well... you know."

Memories of dozens of photos of Jonah with different women on his arm flitted through her mind, courtesy of the paparazzi and gossip columns. Fear that she'd become just another notch on his belt hurt her to the core.

"You must go through a lot of those cards." Her retort came out sharp.

"Hey, I'm not gonna apologize for living my life," he snapped back.

"I never asked you to. At least you know I don't have any diseases, which is more than you can say to me."

"I'm totally clean. That's the first time I've not used a condom. Ever."

While that gave her a bit of relief, she really didn't want to think of the details of his hundreds of trysts over the years they'd been apart. The thought of him lying in other beds like he was in the moment, sharing intimate time with women more beautiful—more famous—than her stabbed at her heart. A jealousy she had no right to feel washed over her.

"Let's change the subject," she suggested flatly, trying not to ruin the short time they had together feeling angry with him.

"I agree." Sam started to relax a bit until he hit her with, "Why did you start cutting?"

"I don't want to talk about it." She tensed.

"Tough shit."

"I promised I wouldn't do it again. Let it go."

"Fine. Why don't you have any food in the apartment?" He wasn't letting up.

"I have food," she groused.

"Ketchup doesn't count." She couldn't help but giggle. "Seriously, Sami. What's with the poverty routine? I'd have expected you to be living in one of the cool new lofts with your apartment full of expensive things. What gives?"

She wasn't even sure she could verbalize it. "You wouldn't understand."

"Try me."

"Dad doesn't want me working. He wants me to be able to focus on law school." It was the truth, although not even close to the full story.

"Listen, I may hate the bastard, but there is no way he knows you're living like this. He's the same guy who bought you a brand new Audi a month before you turned sixteen. He showered you with everything you asked for, and a bunch of shit you didn't even want."

She hesitated, unsure how to verbalize her actions.

"He still does," she admitted reluctantly.

"I don't buy it. What are you doing with the money then?" He hesitated before squeezing her as if to hold her hostage. She wished she could see his face until he leveled his accusation. "You aren't spending the cash on drugs, are you?"

Samantha slugged his chest with her free left hand, and not in a playful way. "I can't believe you'd think that."

"Yeah, well the money is going somewhere."

She didn't understand why, but she didn't want to explain it to him. It felt too private and she suspected he'd think she was being naive to think she could make a difference.

"Samantha."

Damn, she'd forgotten that tone of voice. She'd missed it. It told her he was in control. Instead of revolting like a normal 21st century woman, she relaxed into his dominance, letting his safety net blanket her if only for a few minutes.

"Fine. I choose to donate it to a good cause. I don't need so much."

"What kind of cause?" He probed skeptically.

He was the only person in the world who could possibly understand her motivation. Would he ridicule her?

"I'm a sponsor of disadvantaged women and children at Dallas's newest domestic violence center. I know they can put Dad's money to better use than to buy me another pair of shoes or piece of jewelry."

Jonah started to press her away from his chest, moving to separate. Sam fought the urge to cry that he might be preparing to leave.

She shouldn't have mentioned the shelter.

He pressed her to her back as he rolled towards her to lie on his side facing her. He propped his head up in his left hand so he could peer down at her from a just a few inches away. The only illumination in the room was the dim lamp light from the street corner beyond, which cast intimate shadows.

For a moment, it was hard to reconcile the handsome man with shoulder-length hair and a few days scruff on his face with her friend Jonah. He'd left when he was eighteen. She'd only had the ability to watch him aging through social media and the gossip rags. But his eyes, intense as ever, were the same as he peered down at her.

They'd remained quiet for over a minute as each of them luxuriated in memorizing the other's changed features.

When he spoke, it was with awe. "You did that for my mom and me, didn't you?"

He'd put it together. She didn't trust her voice, choosing to nod her yes instead.

Sam was a bit surprised by Jonah's chuckle. They weren't discussing anything remotely funny. She waited for his explanation, praying he wasn't making fun of her.

"We are quite the pair." He paused. She liked being part of his pair again. "Even back when we were kids, you always tried to hide your wealth from me. I always knew you were embarrassed by it. Like you expected me to think less of you because you came from money."

"Didn't you?"

"Not really. It was more…" Jonah paused, choosing his words carefully. "I'd get mad at myself for being jealous of you. And I was mad at myself for blaming my mom when I knew it wasn't her fault my old man was a drunk bastard who beat on her. But mostly, I hated always feeling vulnerable. Like I never really knew if we'd have enough and I was helpless to help her at the time. I'm so glad Mom got to live the last few years of her life without that worry."

She heard a vulnerability in his voice that scared her. Her larger than life Jonah was laying himself bare, something she suspected Cash didn't allow very often. She was humbled by it.

"I'm glad too. She loved you so much. I'm sure she was proud of your success."

"Yeah." Jonah reached out with his right palm to caress her

cheek. Sam leaned into his touch, absorbing every second she could of his attention. When he grinned, his face lit up.

"All these years later, and what a mess we both are. You, giving away everything, feeling guilty for being one of the lucky ones. Me, hoarding cash. Carrying it around with me like a goddamn safety blanket to prove I have more than enough."

A puzzle piece fell into place for Sam in that moment. "So that's how you got your stage name."

He nodded. "I never leave home without at least five grand on me."

She smiled a sad smile. "Maybe you could send some of it to the shelter. It might help you and I know it would help them."

The tension in the room was shifting as the old friends looked into each other's eyes. It was in that moment Samantha became more aware than ever that they were both still very naked. Feeling embarrassed, she glanced away. What she found on his right shoulder took her breath away.

"Is that Rocky?" she said, reaching out to trace the tattoo of a shaggy dog that looked exactly like her old family pet.

He nodded.

She glanced back into his eyes as she broke the news. "He died just over two years ago."

"That sucks. I loved that pooch," he admitted.

"Do you have a dog now?" she asked, genuinely curious about any scrap of private information he would share with her.

"Naw. I travel too much. Work too much."

Sam went back to examining the mosaic of tattoos across Jonah's body. Musical references. A shout-out to his favorite songwriter. She got a lump in her throat at the beautiful rose with a dedication to his mom.

She rolled slightly so she could examine his other arm, following his art until her heart literally stopped at the sight of the small tattoo on his inner forearm. It was mixed in with a waving flag.

Maybe I'm wrong.

She reached out to trace the simple "*9/11/01 - I Remember.*"

When her heart started beating again, it pounded hard in her chest. She let her gaze return to his face, but he swam before her from the tears forming. Their eyes locked and then he nodded.

"You're the only person in this world who understands what that day really means to me. Everyone just thinks I'm a patriot. They don't stop to figure out I was just a ten year old kid that day."

"Why?" she managed to vocalize.

"Do you have to ask that? It was the day I met my best friend." Sam's heart thumped with hope. He prodded her. "Why did you keep the locket?"

"You know why. The same reason."

She saw agitation in his eyes and it confused her. "I need to ask you something, and I need the truth."

"Anything. I'd never lie to you, Jonah."

He was struggling to form his question. "Are you or were you ever engaged to be married?"

Where the hell had that question come from? He'd asked her about being married before. "What?"

"You heard me. I need to know."

She reached out with her fingers to touch his face. She didn't understand why, but this felt like an important question.

"You know I was a virgin. Not only have I never been engaged, I've never even had a serious boyfriend."

She'd thought the news might make him happy so the fire of anger she saw in his eyes confused her. "What's wrong?" she followed up.

He struggled to compose himself. He looked away, taking several deep breaths and when he turned his face back to her, the anger was gone, replaced with the vulnerable longing he'd reserved for her and her alone.

Their years apart faded. In that moment, it was as if no time had passed. They were exactly where they belonged.

Together.

Jonah leaned in, capturing her mouth in an open mouth kiss meant to reaffirm his possession of her. Sam melted into his embrace as their bodies ground against each other. His free hand explored her body as she held onto him for dear life. She was glad she had when he pulled out of their kiss, breathing heavy as he informed her, "I should go."

"What? No!" Her panic returned in a whoosh. She clung to him with all her strength. "I can't lose you again. Not yet."

The pain in his eyes told her he didn't want to leave either, but his words didn't match. "Sami, I'm no good for you. By some miracle, you are still this perfect, shining light. I'm dark and dirty."

"That didn't bother you when we were friends."

"It always bothered me. I hated to see you ostracized by the cool kids for sitting with me at lunch."

"That was nothing compared to the bullies that bothered you for selling out with the mayor's daughter."

His voice was melancholy, but she could feel him slipping away. "We really have been swimming upstream since the day we met."

She was determined not to lose him again. Not now that she'd seen the real Jonah was alive and well. Samantha pressed him. "What is it you think you've done that's so irredeemable?"

"Sam, you are too innocent. You won't understand."

His condescension pissed her off. "Is it just about the sex? That I was a virgin?" When he didn't answer her right away, she started grasping at straws. "Fine. Then let's go back to just being friends again."

"That's not possible."

"Why? Do you hate me?"

"Of course not, but I do hate your father and your uncle."

Just the mention of the other men in her life had Jonah pulling away from her physically. As he rolled to his back, Samantha let her instincts take over. In her desperation to hold onto the tenuous last thread she had to the man in the room, she pushed to her knees and threw back the sheet that had been hiding their bodies.

His muscular physique was a work of perfection. Muscles rippling in all the right places. She prayed she'd have time to become intimate with each and every inch of him, but in that moment, she knew she had one chance to keep him there. She wasn't too proud to use it.

While she may have remained a virgin, they'd done plenty of heavy petting as teenagers. Jonah had instructed her on the art of oral sex as they'd experimented as teenagers. While she was a bit rusty having had no practice since he'd left her almost seven years before, she was determined to show him she had been a very good student.

His cock was larger than she'd remembered. A nest of course hair surrounded his phallus, merging with the line of masculine hair pointing down from his belly button. Sam reached out and encompassed his girth with her left hand while leaning down to lick the head of his shaft.

His groan of pleasure encouraged her to proceed. She placed the tip of his expanding manhood in her mouth and sucked gently like he'd taught her so many years before.

"Christ, Sami." She felt his half-hearted attempts to pull away and doubled her pressure. "You need to stop, baby."

She moaned 'uh-ha' as she took him deeper into her mouth. His corresponding groan made her feel powerful. She knew that soon he would be helpless. His erection was like flesh covered steel in her pumping hand and she yearned for it to be inside her again. Surely she would die if he didn't make love to her.

In one fluid motion, Jonah regained control over their tryst, pulling her off his cock and rolling them both to the other side of the bed where she ended up flat on her back, him towering over her with a pained yearning on his face.

"Are you sure?" he asked.

"Never more sure of anything in my life," she answered truthfully.

She'd expected him to resume their kiss, but instead, his lips found her neck, nibbling and sucking his way across her body. When he got to the now dark bruise where he'd bitten her two nights before, he kissed her lightly, as if his kiss could take her boo-boo away.

Down her body his mouth went. Kisses... nibbles... sucks... He moved slowly, leisurely, as if he were memorizing every inch of her. As he got lower, he moved so he could spread her legs wider. She fought the urge to close her eyes and just enjoy the sensation of Jonah's lips and tongue caressing her, not wanting to miss watching him as he worshiped her body.

Like after the shower, he took the time to kiss her self-inflicted scars covering her flesh. He situated himself between her legs, opening her up so that her pussy was laid bare for him. She expected him to kiss her there so his words startled her.

"I mean it Samantha. You will never hurt yourself again. Promise me."

"I told you..."

"Promise!"

Their eyes met as she pledged. "I promise, Jonah."

Satisfied with her agreement, Jonah leaned down to spread the lips of her pussy open like the petals of a flower. Sam was self-conscious because she suspected she was very wet. Her suspicions were confirmed when Jonah leaned in, dragging his tongue from the bottom to the top of her slit, ending at her sensitive nub which he took into his full mouth, sucking hard enough that it brought her both pleasure and pain.

Sam closed her eyes, letting the sensations of his mouth and hands roaming over her most private anatomy take her higher and higher. She felt as if she was about to explode when his attention stopped.

Her eyes flew open, trying to understand why he'd aborted. There was a look of desperation in his eyes. "I don't suppose you have a condom, do you?"

"Yeah, right. I stocked up on the off-chance you'd stop by." Her snarky response won her a tiny slap on her inner thigh. The contact had been light, yet the impact drove deep to her core and it confused her.

Jonah tried to hide the guilty glare he was giving her, but he failed miserably as he admitted, "I need to confess. Do you hate me for being glad you were a virgin for me the other night?"

Sami shook her head no, not trusting her voice in that moment.

Jonah added on, "God knows, I didn't deserve that gift."

Samantha answered truthfully. "It was always yours, Jonah."

"Ah, Sami." Jonah maneuvered himself so that he could blanket her body with his own. He was just heavy enough to make her feel more secure than she could ever remember feeling.

Samantha threw her legs open wider, letting him settle in between her thighs until she could feel the tip of his cock at her entrance. He waited there so long she thought he might back out. Finally, she begged him with a simple, "Please."

When he entered her, it was so different from two nights before. Gone was his anger, replaced with a gentleness that kind of pissed her off. He was being careful. Treating her like she was a breakable china-doll. She didn't know how, but she knew he was holding back. She wanted all of him. Every unbridled inch, not this watered-down version who was trying to give her what he thought she needed, when in reality what she needed was for him to lose control. Only then would she know he'd given her his all,

The slow, steady pace of their lovemaking helped in one way— it allowed her the time she needed be aware of every inch of him. Her hands raked down his muscular back, holding onto him for dear life as she took him inside her again and again. Their intimacy brought out complex feelings, and tears formed in her eyes as Jonah's face began to swim before her.

His rhythmic possession of her got more erratic as he neared completion. She welcomed his strong thrusts as he fought to bury himself deeper inside her. Their eyes met and she saw him struggling to extend their tryst. It was the final straw for Samantha. His increased pounding of her pussy pushed her over the edge into a glorious orgasm unlike anything she'd ever imagined.

Recognizing he'd brought her to completion, Jonah's technique took on a desperate quality as if he were chasing something he couldn't quite catch. Her body responded to his possession, never wanting it to end.

Samantha was disappointed when Jonah pulled out of her completely, choosing to deposit his load of cum on her tummy in warm spurts.

As soon as he was able, he rolled off Samantha to lie back on his back, pulling her along with him to end up in the same position they'd slept in for their earlier nap. Her right ear was pressed against his chest. His pounding heartbeat reassured her. It reminded her that he was really there with her and this hadn't been just one of her dreams.

Three words sprung to the tip of her tongue. She didn't want to scare him away and she certainly didn't want to embarrass herself, but since she didn't know what their future held, she knew she'd regret it forever if she didn't say them.

Sleep was closing in on them both in the aftermath of their lovemaking. She managed to say the words just before she nodded off.

"Jonah... I love you." She wasn't sure he'd heard her. She'd tell him again, next time when she could see his eyes for a reaction. For now, she enjoyed his embrace. They'd been best friends once, but she'd been naive. As close as they'd been, they'd never shared the kind of intimacy they just had. Samantha closed her eyes, letting the first seed of real hope for a future with Jonah take root.

Surely, he had to feel their connection as strongly as she did. It comforted her as she fell into a deep sleep, surrounded by his unspoken love.

When she awoke alone just a few hours later, she knew that he'd done to her what she'd done to him just two nights before. It felt like a lifetime ago. The moment she opened her eyes, she knew she was alone in her apartment. Regret for not making him promise to stay again like she had earlier consumed her.

Samantha reached her hand out to touch the now empty bed where he'd been just a short time ago. She could still smell the evidence of their sex hanging in the room as she leaned up high enough to look at the alarm clock on her nightstand.

Almost midnight.

How long had he held her? As she reached out to the empty pillow, her hand came into contact with a piece of paper. She rolled to turn on the small lamp next to the bed, giving her enough light to see Jonah's erratic handwriting on the front of a folded sheet of paper he'd stolen from her desk.

Her hands trembled as she opened the note and her worn locket and a huge wad of hundred dollar bills fell into her lap. With dread she began to read his note to her.

DEAR SAMI,

The locket, like my heart, will always belong to you. Keep them safe.

I'm not the right man for you, Samantha. We have to let each other go.

I suspect you'll be pissed I left you my cash, but I'm serious about this. Use it to take better care of yourself. Even though we are apart, you are important to me.

Love,

Jonah

P.S. I think it's best that we make a clean break, but you can always reach me for any emergency through Jaxson, Chase and Emma.

He'd left her without even leaving his contact info. Pure anguish closed in on her as she crumpled the note, hugging it to her heart as she burst into broken-hearted sobs. How could he do this to her again? This time would be worse, because she already knew firsthand how lonely life could be without her other half with her.

She didn't think it was possible, but she felt worse now than after leaving Runway two nights ago after Cash had forced himself on her. At least then she'd had some righteous anger to sustain her. He'd torn down her anger, laying her completely bare. His desertion this time would surely kill her if she let it.

The siren's call of a sharp blade called to her, exactly like a glass of bourbon to a recovering alcoholic. She'd promised him and she intended to keep her promise. She would not hurt herself. Not this night. No. If she was going to hurt anyone, it would be the man who'd deserted her.

CHAPTER 9

"*I*'m sorry, Mr. Carter, but I can't serve you any more drinks. You're already past our per-guest limit," the bartender in the skimpy corset squeaked. He was glad Spencer had hired wimpy subs as bartenders. They may be decent eye-candy, but there was no way this submissive server would ever stand up to a dominant when they needed to.

His words slurred slightly as he worked his magic to get his way. "I'm sure your boss wouldn't mind," Jonah pressured her, holding his wrist out towards the black light scanner to put his next drink on his tab. He didn't get the chance.

"Actually, her boss does mind," came the answer from Master Spencer Cook who'd come to stand behind him. "You're cut off or there will be no playing for you tonight."

"Fine by me. No desire to play." No truer words had ever been spoken. The only reason Jonah had beelined it to Black Light after leaving Samantha's apartment was that he knew he could get shit-faced here and no asshole reporter could get a photo of him that would end up posted on social media within an hour.

His friend Chase was perched on the bar stool next to him and came to his defense, well, sort of. "Pour him another drink,

Chrissy, but Spencer, I think you need to knock some sense into him again. The whipping from a few nights ago didn't take."

Jonah watched her pour another and then took a swig of his newly filled rock glass before retorting, "You don't know shit about it, Chase."

"So try me," Chase interjected.

"You have no idea what it's like." Christ, he felt lame feeling sorry for himself.

As usual, Chase knew how to cut through his crap. "What? To be famous? To have women throw themselves at you everywhere you go, yet you can't feel close to any of them? To question your goals in life, wondering if you've been fighting for the right things? To work non-stop because you have so many people depending on you so you work yourself into exhaustion?" His friend finally stopped his lecture to pin him with a knowing glare.

Despite how low he felt, Jonah managed a small smile. "Okay, so maybe you understand a little."

Chase grinned at his small victory before taking a drag on his own adult beverage.

"Okay, smartass. What do you think I should do? So far I've had Frank, Ryan and Spencer offering up advice. I'm guessing you'll be the fourth person to tell me to get back to work and stay busy to keep my mind off her."

"Nope. Not even close." Chase paused long enough to ensure Jonah was paying attention before adding on. "You need to cancel your concert schedule for the rest of the year and then go pick her up. Drive to the nearest airport and fly to a remote island resort. Stay there for a month without any intervention from the outside world and at the end of the month, either walk away knowing for sure it's the right thing to do or take her to the first church you come to and marry her."

Jonah's pulse spiked at just the mention of marriage. He tried to laugh it off. "That's it? Nothing in between? Like maybe dating?"

The normal jovial Chase got serious. "I thought you said you've known her since you were ten." Jonah nodded. "So you think there's something left to learn?"

Jonah struggled to articulate how he just knew he was all wrong for Samantha. All he could come up with in the pinch was "She's an innocent. I'm… not."

Chase was not impressed. "You're a Dom. So teach her."

"It won't work. I'm too…" What? He finished with a lame, "fucked up."

Spencer had taken a seat on the bar stool on the other side of him. He held out his wrist for the bartender to use her black light scanner to scan his barcode to charge the drink she had just poured for Jonah to the house account.

The master Dom ganged up on him. "Have you looked around? You're so buried in your woe-is-me shit, you aren't even into the dynamics going on around you."

Jonah looked over his friend's shoulder to take in the closest scene underway to the left of the bar. A naked submissive was restrained in the middle of an eight foot round tiled space with a drain under her. Two Doms had stepped up to whip out their dicks and were in the process of pissing all over the submissive's body as if she were their personal urinal.

Beyond them, he could make out a breath play scene getting pretty intense.

"Okay, so I hang out with fucked-up people."

Chase pulled a buzzing cell phone out of his pocket and looked down at a text.

"Hey, why the hell do you get to bring in a phone and no one else does?" Jonah complained.

"Perks of being the owner. And, it has no camera or recording capabilities." When Chase looked up, he had a shit-eating grin on his face.

"What the hell are you smiling at?" Jonah's words slurred. His newest cocktail was doing a nice number on numbing him.

"Jaxson and Emma just got here. Check it out." Chase turned around on his stool to look across the dungeon. Jonah didn't really give a shit so he took another swig of his drink instead.

Chase nudged his arm to get his attention. "You really should check them out."

Jonah reluctantly turned on his stool just in time to see Samantha standing between Jaxson and Emma near the entrance. She was searching the dimly lit dungeon looking for something. Her search ended the second she saw him across the room.

Jonah's heart was pounding fast like a running jackrabbit. That she'd tracked him down was amazing enough, but she was clearly a woman on a mission. She'd taken off like a bat out of hell, weaving herself across the dungeon, cutting directly through a punishment scene already in progress without paying any attention to the freaky shit underway.

Samantha didn't stop until she stood a foot away from his bar stool. Even without a stitch of makeup on, she was beautiful. She'd thrown on a pair of worn jeans and a frilly blouse that was cut low enough that he could see she hadn't even taken the time to put on a bra. When his assessment got to her face, he could see anger rolling off her.

"What the hell was that?" she accused.

"Hi." His greeting was feeble.

"Don't Hi me." He was surprised he couldn't see steam coming out of her ears she was so upset with him. She'd never looked more gorgeous.

"I tried to say goodbye," he tried to soothe her ragged nerves.

"You didn't say shit. You snuck out. I've never thought of you as a coward before." Samantha reached into her front pocket and came out with his wad of hundred dollar bills. She threw them at him and they flitted to the floor in disarray. "And what the hell was the leaving me money? I'm not a paid whore, you know."

He ignored her paid whore accusation and focused on her claim of his being a coward. "I didn't sneak out. I left."

"Yeah, well you are fucking great at that. It's the staying you have a problem with."

He leaned closer, shouting in his rising anger. "You say that like I have a choice." When she looked at him skeptically, he added. "Maybe tonight I had a choice, but seven years ago I sure as hell didn't."

"Like hell you didn't. We all have choices, Jonah. You could have stayed long enough tonight to at least tell me why you really left me seven years ago. You decided to slink away without even leaving your number. I had to call Jaxson and Emma to help track you down. I came here tonight knowing it would piss you off. I'm sure I'm messing up your normal hook-ups."

Jonah had never seen Samantha like this. In so many ways, she was the same old friend he'd known for most of his life, but about half way through her shouting rant, he realized his Sami had grown up. She was this complex mix of vulnerability and strength, qualities so rare in his world. It intimidated him, reminding him no matter how rich and famous he became, he would never be good enough for Sam.

Their shouting match had gathered attention from around the dungeon. Jonah hadn't noticed his friend Ryan was there with a sub until he joined their little group.

Ryan pushed his way into the center of the gathering of Jonah's friends, placing his back to Jonah and facing off with Samantha who had to take a step back. "You have some nerve coming here after all you and your family have done to Jonah."

Samantha froze, stunned after being verbally attacked by their mutual friend.

Jonah stood and confronted his band mate. "Let it go, Ryan. It isn't her fault."

Ryan turned on him. "The hell it's not! It took you years to recover from their bullshit. I'm not gonna let the Stones do this to you again, goddammit."

Jonah tried to pull Ryan away from Sam, but she wasn't helping. She held Ryan's other arm, attempting to hold him back while she pelted him with questions. "What is it you think we did to him? He won't talk to me. Please, tell me Ryan."

Ryan looked at Sam like she was from outer space. "Are you fucking kidding me?"

Jonah succeeded in pulling Ryan from Sam's grip. "Let me handle this." When Ryan stopped to look at Jonah, he added. "They fucked with her too, man."

Ryan looked skeptical. "Are you sure you aren't just thinking with your johnson?"

"Fuck you."

Ryan glanced between Jonah and a shell shocked Samantha before backing down. "I sure as hell hope you know what you're doing. You're not some broke eighteen-year-old with nothing to lose anymore. You're playing with fire. You hurt their little girl and they'll come at you with everything they've got."

Unfortunately, Ryan was right. Frank was a good lawyer, but he'd be no match legally if the Stone men decided to take Cash Carter on. For a brief moment, teenage insecurities surfaced, but Jonah pushed them down.

What good is being a millionaire if I can't buy a good lawyer?

"I'll be ready this time," he reassured Ryan.

"You're really gonna do this, aren't you?" When he didn't answer, Ryan added. "Are you ready to walk away from all this?" He waved his hand around to indicate Black Light. Jonah knew he meant their BDSM lifestyle.

He answered truthfully, knowing Samantha was listening. "Honestly, I don't have a fucking clue how this is going to shake out. All I know is that for once, Sam and I are going to try to figure it out without any outside intervention." He felt her hand on his arm and when he turned to look at her, she had tears streaming down her face. He spoke directly to her. "You're probably gonna regret coming here."

"Never," she whispered.

"There are so many things you don't know about me," he warned.

She smiled through her tears. "But there are so many things I *do* know, and honestly, I can't wait to learn all I've missed."

"I'll remind you that when you're freaking out."

For a moment, he'd forgotten they weren't alone. Ryan reminded him. "Fucking great. No offense, but I can't stay here and watch this. I'm going back to New York ahead of you. I assume you'll be back in time for us to leave on Tuesday night?"

Jonah saw Samantha's fear when she realized no matter what, he had responsibilities that would take him away from her in only two days.

"Yeah, man. I'll be there," Jonah confirmed.

Ryan left without saying goodbyes.

Jaxson and Emma had arrived to stand next to Chase throughout the earlier soap opera style reunion. Jonah was very aware his friends had been listening to the entire interaction. It would have been impossible for them not to.

He had been so focused on Sam that he'd blocked out the sounds of the dungeon, but as he widened his view, he realized Samantha, the innocent, was standing in the middle of a BDSM club that would most likely have her running in horror within minutes. He was also very aware they'd attracted attention. It wasn't every day that the famous Cash Carter was dressed down by an unknown woman who was acting the antithesis of a submissive.

Well duh. That's because she isn't a sub. She's total vanilla. She doesn't belong here.

Before Jonah could think fast enough to get her out of the dungeon, Jaxson held his hand out to Emma. She went into his arms, but they didn't try to hide their conversation from their friends around them despite the fact they were discussing something very private.

Jaxson informed Emma, "You've earned a punishment, you know that, right?"

Jonah could see Emma was on the brink of tears as she replied with a quiet, "Yes, sir."

"And you remember what I told you would happen the next time you broke your most important rule?" Jaxson's voice brokered no argument. He was in full Dom mode.

"Oh God, not that. Please. Can't we go upstairs or home to the loft?"

"Emma, I made you a promise and I'm going to keep it. I caught you red handed putting yourself down and calling yourself fat again. I won't put up with it. You'll be punished at the club tonight."

The salacious scene had stolen all of Samantha's attention. Jonah, on the other hand, didn't take his eyes off Sami. He could see her breaths starting to become erratic and short as she watched with wide eyes as her friend Emma was drawn into a new and scary reality from Sami's point of view.

Jonah detected Emma's genuine fear and wasn't surprised at all when Jaxson reminded his submissive, "You know you can always safeword if you really want us to stop, right?"

Emma stood stock still, pondering her fate until Jaxson prompted her again. "Are you safewording?"

Emma hesitated, but eventually added her quiet "No, sir."

"Good girl. Chase, take our girl to the spanking bench and start to get her situated. I'll be there in a few minutes."

"Yes, sir." Chase knocked back the last of his drink before standing, taking Emma by the arm lightly and navigating her a short way away to a raised platform where a wooden spanking bench awaited them.

Jonah was off kilter as his worlds were colliding. Jaxson stepped in, moving closer to Samantha so their conversation was more private.

"How are you doing, Samantha?" Jaxson asked softly.

Sam hesitated, more subdued as she took in her surroundings. "I'm okay, I guess."

Jaxson pressed her. "If you're uncomfortable, just say the word and you can leave."

She glanced up at Jonah nervously. "I'm not going anywhere until Jonah and I get a few things sorted out."

"Maybe you'd feel more comfortable sorting those things out upstairs instead of here at the club."

Jonah watched Sam scan the area, keeping her eyes on Chase and Emma across the room for a long minute. He reached out for her hand, ready to pull her out of Black Light. She didn't belong here.

Jaxson didn't give him the chance.

"Samantha, this is the part of my friend's life that he doesn't want to show you. He doesn't think you can handle it. I'm not so sure." Jonah wanted to punch Jaxson's front teeth out as he grinned a comforting smile down at Sam. "If he is right, all you need to say is the word 'red' and Jonah will take you out of here. It's called a safeword. It means you want to stop. You also need to know that no matter how it looks to you, everything happening in this room is consensual. Every submissive, including Emma, has a safeword. They can stop play at any time. Do you understand?"

Samantha's eyes were wide. "Yes."

Jaxson corrected her. "That's yes, sir. In the dungeon or in negotiated scenes, when a dominant gives you instructions or asks you questions, you answer with a sir out of respect."

She hesitated, answering softly as if trying on the new words for size. "Yes, sir."

An odd feeling of jealousy invaded Jonah that Samantha had just addressed someone other than him as sir. He didn't like it, but he suspected he'd love hearing those words on her lips when they were directed his way.

"Good girl." Jaxson paused, glancing for the first time at Jonah before turning back to Sam and adding. "Everything else you'll ever need to learn about our lifestyle, this guy here is gonna teach you, that is… if you consent to him. He's a good dominant when he gets his head out of his ass." Jaxson smiled at Jonah's expense before adding a friendly. "I have a feeling he'll take very good care of you, if you let him."

Samantha's face was glowing. "Oh, I'll definitely let him."

He let her words sink in. She hadn't freaked out yet. She hadn't demanded to leave. Maybe there was hope.

Jaxson nodded his way before turning and heading toward his lovers, leaving Samantha and Jonah in relative privacy for the first time since she'd arrived. He wished he hadn't had the last drink. It was clouding his judgment. He and Sam had a thousand other things they needed to talk about before dragging the weight of a D/s lifestyle into things. Yet he stood still, helpless to whisk her away because all he really wanted to do was get inside her again.

Their time together back at her apartment had been like magic. He'd never dreamed he could feel so close with another human being. That she was standing in front of him, looking at him with love in her eyes amazed him. Sure, fans looked at him that same way every day, but they didn't count. They were in love with an illusion—the Cash Carter persona his publicist had helped craft.

Samantha saw Jonah. She knew his history. His dreams. His weaknesses. Yet she looked at him with a love he didn't deserve.

He closed the distance between them, taking her into his arms and holding her close. He leaned in to whisper into her ear. "Say it. Tell me you want to stay here."

"I want to stay here… with you," she answered with confidence.

"You aren't going to like it," he warned.

"How do you know that?"

The truth was he didn't know. Jonah pulled out of their embrace just enough to look down into her expressive caramel brown eyes. "I guess there's only one way to find out."

Jonah took Sam by the hand and led her through the dungeon to a seating area closer to Jaxson, Chase, and Emma. They'd have a good view of the scene about to play out, yet would be able to exit quickly if Samantha freaked out as he suspected she might.

Jonah sat first, pulling Sam into his lap, hugging her to him and enjoying having her in his arms. Samantha didn't even blink as she watched with great interest as her friend Emma was stripped down to her panties by the men in her life. Jonah could see Emma's genuine apprehension of what was about to happen and wasn't surprised that Sam had tensed up, becoming concerned for her friend.

Chase and Jaxson took the time to sandwich Emma between them in an embrace. The spectators couldn't hear what they whispered to her, but she relaxed just a bit.

They led Emma to the wooden spanking bench. Jaxson had purchased several of the high-end custom designed pieces of BDSM furniture for the many different sections of Black Light. It was just one of the many reasons members loved their new club.

It only took a few minutes for the men to situate their curvy submissive across the bench. She kneeled on the leg braces, bending over the padded railing at the top and reaching down and forward for the hand grips that spread her arms wide, closer to the floor. The men adjusted the bench to spread Emma's legs wider to match her arms and then started to use the leather belts to secure her in place at the wrists, ankles, knees and waist cinch. By the time they were done, Emma was completely immobile, her ass high in the air, a ready target to receive her punishment.

Their final adjustment was to pull out an adjustable neck brace that would hold Emma's head up and in place so that they, and other patrons, could see Emma's expressions as she received her discipline.

Jonah had to hand it to his friend, Jaxson. He had formed an extraordinary trio with Chase and Emma and from the time he'd spent with them in the recent days, Jonah suspected they would stand the test of time as relationships went. As he felt Samantha trembling slightly in his lap, he wondered if they'd find a way through their own rough times ahead as they sorted through all of the drama from seven years ago.

Sam burrowed in closer to him after watching Jaxson unbuckle his thick leather belt and pull its from its loops. But still, she didn't look away.

Sam self-consciously clutched at his black T-shirt as she watched Chase walk to the wall full of punishment implements, reaching up to pull down an eighteen-inch long wooden paddle with three holes drilled down the middle of the four-inch wide surface.

When Jaxson stepped close to Emma and began paddling her bottom with his open palm as a warm up, Sam relaxed a bit into his arms. He couldn't have stopped the blood from rushing to his cock if he wanted to, and he certainly did not want to. Sami started gently rocking to the rhythm of the spanking, unwittingly grinding against Jonah's growing erection until he sat there in his now uncomfortably tight jeans, desperate to be inside Samantha again.

When the warm-up ended, Sami scanned the rest of the room for the first time. He followed her gaze, taking in the Dom fucking his submissive's mouth while she knelt before him less than ten feet away from them. He heard her sharp intake of breath as she saw the submissive hanging from the ceiling, wrapped in an intricate labyrinth of ropes, leaving her sex exposed for her Dom to latch over a dozen brutal looking clamps onto her labia. Even from the distance, Jonah could see the tortured submissive's trembling under the strain.

Their attention was drawn back to Emma with the first loud lash of leather on flesh. From their vantage point, they could just make out the red splotch just below where her panties ended where her Dom's belt had connected with flesh. Jaxson was in no hurry, delivering ten stripes at a rather leisurely pace before stepping away from Emma. As if the men had choreographed their scene, Chase moved closer, stepping behind Emma and tapping the wooden paddle to her ass lightly. Jaxson had taken position in front of Emma and her stationary position of her head ensured she would stare into her disciplinarian's eyes as her bottom was paddled by Chase.

She must have closed her eyes because Jaxson barked his order, "Eyes open." When his naughty sub complied, he nodded to their lover behind her to continue.

The sound of the first strike of the paddle filled the air with a heavy thud followed by Emma's loud squeal of pain and Samantha's surprised groan as she turned her face into Jonah's chest, burying her eyes from watching. The next loud thud as wood connected with flesh brought a cry from Emma and a grinding wiggle from Sami.

"Look at me, Sami," he urged her. When she didn't look up, he got his Dom on. "Samantha."

Her eyes darted to his with a frantic longing.

"How are you doing, baby? Do you want to go?"

"No!"

"Well, okay then," he chuckled with relief.

CHAPTER 10

*N*othing in her twenty-three years had prepared Samantha for Black Light. While she'd remained a virgin until very recently, she'd actually begun her sexual awakening at a very young age, courtesy of the man whose lap she was presently sitting in.

She hadn't had the words to describe the tingly feelings Jonah could stir in her with just a look, even when they were just kids. As they'd gotten older, their intense friendship had morphed naturally into a physical relationship.

The irony was Samantha would have gladly given Jonah her virginity in high school. He'd been a gentleman who'd insisted they wait until she was a bit older to ensure she was really ready. That hadn't stopped them from their sexual exploration, but then they'd been torn apart before they could truly consummate their relationship.

But here... tonight... the kind of sexual experimentation happening around her blew her inexperienced mind. While she'd seen her share of soft porn on the internet, nothing came close to watching her new friend, Emma, being punished by her two dominant lovers. She should be running from the room as she glanced around, watching the mostly submissive women being dominated in oh-so-many naughty ways.

But instead, it felt more like pieces of a puzzle finally falling into place. She still didn't have the right words to describe her feelings, but at the heart lay her love/hate relationship with control. She'd always struggled and out of necessity and self-preservation, she'd learned to take control of her life after Jonah had left. On her dark days, when she lost her battle with control, she'd cut.

Luckily, her dark days had come fewer and farther in between over the last few years.

Tonight, she recognized the seed of submission that Jonah had planted in her all those years ago had laid dormant, just waiting for him to return and claim his rightful place in her heart and in her life.

With each swing of Chase's paddle, Samantha sank deeper into her memories of struggling to find her way after she'd lost Jonah. Remembering how her father had tried, and for a while succeeded, in filling the gaping hole Jonah had left. Not that her dad had ever crossed any sexual boundary he shouldn't. She was grateful for that. But she'd insisted on going to law school outside of Texas, in part because she needed to put distance between her and her father, knowing he was influencing her life in unhealthy ways.

Thank God I did, or I may have never seen Jonah again.

Real hope for her future filled her heart as she enjoyed the attention of Jonah's roving hands, one currently slipped under her blouse to squeeze her bare right breast while his left hand fumbled with the button and zipper of her jeans. As soon as he had them open, he slid his hand into her pants to grab her pussy through her panties. She was glad he couldn't see her flaming face from his angle or she would die of mortification.

"That's my girl. You're so fucking wet," he growled against the shell of her ear.

Sam renewed her rhythmic grinding as he positioned her to face forward. She laid her head back onto Jonah's shoulder, trying to relax into the growing sexual need the sights and sounds of the room were stirring. His roving fingers exploring in her pants didn't hurt either.

Emma was struggling now against the restraints. Guilt crushed Sam when she realized that instead of being angry on her friend's behalf, she instead felt a pang of jealousy as she watched the two alpha men in Emma's life both dominate and protect her at the same time. On some instinctual level, Samantha understood the rules of this new game and answers to questions she'd never even thought to ask in her past started to fall into place.

Even when he was ten and the new kid in school, Jonah'd been the one in charge. The kid the bullies wanted to control, but were never quite brave enough to take him on. Even before his young, scrawny body had shown visible signs of being a rock king, Jonah's character, drive, and ambition had been larger than life. He had been her whole world.

He still was.

Her breathing was ragged by the time the men stopped Emma's punishment. Jaxson had ripped his submissive's panties away from her scorched ass and was gently gliding the palm of his hand over the blotchy, red skin, inspecting it to ensure no real damage was done. At the other end of the restrained sub, Chase was helping the punished woman blow her nose.

As soon as the men were satisfied Emma had learned her lesson, they moved into action again, this time to each unzip their pants and take out their hardening erections. Jaxson directed the scene, placing Chase at Emma's head as he stepped up between Emma's spread legs. The entire dungeon seemed to pause to watch the trio in action.

Just as the men plunged into Emma's body, Jonah decided to plunge his fingers into Samantha as he sucked on her neck once again. The two women each cried out in unison, surprised need.

"Oh, please. Jonah…" she begged.

"Please, what, baby?" His question was deceivingly soft in her ear.

"You know… I need…" she stammered.

"Tell me. What do you need?"

"You. Inside me," she replied breathlessly.

"Now? In public?" She heard his uncertainty.

"Anytime. Anywhere." In that moment, she meant it.

He sprung to his feet in a rush, scooping her up and placing her boots on the ground long enough to unfasten his own jeans and free his cock. Sami turned towards him as he pulled her closer, fumbling to help push her pants down her legs. She couldn't stop her giggles as they frantically worked to free her from the confines of her too-tight jeans, almost toppling over several times.

Finally naked, save her socks, Jonah urged her as he pulled her back towards the plush chair, "Back on my lap, Sami. I'm gonna take you for a bit of a ride while you watch the show." She followed his directions just as she heard Emma's cries, begging to be allowed to come when Chase's cock left her mouth to let her breathe.

Sam collapsed into his lap, expecting Jonah to guide his shaft into her body. She was surprised when he took the time to situate her so her back was against his shirt so she faced the scandalous scene playing out mere feet away. He reached forward and pulled her legs as wide apart as they would go, looping each knee over their corresponding leather arm rest and exposing her completely to anyone who dared look their way.

For the first time since she'd arrived, Samantha took a minute to really take a look around her. She'd expected to find the crowd riveted to the threesome on the platform, but was uneasy to find at least half of the eyes of the room were on her and Jonah. It reminded her that the man who was Jonah to her was also the A-list celebrity, Cash Carter, to the rest of the world. Sexual excitement mingled with embarrassed reticence, creating a cocktail of emotions she'd never felt.

Jonah's confident voice talking against the shell of her ear helped her stay connected to him when her nerves might have failed her. "Eyes on Emma. Place your hands on your legs. Leave them like that."

Only as she moved to follow his directions did she realize she'd self-consciously covered her sex with her hands to shield herself from the voyeurs in the room. A new thread of excitement shot through her as she moved her arms to obey Jonah's command. It was absurd that her heart physically fluttered at his "good girl" in her ear.

It was hard to focus on the scene in front of her when Jonah's hands began their trek across her body, starting by squeezing her breasts until they almost hurt before moving lower to alternately pinch and stroke her pussy. It was unclear if it was his touch or the smoking hot sex happening only a few feet away that was responsible for her dripping wet condition. Her core clenched, desperate to take him inside her again.

She was transfixed by watching the two alpha men fucking each end of her friend in a coordinated choreography. She was so lost in the moment, she missed Jonah's hands finally clamping into her hips and lifting her up high enough to line her up with his protruding shaft. Precisely at the same moment Chase and Jaxson leaned in to begin making out above Emma's back was when Jonah pulled her onto his rod, impaling her deeper than he'd ever been.

Sweet pain mingled with overwhelming pleasure, making Sam feel more alive than ever before. Her body was beginning to get sore from the unfamiliar intimate attention certain virginal body parts were getting, yet Sam surrendered to the soreness, grateful for it because it proved to her that this wasn't just a dream. Jonah was there. He was inside her. They were finally one.

He was strong, lifting her entire body up off his shaft again and again before releasing her to let her weight fall onto his erection. Each thrust brought her ecstasy like nothing she'd ever felt. She collapsed against him, her back against his hard, muscular chest while her head rolled back to lean against his shoulder. She couldn't resist sticking her tongue out and licking a line along his scruff filled jaw.

I licked him. He's mine.

Jonah's gravely growl in her ear told her how close he was to coming. His thrusts into her as he lifted and dropped her were becoming erratic just as the trio in front of them lost their choreographed rhythm when the men's kiss turned almost brutal as they stilled, buried inside Emma's mouth and pussy until she began to gag and sputter.

Jonah's hard pinch on her clit came as he ordered her to, "Come for me!" Her core hugged his steel-hard rod deep inside her, tipping her into the strongest orgasm of her inexperienced sexual life. That she could feel Jonah's warm spunk being spurt inside her enhanced her own pleasure. That she could see Chase and Jaxson's final cum being shot onto their naked submissive excited her.

It took some time for them to catch their breath. She let her attention rake around the room to take in at least a half dozen other couples in the process of fucking each other in all kinds of perverted positions.

"You really aren't freaking out?" Jonah sounded surprised.

She allowed herself to relax fully into his arms. Despite being on display to a room full of strangers, Sami knew in that moment she was exactly where she was supposed to be.

"Not even a little bit," she replied truthfully. "But…" she shuddered remembering one of the sexual situations she'd observed as she'd scanned the room for Jonah upon her arrival. "Don't you ever try to pee on me."

Jonah's hearty laugh in her ear was exactly what she needed to hear. "Got it." He then added. "Congratulations, Sami. You just gave me your first hard limit."

* * *

THE NEXT HOUR was a bit of a blur for Samantha. The adrenaline she'd mustered to chase after Jonah had been spent in their unconventional time at her first visit to a BDSM club. She remembered Jonah cradling her until she was almost asleep. His cock had softened inside her, eventually slipping out of her allowing the wet sticky mix of their combined orgasms to cover each of them.

Sam felt chilled for the few minutes Jonah left her alone, naked in the leather chair they'd been parked in for the show. He returned with a warm, wet cloth and had gently cleaned her and the chair of their cum before helping her dress. Unexpected tears pricked at her eyes at his tenderness. His attentiveness.

She'd forgotten how she'd loved the feeling of being wholly surrounded by Jonah's larger-than-life persona. He'd always had a way of making her feel as if nothing could ever hurt her as long as he was there. It was why his desertion had nearly killed her. She'd not been prepared to go it alone.

Please God. I don't want to lose him again.

He insisted on carrying her as they left. She didn't fight him. He weaved them to the club exit through a different long, drafty tunnel she'd not seen when she arrived. She burrowed into his arms for warmth as they followed the head of security up narrow stairs and came out at the back of what looked like a psychic's shop. The store was closed, but there were low-level lights on in the space lighting the way to the front door where another security guard waited for them, ready to open the door for their departure.

"Your limo is out on the curb, Mr. Carter. I took the liberty of directing them to take you to your hotel at the Four Seasons."

"Good. Thanks."

"Of course, sir. We'll see you at your next visit."

Jonah nodded to the men as she snuggled in closer, burying her face into the crook of his neck as the cold blast of wintery bluster whipped around them for the dozen feet they had to travel between the building and the held-open limo door.

She struggled to stay awake for the ten-minute drive through the city, not wanting Jonah to have to carry her through the lobby of the hotel. The silence in the small space was amicable between the lovers as they simply enjoyed the relief of being together.

The doorman who opened the door next to their seat in the hotel carport had to reach in and help steady her as she crawled from the back of the car.

"Welcome back, Mr. Carter."

Of course everyone recognized the celebrity. Her Jonah was the world's Cash. She'd almost forgotten, but the knowledge rushed her, waking her up as they stepped through the door being held open for them by another doorman.

She had no idea what time it was. It had to be after two and the lobby was thankfully empty save a housekeeper who was busy in the distance vacuuming. Jonah held her hand, pulling her closer as they waited for the elevator. It wasn't until they were in the lift that they saw the grungy looking guy with a high-powered camera rushing towards them, his camera flashing bright just before the doors slid shut.

"Fuck. That guy has been dogging me since I got to town."

"Is it like this everywhere you go?" She wasn't sure she wanted to know the answer to the question.

"Unfortunately, it's not uncommon, no. You'll get used to it."

His words startled them both. She could tell when she glanced up at him he was thinking the same thing she was.

I hope I am around long enough to get used to it.

Jonah's room was at the end of the long hallway on the top floor of the luxury hotel. By the time he found the keycard in his wallet and got the double French doors open, the ding of the elevator returning down the hall sounded the arrival of the persistent paparazzi.

"God dammit, this is ridiculous!"

Jonah pushed her through the open door just in the knick of time to get in and slam the door closed before they had an unwelcome visitor. Samantha stood stunned near the door while Jonah rushed to the bathroom and grabbed up towels, shoving them along the bottom of the door. He put on the deadbolt then and finally checked to make sure that the small hinged cover over the peep hole was closed.

He answered her unspoken question as he finally led her by the hand into the suite. "Assholes like that stop at nothing. They'll put small cameras under the door jam or use cameras that can attach to the peep hole to take video."

The opulent room was lit with soft lighting. He led her through the living space and into the massive bedroom where the king sized bed had been turned down, several chocolates left on the pillow. Only once he had her seated on the bed did Jonah go to the phone on the nightstand and dial zero.

He didn't bother with salutations, launching directly into his rant. "This is Cash Carter. I need security to sweep my floor immediately. There's an unauthorized reporter stalking me and I need him gone from the building." He barely finished before hanging up.

As soon as one call ended, he dialed the next. She assumed it was room service when he launched into his order.

"I need a large pepperoni and mushroom pizza, a couple beers and a large glass of milk."

Sam must have scrunched her face at the order of what she assumed was her drink. Jonah grinned into the phone. "Make that chocolate milk."

He'd remembered. She pressed her luck. "Can you make it hot chocolate?"

He covered the phone receiver, "No, but I can order both for you." To the phone he added, "and add on one hot chocolate with marshmallows." How ridiculous was it that his remembering her love of marshmallows made her insanely happy?

"Now, I think we have just enough time for a hot shower before the food arrives." Jonah grabbed up her hand, but she tried to stop him.

"Can't that wait until tomorrow? I'm too tired. In fact, just the thought of eating pizza makes my tummy churn."

"That's too bad. You need to put on some weight. You're too thin. Don't think I've forgotten that not too long ago you passed out on your bathroom floor. You aren't taking care of yourself, Samantha," he chastised.

In some sick way, his lecture had her heart fluttering, in part because it meant he cared, but more so because she suspected how Jonah would deal with her lack of self-care in the future. She was pretty sure it might be the same way Jaxson had dealt with Emma's own gaff earlier. It was insane that Sam's ass tingled at the thought.

She was happy when her revelation went over Jonah's head. He was too busy pulling her along behind him by the hand to the luxury bathroom. She hadn't exaggerated how tired she was and when she dawdled at undressing, Jonah was there to help her shed her outfit, placing small kisses along her flesh as he peeled her clothes off.

He was naked in a flash, pulling her into the shower that was large enough for at least another couple. Hot water jutted out from three sides as well as above them, filling the glass enclosure with steam. Rather than actively showering, they merely fell into each other's arms, still getting used to the fact that they were really together... in the same place... alone.

Sam was pretty sure she'd have toppled over if it wasn't for Jonah's strong arms holding her against him as water shot them from all sides and above. She closed her eyes, enjoying the pounding of his heart against her ear she had pressed to his chest.

Only when they could hear the pounding of the room service delivery person did they snap out of their trance. Jonah turned off the water and reached out to the shelf just outside the shower to grab up two oversized towels, taking the time to towel dry her and pull her along to sit in the chair near the whirlpool before throwing on a robe and handling the food delivery.

By the time he came back for her, she was falling asleep.

"Poor baby. We need to get you to bed."

She didn't argue, that was until he led her, wrapped only in her towel, to the dining table instead of the bed.

"I can't eat. Save it for breakfast," her words slurred.

"A few bites. And you need to drink more. You were dehydrated earlier."

She opened her mouth to complain, but he shushed her easily with his finger to her lips. When she was quiet, he sat in the chair next to her and reached out to hold both her hands. The gold flecks shone in his intense eyes, looking serious. "We have a lot to talk about, baby, and I know you're too tired now. But think back to the club tonight. Who was in charge?"

"You, but..."

"Me. Who was in charge back at your apartment?"

"You, but..."

"Me." He hesitated before his next question. "Who was in charge when we were in high school?"

His question shocked her. This one was harder. It hadn't been as obvious back then, but there was no denying the truth. "You, but..."

"I get it, Sam. You've been taking care of yourself, but here's the thing. The cutting. The fact you no longer are prepared with your medication when you had an episode at the club Friday night. The fact that in spite of being dangerously thin, you didn't eat or even drink for two days for Christ's sake. The fact that you've been living in poverty to the point of hurting yourself. It's all enough to tell me you need help, baby, and I'm applying for the job of your caretaker."

The serious atmosphere lightened when he broke into his sexy grin, literally knocking the breath out of her. He was devastatingly perfect. She let his words seep into her heart, trying hard to believe that not only was Jonah really there, but he was sweeping her off her feet, saying the right things. Doing the right things.

God help me if he leaves me again. I will surely die.

As afraid as she was of getting hurt, submitting to his control felt as natural as breathing to Samantha. Without even really thinking about it, she let her relieved "Yes, sir" spill out.

The mega-watt smile he flashed at her acquiescence would have toppled her over had she been standing. Oblivious to the effect he was having on her, Jonah reached for a glass of water, insisting she start by downing at least half before she ate.

She wasn't sure how long it took him to get the large slice of pizza down her, but he was patient, holding the food to her mouth when she'd refused to feed herself. It was absurd, but there was a part of her deep down that reveled in being babied by the man the world knew as Cash Carter.

By the time she'd drank half of the hot chocolate, her tummy was stuffed and her eyes barely stayed open. She snuggled into him when he scooped her up and carried her to the bed, placing her in the middle and pulling the towel away, leaving her naked until he pulled the covers up to her chin.

Samantha enjoyed the soft brush of his fingers across her cheek as he leaned in to kiss her. "Get some rest, baby. We'll talk more in the morning."

"Hmm-mm," she mumbled.

She was almost asleep when fear gripped her, causing her to open her eyes in panic to search for him. He was sitting on the edge of the bed, just watching her sleep, a funny look on his face.

She blurted, "You promise you aren't going to leave again, right?"

He swished her hair out of her face and smiled down at her. "There is nothing in this world that could convince me to leave this room. Not now. Not without you, Samantha."

She let relief spread through her like warm butter, loving the sound of her name on his lips.

CHAPTER 11

*J*onah awoke with a start. It had taken him forever to unwind enough to fall asleep. He'd seen four fifteen on the bedside alarm clock before he'd finally nodded off, exhausted. He'd spent over an hour just cradling a sleeping Samantha in his arms, rehashing every minute of their time together since the second he'd seen her in the crowd Friday night at Runway.

Had it really just been a few days ago? In some ways, it felt like they'd never been apart. The ease at which they'd fallen back into their intimate bond was nothing short of miraculous considering how he'd carried hatred of the Stones around like a fucking badge, wearing it where the world could see. He wove his hostility into the lyrics of his songs and into the decisions he made on everything from where he traveled to what he spent his money on.

As he'd lain awake, he'd tried to convince himself he could just let go of the loathing now that they'd found their way back to each other. Instead of making things better, he discovered his anger flaring hotter than ever before when he realized how the Stone men had not only fucked with him, but they had hurt Samantha in the process, and that was unacceptable to Jonah.

Now in the light of the new day, he recognized a new emotion closing in.

Guilt.

He should have known seven years ago that they'd lied to him. He should have trusted his gut that Samantha wouldn't have walked away from him as easily as they had made him believe. In his immature insecurity, he'd allowed the powerful lawmen to not only destroy him, but to drive the very woman they claimed to be protecting to the point of cutting her own body. He didn't understand the draw to cutting itself, but he sure as hell understood the seduction of self-destruction during times of despair.

Samantha had needed him, and he hadn't been there for her. His failure was a kick to his balls.

He'd been wallowing in his own thoughts when the ding of an incoming text message sounded muffled from the heap of Samantha's clothes on the floor next to her side of the bed. He rolled to see if she were awake to find himself alone.

Jonah shot from the bed in a panic. His brain told him she wouldn't have left him, but their reunion was too new. His emotions were still fragile.

He ran naked out into the living room area first, finding it empty. He glanced towards the entry and was relieved to find the towels he'd layered in front of the door still there.

She hadn't left the suite.

He took a calming breath and headed back through the bedroom towards the bathroom door. He hesitated, knocking softly, but didn't wait for her reply. The sight that greeted him when he opened the door brought a grin to his face.

"Jonah! Get out! I didn't say you could come in!" Samantha's face burned beet red at being caught sitting on the side of the whirlpool tub, razor and shaving cream busy at removing hair from her legs and pussy.

"Hey, I'm missing the show. You should have woken me up."

Sam grabbed a loofa from the top of a nearby basket of bathing supplies supplied by the hotel and threw it at his head. He caught it easily and threw it back at her. While she was busy reflexively catching it, Jonah moved in closer to get a better vantage point to watch the exhibition in progress.

"You're terrible. Can't a girl get a bit of privacy around here?" she teased turning back to her job at hand.

"Nope. Your privacy days are over, my dear," he countered as he took a seat in the same chair she'd sat in the night before. He had the perfect angle to watch the sexy sight.

What started as fun, soon turned dark as Sam's scars were uncovered one razor swath at a time on her thighs.

His guilt returned. In that moment, he knew without a doubt that had he fought the Stone men harder seven years before, there would be no scars marring her perfect body.

Lost in his own thoughts as he stared at her body, he missed Sam's sad look as she looked back at him. When he looked into her eyes, her words made him feel worse. "I'm sorry they're so ugly."

He was on his feet and sitting next to her on the ledge next to the whirlpool in a flash. He pulled her torso close, smearing shaving cream on himself as he made sure she was listening. "Nothing about you is ugly, Samantha, other than your bastard of a father and uncle. I should have been there. You wouldn't have hurt yourself if I'd been stronger."

Her eyes widened at his passionate words. He watched her struggle to know what to say before pressing him. "Tell me what they did, Jonah. I swear to you, I don't understand. I need to know so I can process it."

He agreed she did deserve to know, but, "Later." When she opened her mouth to complain, he held a finger to her lips. "I promise, I'll tell you, baby. But later. We have so many things to catch up on and I want to wait until you're stronger." When she looked like she wanted to argue with him, he added reluctantly, "Until *we're* stronger."

That she seemed to understand. He was relieved when after a few long seconds, she let it drop. "Fine, if you're gonna stay, then you can help. I forgot to bring a wet washcloth with me and I was trying to avoid doing the whole bath thing. Can you get a warm cloth?"

"That I can do."

Jonah walked to the sink to find she'd already used his now wet toothbrush and paste. Seems Miss Samantha had been up for at least a little while before him.

He was handing her the warm cloth when he heard the phone ringing in the bedroom. It had been the sound that had woke him up. "Someone's trying to get ahold of you. Your phone is ringing."

She brushed it off a little too quickly. "Oh, I'm sure it's not important. Just let it go to voicemail."

"Who is it, Sam?"

"How should I know? It's in the other room." She was keeping a bit too focused finishing her job. He became suspicious.

He didn't know how, but he knew she was lying to him. "Samantha."

He didn't need to say another word. His tone told her he knew. She paused, taking a deep breath before finally looking up at him with tears in her eyes.

He guessed. "It's your father again."

She shook her head vehemently. "No! It's not… it's…" She stalled until he raised his eyebrow. "It's Megan's ring. I'm sure she's worried about where I am."

"Why would she worry? Won't she know you're with me?"

"Yes, but…"

"What aren't you telling me, Sami?" he pressed.

"I'm in law school. It's grueling. I've already missed a big test this morning that I didn't even study for and I'm supposed to be at another class where we had a guest speaker coming in. I'm sure she's just worried because… well… it's not like me to skip."

Jonah could kick himself. "Dammit, I should have asked you

what time you needed to be where today, but you should have brought it up, too." Jonah turned to start brushing his teeth, while Sam rushed to finish the last of her shaving. She was hurrying towards him as he rinsed.

"Get dressed," he instructed.

"No. I'm not leaving you," she answered forcefully.

"Excuse me?"

"You heard me. I'm not leaving you until you have to leave for your concert tomorrow."

"Listen, young lady, I thought we discussed this last night. Who's in charge?"

She crossed her arms hiding her perfect breasts from him. "I want to renegotiate."

"Renegotiate?"

"Yes," she confirmed, although a little less confidently.

"And just when is it you think you should be in charge?"

Sam's face lit up, "When you don't agree with me." She giggled, disarming him.

He reached out to pull her against his chest; the feel of her lithe naked body flush against him had his cock filling.

She must have felt it too because she grinned, "See you don't want me to leave either." Sami didn't play fair, roaming her hands up and down his back, squeezing his ass playfully as she leaned into him.

Fuck me.

"You do realize you're being a very naughty girl, tempting me like this." He'd said the words playfully, but when he looked down into her caramel brown eyes, he saw her surprised longing. He trusted his gut and pressed further. "You know what happens to naughty girls, don't you?"

He felt her tense in his arms telling him she did indeed know. He wouldn't press her. Not if she wasn't ready, but desire to explore with her had him moving his own hands down to cup her ass cheeks in his palms. Her eyes widened.

"That's right, you do know. I think you've earned your first spanking."

She shook her head slightly in protest, but she didn't say a word. He could see the conflicting desires warring in her eyes. One day, he'd push her harder, but not now. She was a total newbie and he wouldn't let himself forget that.

"We have so much to talk about, baby. Like you said, we'll negotiate, but until we sort through it all, the most important thing to know is that you always need to be honest with me. What you like. What you don't. What you'll try. What you won't. We'll talk about it all and until we sort through it, you know you can slow anything happening down with a simple 'yellow' and I'll stop with a 'red'. Got it?"

After listening, she slowly nodded her head. "I need to hear you, baby. Say the words for me. What word slows things down?"

"Yellow," she whispered, almost embarrassed by the intimate topic.

"Good. And what word stops everything?"

"Red," she added breathlessly.

Jonah led her to the chair only a few feet away. He moved the seat closer to the whirlpool tub, angling it just right for his plans. After he'd taken his seat, he pulled Sam to stand in front of him between his open legs. His heavy cock and balls hung down between his legs and when he looked up at Samantha, he caught her red-handed gawking at his package in the light of day. With each long second that passed, the blood was rushing faster to his appendage, filling it to a rather impressive length and girth.

Sam looked confused as to what would happen next so he helped her. "You'll always come to my right side and lay across my lap this way. Do you understand?"

She nodded again. He countered with, "Verbal answers only."

"Yes, sir," she rushed to answer, but he noticed her slight tremble.

Christ, she was perfect.

He gently pulled Sam forward, resting her tummy across his thighs and allowing his erection to press into her from below. He upped the ante. "Reach out and place your palms on the tile next to the tub. I want you to keep your hands there and not move them to try to cover yourself. Do you understand?"

She hesitated, forgetting to answer until he tapped her bare bottom lightly. "Yes, sir."

He grinned as she hustled to obey, stretching out, prone before him, crossing her legs, wiggling in embarrassment. She couldn't see what a perfect package she made as he looked down on her from above. He must have taken too long admiring her because she eventually craned her neck to look back over her left shoulder, a questioning look on her face.

"Good girl, Samantha. You just have one small change to make." He moved his right hand lower, pressing in-between her squeezed thighs. "Open them up for me, baby. Place your toes on the tile and spread your legs apart as far as you can without falling off."

Her embarrassed groan was her only complaint as she contorted her body to his specification.

He admired her perfect, pale white skin on her rounded ass, cupping and squeezing her flesh until he felt her relaxing.

The first spank was playful, nothing more than a love tap. He felt her body relaxing further, turning herself over to him. There would be plenty of time in their future for harder games. Kinkier play. Harsher punishments. Today was about building trust. About giving his little newbie sub a juicy taste of the lifestyle he prayed she would embrace. He planned on making sure that first taste would be something she'd learn to crave.

His next volley of spanks were sharper. He spread them around liberally, making sure not to focus on one spot for too long, wanting to give her a nice overall heat versus a burn. When she started to pull her legs together, he stopped long enough to insert his hands between her thighs, pressing until she reopened her legs for him. He rewarded her with several long strokes of his fingers through her wet labia until he again crashed his now wet, open palm harder across her globes. He loved that despite how thin she was, her ass jiggled slightly as it turned a blushing pink.

Jonah thrust his left hand into her thick, long hair grabbing ahold and yanking her hair hard enough to pull a squeak from her as Sam arched her back beautifully, careful to keep her palms on the tile while she lifted high enough for him to watch her breasts swaying as she wiggled across his lap. Each loud slap to her bottom was like a kick to his groin. Despite them having sex several times in the last twenty-four hours, he ached to be inside her again.

What surprised him the most was it wasn't just about the sex. He'd experimented enough to know sex with Sami was the best of his life.

The addicting part was that he felt starved for the unique intimacy he'd only found when inside Samantha, watching her face as he brought her pleasure, knowing he was the only man to have seen how special it was. Being her first was so important, but what scared him was that he suspected he wouldn't be happy unless he was her one and only.

He was losing control just thinking about some other asshole touching her. Old-fashioned masculine dominance invaded his thoughts until he knew it was time to claim her again.

Jonah pushed to his feet, lifting his naughty sub up with him, helping her get her feet under her just long enough to hustle her across the room to the vanity where the sink was located. It wasn't the sink he was interested in, but the huge mirror.

"Place your hands up close to the glass. Lean over and press your ass out for me." He helped position her in her prone position, using his bare foot to tap the inside of her feet until she moved her legs apart. He didn't stop when they were shoulder width. No, he needed her off balance.

"On your elbows, baby. Lean up." After she'd obeyed, he pulled her legs wider until her entire now bare pussy was peeking out at him along with the tight little pucker of her asshole. He hadn't even thought about how much fun he'd be having exploring that uncharted territory on Samantha's beautiful body. Her spanked ass blushed as bright as the line of blush across her cheeks as she realized he was inspecting her most private part.

As Jonah stepped closer, he could see the reflection of her perky breasts poking down towards the counter. Their eyes met in the mirror as he stepped up close enough to rub his erection against her punished bottom while he reached forward to pinch her nipples, playing with them until he felt her tits magically hardening.

She licked her lips nervously watching him in the mirror as he moved his right hand from her tit to slide it between them. The slickness he found confirmed her body was ready for him, but he teased her, dragging his now wet digits back and up. Her eyes widened with shock when he grazed her pucker.

Sam totally broke pose, shooting to an upright defensive stance in a flat second. He shook his head, clucking disapprovingly. "You broke position. That's a bad girl."

Her eyes dilated at his chastisement, but she didn't argue. He waited for her to deliver a hard limit for their play, but it didn't come. Sam looked like she was biting her tongue. He tested her.

"I won't be playing with that body part today, but make no mistake. Your ass—every single part of it, inside and out—it's mine, Samantha."

"But…"

"Yes, your butt," he agreed with cheer, unable to hide his smile.

"No, that's not what I meant."

"I know, baby, but it's what I meant. It's mine." Jonah wrapped his arms around her, his hands palming her ass.

"You mean…" her voice trailed off.

"Yes, my little innocent. When you're ready, and it won't be too long from now, I'm going to stretch your bottom hole until I know you'll be able to take me fucking you there just like I do your pussy."

"What if I don't want that?" she quizzed him.

He paused, pretty sure she was just testing him. "What do you think?"

"I think I'd need to say red if I wanted you to stop."

He grinned, "Good girl."

"You mean you'd stop?"

"Sam, I'd be disappointed and I'm going to do my best to convince you to at least give it a try, like I will many much more kinky things, but yes, baby. You say red, I stop. That's how it works."

She let the words sink in before grinning. Without another word, she turned, returning to her splayed out position, a look of excitement on her face.

Their intermission had done nothing to squelch his need. On the contrary, talk of kinks and ass play had him on the edge. To date, save the night of their reunion when he'd—fuck, raped her— he'd been trying to ease Samantha into his lifestyle. He'd let his Jonah, more gentle, persona resurface to reconnect with his long lost love.

This morning, he would be introducing Sam to a signature Cash Carter fuck.

Jonah closed the last inches between them, reaching out with his left hand to yank her head back with his handful of her hair. Sami arched her back giving him a better view of her swaying tits as he lined up his shaft and rammed into her body hard enough that he sent her forehead bouncing into the mirror.

They both chuckled, but all humor fled as he pulled out and pressed forward harder, deeper. He loved holding her head back far enough that he could see her beautiful neck, bare and laid out for him to lean in and nip at her neck as if he were preparing to bite her and leave his mark.

It was then that he remembered that once again, they were

about to have unprotected sex. He'd lost track of how many times now. He knew they were playing with fire, but he didn't have the self-control to stop long enough to find a condom in his bag.

More importantly, he recognized that he didn't want anything, even a thin barrier, between them. He'd talk to her about birth control pills later.

Their bodies slapped together hard and fast. He didn't play fair, reaching his free right hand around her to find her swollen clit as his cock pistoned at a fever pace. Several light taps. A few harder swipes. Sam rocked in his arms, trying to get enough pressure to tip her into her orgasm. He obliged her by pinching her clit so hard she cried out his name just as he felt her cunt squeezing his rod still buried inside her.

Once she'd come, his thrusts moved to double time. He grabbed her right hip, using his grip to pull her body hard as he thrust forward. Their bodies crashed together, loud slaps and wet suction sounds reverberating off the walls of the bathroom.

He should pull out, but his need to mark her was too great. He felt his balls constricting and knew it would only be seconds now. He took them across the finish line by lifting his right hand and while he pulled her hair harder, proceeded to crash his palm down on her right ass cheek in time to the beat of their fucking.

He was too far gone to be playful. He cracked her ass hard, again and again, watching her eyes in the reflection, looking for her panic. He watched for the discipline to be too much, only that never came. What did happen was Samantha's overwhelmed sexual rant.

"Holy shit, Jonah!" She was panting, out of breath despite the fact that he was doing all the work. He didn't think it was possible to be more turned on than he was in that moment, but he was wrong. Her nonsensical mumbling of "yes" and "more" spurred him on. He fought to fend off his eruption as long as possible, enjoying her added chanting of "harder" and "faster" as she chased her next climax.

Samantha screamed his name when she crashed into her next orgasm. He didn't hold back, shooting jets of warm jizz into her spasming core.

As soon as he released her hair, she let her upper body fall to the vanity, resting her right cheek on the cool marble while she gasped to catch her breath. He could see how tired she was, yet he enjoyed staying locked inside her as they each came down from their high.

"Don't move." She held her position, watching him in the mirror as he pulled his softening tool out of her sloppy sex, leaving her to go to the sink to prepare a warm cloth. Only when they were cleaned up did he scoop her into his arms and carry her back to bed where she tried to burrow into the covers for a nap.

Jonah retrieved the remaining cold pizza from the night before, hand feeding Samantha small bites. After the first few, she protested.

"I'm not hungry," she groused as she slapped his hand away from her mouth.

"That's enough. You can take a nap when you eat one slice."

She grumbled but obeyed. When she'd finished her slice, she announced victoriously, "I don't want any more pizza."

Jonah set the plate aside and slid under the covers, pulling her against him so she could use his chest as her pillow. He sure as hell could get used to this.

He felt her relaxing into her nap.

"Get some rest, baby. I'll have a proper breakfast of eggs, bacon and pancakes waiting for you when you wake up."

Her mumbled groan against his chest made him smile, hugging her closer.

Yep, I sure as hell could get used to this.

* * *

THE POUNDING on the hotel suite door was new.

Jonah and Samantha had been holed up in the penthouse suite of the Four Seasons for thirty-six glorious hours, but their attempts at shutting out the rest of the world were becoming increasingly difficult.

It had begun with Samantha's cell phone starting to ring first thing Monday morning when her friend Megan had been concerned that she'd missed her first class. Unwilling to cut their time short, Jonah had let Sami convince him her grades could withstand missing two days of classes. He suspected she'd quit school that very day if he asked her to, which he was ashamed to admit had crossed his mind. Only the fact that he had a full concert schedule until Christmas Eve helped him force down his urge to drive them to the airport to board a plane to run away to Tahiti.

By Monday afternoon, Frank's calls had started. Reports of Jonah being holed up in his suite with the woman he'd jumped from the stage for on Friday night had made it back to Frank. His manager was in full lawyer mode, adamant that Jonah get Sam to sign an NDA and even better, a copy of the relationship contract Frank had created over two years before after one of Jonah's casual BDSM partners had tried to sue him for abuse after he'd caned her. That little escapade had cost him a pretty penny to legally extricate himself before the police had been brought in to complicate things.

The only interruption that had been welcome was the stream of in-room dining deliveries that had brought them breakfast, lunch and dinner on Monday along with a hearty breakfast hours before.

Despite Samantha's assurances that she was about to burst from eating and drinking too much, Jonah was determined to keep stuffing her to try to put a few pounds on her too-thin frame. He had made it abundantly clear that her days of starving herself to send every penny she could spare to the women's shelter were now over. She'd resisted until he'd called his financial advisor and authorized a transfer of $50,000 to the shelter in her name. He grinned remembering how she'd then spent the next hour showing her appreciation for his generosity.

As it was now after noon on Tuesday and past his checkout time, he suspected the knocking on the door was the housekeeper, desperate to get in to clean the suite to prepare it for the next VIP.

Samantha clung to him harder the longer the knocking went on. He'd put on the deadbolt to ensure no one would inadvertently let themselves into their room.

"I need to get up and see who it is," he finally said, reluctantly.

"No you don't," she hugged him tighter.

"Sami."

"Jonah." He could hear the emotion in her voice. "I don't want you to leave."

Shit, he understood. For the first time in his musical career, he dreaded having to leave for a concert. He'd already blown off stopping in New York to meet up with River and the rest of the band. He'd texted them to let them know he'd meet them in Boston in time for that night's show. The crew had driven up over the weekend after Friday night's Runway show and he didn't look forward to being back on the tour bus that night.

He got a reprieve when the knocking stopped, but he knew it would be short lived. He'd put off talking about what came next, but they were out of time.

"We need to get up and shower. Frank will have a car downstairs waiting for me. I'll have the driver drop you off at your apartment on the way to the airport." He felt her trembling and suspected she was fighting off tears. He hugged her harder. "But I'm gonna call you as soon as I get to Boston. It'll be too late to call you after the show and there'll be a bunch of people around on the bus anyway, but I promise, I'll call you as often as I can."

He felt wet tears spilling onto his chest where Sami clung to him like a body pillow. He let her cry, trying to comfort her while swallowing a lump in his own damn throat.

Can I really walk away from her again?

Leaving her would be so different this time. He had a choice now. He wasn't a scared teenager with no means to fight back. He wasn't afraid the men in Sami's life could hurt him again like they had last time he got too close. What scared him the most was that he knew she would soon have to choose between the men in her life. Despite being confident she'd choose him, he knew she'd be the collateral damage as the drama played out between Jonah and her family.

For years he'd survived on revenge when that was all he had to his name. Had Jonah doubted for one minute that he was in love with Samantha, his doubt was gone when he realized that her happiness meant more to him than exacting his own sweet revenge. That revelation left him confused. He prayed the next few weeks spent apart would help him sort through those complicated feelings.

They somehow made it through showering, silently clinging to each other as they let their soapy hands roam over the other's body in an effort to memorize every inch to recall in their coming weeks apart. Jonah's resolve wavered when she kissed his 9/11/01 tattoo, but he knew he had to be strong enough for both of them.

"It will only be three weeks," he tried to reassure her. "We can make it three weeks."

"And then what?" She pressured him for answers he didn't have. "You finish on the twenty-third. Why can't you meet me then?"

"We've been through this. I'm never stepping a foot in Texas again. Ever." His tone was harsher than he'd intended and Samantha flinched.

"You still haven't explained it to me." He knew what she was asking, but he held his tongue.

He'd pieced together that the Stone men had fucked with Samantha as much as they had him. She still clung to the delusion that she came from Texas elite. Jonah hadn't quite figured out how to explain to her exactly how corrupt the men in her family were. As soon as he left Samantha today, he'd be hiring the best private investigator he could find to get the newest dirt on his oldest enemies. He'd need all the facts before he broke Samantha's heart.

"We'll talk about it when I see you after Christmas. We need more time than we have now."

"But,"

"Samantha." His Dom voice did its magic. She didn't push him further.

After the shower, they finally put on clothes. They'd been naked since arriving at the hotel late Sunday night. Since she had no other outfit with her, Sam was forced to put back on the jeans and frilly blouse she'd worn to Black Light.

They were at the door, ready to leave their private haven when panic hit Jonah. He stopped short, turning to Sam and seeing tears in her eyes. Despite her wet hair and having absolutely no make-up on, she took his breath away. Her vulnerability. Her trust in him. It was there, pouring out of her adorable face.

He couldn't lose her again.

This time, it was Sam who comforted him with a wan smile on her lips. "Three weeks." She said it like a promise.

He hadn't expected Frank to be waiting outside their door. His manager sat on an uncomfortable looking chair looking pissed as hell.

Jonah could feel Samantha shrinking against his side when she saw they weren't alone. He wrapped his arm around her to give her comfort and to signal to Frank to back the fuck up.

"There are over a dozen news outlets in the lobby and on the sidewalk outside of the entrance to the hotel. They sent cameras and reporters. The works," Frank reported with a bit too much glee to suit Jonah.

"We'll go out the back then," Jonah reasoned.

Frank couldn't hide his agitation. "Since when? This is publicity, Cash."

"No, Frank. This is my life."

"Since when are those two things separate?"

"Since today." Jonah knew what he needed to do next. "Frank, you've met Samantha Stone." Jaxson had shared with Jonah how poorly Frank had treated Sam backstage on opening night. He needed to make sure nothing like that ever happened again. "She is important to me. She's to be protected at all costs."

"Fine. Fine. But she still signs the NDA."

"Nope."

"But…"

Jonah separated from Sam and got in Frank's face. "Let me be clear. No paperwork. No publicity stunts. Not with Sami."

"Sami? We're at the nickname stage already? It's only been three fucking days."

"That's where you're wrong. It's been over fifteen years. She's my oldest friend."

Frank couldn't hide his alarm. "Wait. Stone… as in…"

Jonah cut him off. "Enough. We'll talk later. Now, can you get the car around to the back or do I need to order an Uber to meet us there?"

"Give me a few minutes," he groused before pulling his cell phone out of his pocket and making a few calls.

Jonah pulled Samantha into his arms while they waited. He could feel her trembling. "Shhh. It's gonna be okay, baby."

"Promise?" she pleaded.

Fuck. Could he promise? Knowing the fight they'd have on their hands, he felt like an ass answering her confidently, "I promise."

Five minutes later, the threesome was in the employee elevator on the way to the back exit of the luxury hotel. They were met by hotel security on the ground floor who helped them weave through the back of house corridors, exiting into the back alleyway next to the hotel loading dock.

Jonah held Samantha's hand as they approached the limo with

the smoke tinted windows. They were only a few feet away when the persistent photographer jumped from behind the nearby dumpster and started snapping photos like the paparazzi he was. Jonah jumped in front of Sam, shielding her as best he could, hoping to delay her being identified by the press as long as possible.

Only once they were safely inside the car did Frank yell to the driver to take off. Jonah pulled Samantha into his lap, both of them wanting to enjoy their last minutes together, at least for a few weeks.

Sensing they needed their privacy, Frank held his tongue as Jonah reassured Samantha one last time. "The next few weeks will fly by. You'll see. You need to focus on catching up on the work you've missed and getting good grades on your finals in a few weeks."

"Why? I'm not going to finish grad school," Samantha argued.

"You don't know that."

"Yes, I do. I never wanted to be a lawyer. I want to help people instead."

Jonah chuckled. "Well, I don't disagree that most lawyers don't do much to help." He paused, shooting his lawyer/manager a humorous grin. "But, I'm sure you could do a lot of great work to represent the shelter and other causes like it as a lawyer. Nonprofits always need good legal help." He could see her processing that idea as they went through one of D.C.'s many roundabouts.

The drive to her apartment was too fast. They were already pulling up in front and the doorman was coming to open the door beside them before he could catch his breath. Jonah wished they had some privacy for their goodbyes.

She clung to him, only agreeing to get out when he offered to walk her to the door. They moved slowly as if walking to a funeral dirge. Once inside the small lobby, he held her close for one last hug.

"It's going to be okay, Sami," he reassured her.

"How do you know?" she questioned.

Jonah said the only words that mattered. "Because you love me, and…" their eyes met before he finished his sentence. "And, because I love you."

His words brought renewed tears, but this time from joy. He loved the feeling of her body melting against him and for the briefest of moments, he considered canceling the concert that night. Only the sound of the doorman clearing his throat snapped him out of his wishful thinking. He had responsibilities. People counting on him. Fans who'd spent their money on tickets. Band members who needed their leader. No matter how much he personally wanted to run away, obligation won the day.

He leaned down to kiss the tip of her nose affectionately like he'd done dozens of times when they were kids. "I'll call you when I land," he promised.

Only when he was pulling away in the limo did he see the paparazzi across the street, waiting to pounce on Samantha when she left. So much for shielding her from being identified.

This complicates things.

CHAPTER 12

"I'll have a latte, skinny." Samantha placed her order with the waitress in the restaurant of the luxury hotel where she'd agreed to meet her new friend Emma Fischer.

This was the third time the women were having coffee in the two weeks since Jonah had left D.C. The two undercover security guards, one assigned to each of the women, shared their own cup of coffee at the table next to them while keeping their eyes and ears peeled for intruders.

Emma and Sam had learned their lesson at their first meeting at the local Starbucks just a few days after Jonah had left for Boston. Excerpts of their very private discussion that day had made it into the national gossip rags thanks to the industrious journalist who'd gone undercover as a fellow grad student, getting close enough to the women to snap a few grainy photos and record salacious details about their love lives with their A-list celebrity lovers. Ever since then, Jonah had insisted on a guard being with Sam at all times when she left her apartment. It was an inconvenience to be sure, but if it was the price to be in Jonah's life, she didn't mind.

Once the waitress delivered their drinks, the women enjoyed their first moment of privacy.

"I hope I'm not driving you crazy inviting you for drinks too often." Samantha was letting her insecurities shine through.

"Are you kidding me? I'd meet every day if we could. You have no idea how nice it is to have someone who really gets it," Emma countered, sipping her hot beverage gingerly.

Sam was so relieved to have someone to talk to who really did understand what she was going through. Emma, a grad student from Wisconsin, had been walking the same path Sam now found herself on for over a year. Not only could Emma share advice, but she could empathize when all Sam wanted to do at times was have someone listen.

Jonah had been true to his word, calling her daily. They'd spent hours talking about everything and nothing, just like they had in the old days. Yet, each day they hung up the call without discussing the eight-hundred pound gorilla that stood between them. They had yet to tackle the details around why he'd left seven years before, and the conspicuous avoidance placed a growing wedge between them that was beginning to feel insurmountable.

"We'll be in Wisconsin for almost a week at my parents. How terrible is it that I'm dreading it?" Emma looked miserable as she shared her Christmas holiday plans.

"I thought you said your parents loved Jaxson and Chase?"

"That's just it! They do all love each other and get along great. It's just that... well..." Her friend blushed before continuing, "It's a bit difficult to spend quality time together when we're at my parent's. If we aren't helping Mom in the kitchen, Dad has the guys going out on hunting expeditions, or riding the ATV's or cutting down the Christmas tree. And don't get me started on the sleeping arrangements."

"Do your parents worry about you considering how many

stories the press put out about you, Jaxson, and Chase?" Samantha was more than a little curious.

"In the beginning, when the scandal after Jaxson's father's fundraiser broke out, sure. They weren't crazy about their daughter's name being dragged through the mud in conjunction with politics and even LGBT rights. Even now, activist groups still try to use our relationship as their poster child to draw attention to the lifestyle, both for it and against it."

Samantha shuddered. "I can't even imagine how my father would take news like that."

"Yeah, it got a little tense there for a bit, but the guys have done so much to protect me from anything like that happening again that Mom and Dad adore them as much as I do. It also helped that the guys invited my parents to Europe last summer while we were in Rome for a few weeks. They spent quality time getting to know each other. I think Jaxson, especially, appreciates having parents around that aren't whacko like his father."

"You are so lucky," Sam reminded her with envy.

"You're right. I should just shut up. It could be so much worse." Emma looked at her sympathetically. "So you still haven't talked to your Dad about Jonah yet?"

Her heart rate went up just thinking about that confrontation coming as soon as she got home in less than two days. "Honestly, I'm surprised my dad hasn't ripped into me already. I'm pretty sure the stories of Jonah and me are making national news. I keep waiting for him to confront me about it, but so far Dad hasn't even mentioned knowing we've reunited."

"Why do you think he won't be happy?" Emma questioned, sipping her hot coffee.

"It's complicated," Sam replied, unsure where to even start.

"We love celebrities. The most simple things in life become complicated when they're involved," Emma reasoned.

Considering she now had a shadow to attend class or even have a cup of coffee, Sam had to agree with her friend. As she tried to formulate her answer, the truth was, Sam still didn't really understand what had gone so terribly wrong seven years before either. She shared what she did know.

"My father never liked Jonah. I was too young to understand at the time. We lost my mom the year before Jonah moved to Texas. It started with Dad thinking he was protecting me from mixing with what he considered the wrong sort of crowd, but looking back, I think he was jealous of the influence I gave Jonah over me, even as a kid."

Emma agreed. "Men can be so weird. My dad had a harder time accepting Jaxson especially for the same reason. Do you think they will argue when they see each other over the holiday?"

Renewed sadness hit Sam. "They won't get the chance. Jonah refuses to step foot in the state of Texas he hates it so much. I'm flying home Friday and will spend through the day after Christmas with Dad before I fly out to meet Jonah in Colorado for some skiing. How terrible is it that I'm dreading going home and just want to spend the holiday with Jonah instead?"

Sam felt guilty even thinking that. Her dad, Robert, didn't have anyone left other than Sam and his brother, William. She worried that she would soon be forced to choose between the two men in her life and wished more than anything it didn't need to be like that.

"It's only natural. You've been separated from Jonah for a long time. Of course you want to spend time with him. How old were you again when he left Texas?"

"I was a sophomore. He was a senior. Our last date was the night of his senior prom." Sam blushed at the memories of that night. She glossed over them, giving Emma only the highlights. "He left right after his senior year. He'd never hidden his dream of starting a band, but I just couldn't believe he'd leave without staying in touch, or at least saying goodbye." Familiar anger stirred as she remembered her confrontation with her father a few months after Jonah had left. "I wouldn't let it drop. I knew he wouldn't just leave like that. My dad and uncle finally admitted that they'd offered Jonah fifty thousand dollars to help him get the band started if he'd leave town and never come back."

Emma whistled in surprise. She sat in silence, unsure how to respond.

Sam had never, not once, said those words out loud. Hearing them made the pain flood back, but this time, the ache felt different. As a kid, she'd placed most of the blame on her parent, giving Jonah a pass for not being able to resist what was a life changing amount of money for a poor kid from the wrong side of the tracks.

Today, seven years later, she was finding it hard not to resent his celebrity status, knowing he'd chosen it over her all those years ago. Panic gripped her as she realized confronting her father wasn't the only uncomfortable conversation in her near future. She and Jonah would need to have a long talk about why he'd chosen fame and money over her if they had any hope of making it for the long haul.

"Needless to say, things were rocky between me and Dad there for a while, but eventually he wore me down and I forgave him, knowing Jonah hadn't been forced to take the money. It was his choice, only now..." Sam stalled, playing self-consciously with the sugar packets on the table to avoid making eye contact with her friend.

"What?" Emma questioned. "Has Jonah talked about it?"

Samantha was frustrated. "No, and that's what's so weird. Instead of acting grateful for the help, he seems to hate my dad and uncle. I've tried to bring it up a few times, but am so afraid of losing him again, I decided to wait until we were together before I try again. I want to be able to see his eyes."

Emma agreed, "That sounds like a smart plan. So you'll have to confront your father first, then."

"Yep, unfortunately I cannot put it off any longer. I'm dreading it, but while I'm furious that Dad intervened back then, I'm really hoping he won't continue to hold a grudge. Surely he can see how successful Jonah is and be happy for him now."

"I hope so. Men. Sometimes they don't make any sense," Emma reasoned.

"You should know. You live with two of them."

Emma grinned, "Don't tell the guys, but I'm grateful for the power dynamics in our relationship. Sometimes I feel guilty playing the role of a submissive when society has raised me to be a career minded, Type A, always in control professional." Emma paused to make eye contact. "You know what I mean?"

Boy, do I ever.

"Totally. I've had a long time love/hate relationship with control." Samantha hadn't been brave enough to share her past history with cutting with her new friend yet.

"Well, if you stick with Jonah, it will continue to be exciting. I'm guessing he won't be the type to share control, at least not in some of the more intimate parts of your relationship, if you know what I mean." Both women blushed having witnessed some of those intimacies first hand.

The women enjoyed their visit for another half-hour, talking non-stop, until Samantha had to head out. "I wish I could stay, but I need to see the campus OBGYN before I go home."

Emma looked concerned so Sam put her mind at ease. "Oh, nothing's wrong. I just want to get a prescription for birth control and would prefer not to do it with my doctor back home since he goes to Daddy's country club. I'd like to think he'd be discreet, but Texas, you just never know."

"But you're twenty-three. Does your father really think you're still a virgin?" Emma asked incredulously.

Samantha's cheeks burned from embarrassment before she reluctantly admitted. "Honestly, I was a virgin until that first night at Runway."

"What?" Emma's face registered her shock. Samantha silently gave Jaxson kudos for keeping her secret, even from his lover.

"Hard to believe, I know, but I was."

Emma whistled. "Wow, and then a few days later you were already at Black Light. You're making up for lost time pretty quickly."

Sam chuckled, "How could I not with Jonah as my teacher?"

Emma grabbed the check and put down a ten dollar bill to cover it. "Hey, it's my treat this time. You save your cash for your prescription. That's a hundred times more important. As much as I love Jaxson and Chase, I can't even think about getting pregnant right now. What a nightmare."

A sliver of anxiety slithered through Samantha. Her and Jonah had already played with fire having unprotected sex multiple times. She had enough stressful things happening in her life. At least handling birth control could be easily fixed.

The ladies hugged goodbye before parting. Emma prodded her friend. "Keep in touch over the holidays. I can't wait to hear how everything works out."

As Sam walked the few blocks to the campus medical center, she started to mentally prepare for the coming long weekend with her father. She wasn't sure which would be harder to break to him: that she and Jonah had been reunited and no amount of money would keep them apart this time or that she had just taken her last class in law school.

* * *

"CASH! CASH! OVER HERE!" Jonah pushed through the throng of fans gathered outside the stadium. They'd be playing to a sold out crowd in less than two hours. The men of the band pressed forward slowly, stopping to sign a few autographs and allow fans to touch their favorite rockers as they moved into the building. The flash of cameras bounced off the falling Colorado snow until they made it into the back hallway, finally free of the rabid crowd.

As soon as the door was closed behind them, he turned around to confront Frank who'd been right behind him as he'd left the limo. Jonah wasn't happy with his manager.

"What the fuck was that? I told you in Omaha that you needed to tighten up security. It's getting out of control again."

Frank was defensive, "Hey, I can't help it that everyone is going batshit crazy to get a piece of you, worried you're going to be off the market soon."

His manager had not hidden the fact that he was against Jonah making his relationship status change become public record. They hadn't exactly taken an ad out in the newspaper to announce Jonah was in a committed relationship, but the rumor mill was coming unhinged with speculation. So far, the lead singer of the Crushing Stones had neither denied nor confirmed the rumors officially.

Christ, he was tired.

The last two weeks he'd spent apart from Samantha had dragged by at a snail's pace. They had so much unfinished business. Each day that passed, the pressure to confront all of the bullshit from their past grew until it felt like it was strangling him. The only things getting him through the added stress were his hard workouts that helped burn off his aggression and daily phone calls with Samantha herself.

Those calls, unfortunately, both helped and hurt. Just hearing her voice calmed him in ways nothing else could, yet every day they hung up without talking about why he'd really left her years before added more bricks to the wall that was forming between them.

Having nothing new to say, he eventually turned his back on his manager and continued stalking into the underbelly of the auditorium that doubled as the home to the city's professional basketball team.

That they would soon be performing for over twelve thousand Crushing Stones fans should make him nervous, but it didn't.

Music, he could handle. Navigating through the tricky relationships in his life was proving to be a bit more difficult.

When they got to their backstage dressing room, Jonah relaxed a little. He and the band would at least have a few minutes of relative privacy to regroup as they ate a light meal and got ready.

The band members were usually quiet before a show, focusing on the mental preparedness required for a successful concert. Jonah took advantage of the subdued environment to collapse into one of the many couches in the space. He took a few minutes to close his eyes, remembering Samantha and how beautiful she'd been their last afternoon together.

Only a few more days and then we'll be reunited.

He was on edge. He knew he wouldn't truly relax until she'd returned to him. He'd be lying if he said he wasn't concerned about her traveling to visit her father and uncle for the Christmas holiday. It took all of his self-control to stop from forbidding her to visit the men in Texas. Jonah was almost sure she'd agree to fly to Colorado early if he asked her, but he also knew it would be a gross misuse of his influence over her if he played that card. It was the kind of shit the Stone men would pull and he was determined to be the better man in her life.

The vibration of his cell phone in his front pocket pulled him from his memories. A quick glance at the screen cheered him up in a flash. It was Sami.

"Hello! I was just thinking about you," he answered with the genuine surprise he was feeling.

"I was hoping to catch you before the show. I miss you so much," she answered quietly, sounding as conflicted as he had just been.

"Hey, it won't be long now. How was your last final today?"

"Okay. Not great, but I should be able to hold my B average," Sami informed him.

"That's my good girl." He was so impressed by all she could accomplish.

Sam perked up a bit, adding, "I think I deserve a reward."

"Really? What did you have in mind?" Jonah flirted, expecting her to talk sexy to him like most nights when they talked late into the night.

He wasn't prepared for her more serious request. "Please, Jonah. Come home with me for Christmas tomorrow."

He was agitated that she wouldn't let the topic drop. "We've been through this, Samantha. I'll never go there again."

"When are you going to tell me what happened between you and Dad before you left?" Tonight's call was taking a darker turn. One he wasn't ready to discuss yet.

Agitation grew to anger. He fucking didn't want to talk about the bastard, especially over the phone. They'd done so well with avoiding the hot button topics. He didn't understand what had changed to make Samantha want to confront the subject this close to being back together. He let his mind wander, avoiding talking to her.

He'd put enough together to know that she'd been duped as much as he had by the men in her life. She had no idea the Stone men had had him arrested for statutory rape of their under-aged Sam the night of prom. With their extensive legal contacts, they'd literally been able to incarcerate him in a juvenile detention center and throw away the key for what had seemed like an eternity to a teenage Jonah.

Five months to be exact.

Five months behind bars without access to a lawyer that hadn't been hired by the Stone men themselves. A lawyer interested in only one thing—securing Jonah's cooperation in leaving Samantha alone.

Five months without access to his mother who'd been frantic with worry for her only son, not knowing what had happened to him and being told lies by the Stone men making her afraid to go to the police for help.

Five months to be worn down until he'd have signed anything

to get away from them. Even a piece of paper that would give them the power to arrest him the second he stepped foot in the good 'ole state of Texas again. Even a paper that had him promising not to contact Samantha again. It had spelled out how she'd been promised in marriage to the wealthy son of one of their cronies from the country club and she didn't need to have her questionable friend showing up to confuse her.

When he'd balked at signing that last piece of paper, they'd sweetened the deal, throwing in a diploma to show he'd graduated from high school, even though he'd been in his cell the night of the ceremony, along with a sealed envelope that contained a check made out to him in the amount of fifty thousand dollars.

That's the price the bastards had put on Samantha's worth. A measly fifty thousand dollars out of their millions. It was a fucking joke.

"Jonah?" He'd zoned out in his little trip down memory lane.

He scrambled to salvage their conversation. "You're still planning on coming to Vail on the twenty-seventh, right? I'll meet you there. You'll see, everything will turn out fine." He felt slimy promising her that when they had so many big topics still hanging between them. He tacked on, "We'll get to spend ten whole days together, including New Year's Eve. It will be great."

"But that's almost a whole week away."

"Baby, we went almost seven years. You don't think we can make it another five days?" Even as he said it, the precarious wall of confidence he'd been trying to prop up between them felt like it was crumbling. His sixth sense was telling him not to let the Stone men get their hands on Samantha again.

What if they could make her disappear as easily as they'd made him go poof years before?

The stage manager was calling out pre-show orders. Frank was waving at him to wrap up the call and change his clothes for the show. River was giving him the evil eye from across the room, knowing who he was talking to and still not trusting a Stone. Not even Sam.

"Sami, I gotta go, baby. I'm gonna call you later after the show. We'll talk about this more then, okay?" He waited for her reply that didn't come. "Sam?"

"Yes," it was a whisper. If he didn't know better, he'd swear she was crying.

"What is it? What aren't you telling me?" He couldn't shake that something bigger was going on tonight.

"I just… need to… see you…" she stumbled through her words, too full of emotion.

"Ten minute warning," the stage manager yelled out to the crowded room of musicians.

Fuck.

"I'm sorry, baby. They're calling me. I really do need to go, but I'll call you later. I promise."

"It's okay. I'm just being silly. I have an early flight in the morning and still need to pack. Why don't we talk tomorrow?" He could tell she was trying to put on a brave face. Jonah wished he had more time to get to the bottom of what was bothering her, but it would have to wait a day.

"Okay. Sleep well."

He didn't have time to worry about the heavy shit hanging over them. He had a job to do. Jonah got up and got to work turning himself into Cash Carter.

* * *

TWO HOURS LATER, Cash Carter's shirt was soaked through with perspiration from his exertion on stage. Like the consummate professional he was, he'd turned off all of the distractions to focus on delivering a kick-ass concert the fans had paid big bucks to see.

Adrenaline pumped through his veins as they took their final bows, giving the sold-out crowd not one, but two encores. By the time the band headed down the back steps and towards their dressing room, he'd almost forgot about the heavy problems waiting for him.

The back corridor was crowded with groupies and VIPs with backstage passes, all pressing in to touch the band members. He was going to be having another discussion with their head of security. It was bullshit how each night they'd had more and more unauthorized fans to deal with. It was a huge security risk.

He was almost at the end of the gauntlet when he noticed several news cameras rolling. Frank usually warned them when he'd set up interviews. He was exhausted and never would have agreed to do an interview tonight, this close to Christmas. He didn't need reporters questioning him again about who the woman was in D.C. or where he'd be spending his holidays.

He had just turned to find Frank as the glow of the nearest camera pointed his way. In the glare of the bright lights and the commotion of the pressing crowd, he totally missed the woman throwing herself at him from the right until she was draped all over his sweaty body. Her arms wrapped around his neck in a choke-hold and before he could throw her off, her lips latched onto his in an open mouth kiss.

He was only a second into the kiss when he recognized the body molded against him. Cash reached up to grab her by the forearms and started pushing her away from him, but the pressing crowd was working against him. In the chaos, she managed to rub against him in what would look like an intimate embrace to anyone paying attention.

Jonah wrenched his head away far enough to sound his warning. "Goddammit, Caroline."

The blonde bombshell who he'd dated months ago for a few weeks flashed her sexiest smile. He'd seen it many times before, just before he'd fucked her brains out. They'd gone their separate ways, and she'd joined the long list of his tossed aside dalliances.

He pressed her for answers, even as the paparazzi moved in closer. "What the fuck are you doing here?" He had to shout over the commotion.

"I missed you," she purred.

"Since when?"

Jonah tried to move around her, desperate to get out of the throng of groupies groping him as he tried to distance himself from the woman intent on making a scene. Caroline latched onto his arm as he moved past her, acting like she would be tagging along with him. He moved to extricate himself from her clinging as she added confusing words. "I forgive you."

Jonah stopped in his tracks, turning back to her. "For what?"

She didn't answer, instead smiling a sexy smile as she leaned in closer. "We aren't over."

Jonah lost his temper. "Honey, we never started. Fuck off."

He succeeded in extricating himself from her clutches and pressed through the remaining crowd to finally make it to the door to their dressing room. His security detail was there and helped to hold back the crowd who tried to follow him.

Only when he got into the relative quiet of their private sanctuary did Jonah's pulse finally return to normal, allowing him to think through all that had happened. His gut was screaming at him, and at first, he didn't figure it out. But with each passing minute, it became more and more clear to him.

"You mother fuckers," he said to no one in particular.

He needed to find Frank and Ryan.

CHAPTER 13

"*S*amantha!"

Sam was standing next to the luggage carousel, waiting for her bag when she heard her father's voice calling her name. She turned in time to see him striding her way.

"Daddy? Since when do you come pick me up at the airport yourself? I was expecting to see Miguel." Despite her nervousness about the upcoming difficult discussions she'd be having with her father, she had to admit she felt nothing but relief when he hugged her tight.

"I've missed you so much. I didn't want to miss welcoming you home. Miguel is making laps with the car. I told him I'd text him when we had your luggage."

His hug was a bit too tight. It was on the verge of hurting, but she reciprocated. When he pulled out of their embrace to look down into her eyes, she was concerned to see bags under his eyes. Her only parent looked exhausted.

"Is everything okay, Daddy? You don't look so hot."

"Gee, thanks." He feigned hurt feelings and she didn't know how to tell him she'd meant it. He surprised her with his own assessment. "You don't look so hot yourself, there, missy. You've been working too hard out there in D.C. I'm glad to have you home where I can take care of you again."

Sam didn't have the heart to break the news to him that she wouldn't be staying long. He thought she'd be home for five weeks over Georgetown's winter break. He'd be in for a surprise when he found out she'd be leaving in just a few days to join Jonah.

The baggage claim carousel at DFW airport wasn't the place to have that conversation.

It wasn't until they were seated in the back seat of her father's Cadillac SUV while his driver weaved through the heavy holiday traffic that the awkward silence fell over the small Stone family. Sam knew why she was struggling to make conversation, but then it hit her that her father wasn't acting his normal self either. With each passing mile they drove, the silence dragged heavier. By the time her parent finally spoke, it startled her.

"Your uncle is at our house waiting for us. He is anxious to see you, too." Sam heard the edge in his voice. He seemed as agitated by the news as she did.

"That's too bad. I was hoping to have some time to catch up with you alone before we saw him."

Her father scoffed, "Wouldn't that be nice." Her parent looked out the far window, avoiding making eye contact.

"Daddy. What's wrong?" She knew there were so many things. He could take his pick where he'd like to start their conversation.

But he didn't take the bait. Mayor Robert Stone sat frozen, watching the Texas skyline pass by as they made their way towards their little suburb where he was the biggest fish in the smaller pond.

When he finally spoke, his words were cryptic and confused her more than anything. "I've been thinking a lot lately. I want you to know that no matter what happens, I love you more than anything else in this world, Samantha." Her parent hadn't taken his eyes off the sprawling Texas landscape as he'd pledged his love.

As she watched him, she could see him swallowing often as if he were choking back emotion.

"I love you too, Dad." A sudden urgency to purge herself of her secrets overcame Sam. "How about we stop for a late breakfast and catch up... before we..." The words *have to see Uncle William* hung in the air. Talking to her father about Jonah would be hard enough. It would be ten times harder with her uncle there. The powerful judge was like a tornado to be around. He'd sweep in, leave his mark on anyone and everyone he encountered, and then be gone before you knew what hit you.

Sam didn't know why she didn't see it before, but in the back of that car, making eye contact with her father as he contemplated her request, she saw something she'd never seen before.

Fear.

Her father was afraid of his brother.

The elder Stone glanced down at his high-end watch before replying. "I wish we could, sweetheart, but I'm afraid we don't have time."

"Of course we have time. It's Christmas Eve. Surely you're taking today off."

He looked uncomfortable and in that moment, she was sure he was hiding something from her.

"I'm not going into the office, no, but we do have some appointments we need to make."

How different this visit was for Samantha. Gone was her childlike trust in her parent. She'd grown up in her months away. Had become a woman. It changed how she looked at everything, including... no *especially* in how she viewed the Stone men.

"Please, Dad. There are some things I'd like us to discuss in private."

He answered with an air of resentment, "There is nothing we can't talk about in front of your uncle. He knows everything that's going on around him anyway, so there's no chance of hiding anything," his words sounded like a warning. A self-fulfilling prophecy.

He knows everything going on around him.

Her father had just told her the men knew she'd been reunited with Jonah. Why wasn't her father pressing her for details?

"Maybe I don't want to have Uncle William involved in everything anymore," she retorted.

"Yeah, well we don't always get what we want, Samantha. The sooner you accept that, the better off you'll be."

His cryptic words were a premonition. She fought the urge to order Miguel to turn around and return her to the airport where she could board the next flight she could find to Denver. Oh how she wished Jonah were there with her. It would be so much easier to tackle their problems together.

The twosome fell into another awkward silence. With each mile they drove, it became more uncomfortable until she wanted to jump out of her skin by the time they pulled through the security entrance of their gated community in Plano.

Samantha took a calming breath before exiting the SUV. She grabbed her carryon bag, unwilling to part with her phone and laptop, her only connection to Jonah. Miguel would bring the rest of her things.

The second she opened the front door, she was tackled by a fluffy puppy she'd never seen before. She bent down to lift the little fur ball with a laugh as her father stepped close and kissed her on her cheek. "Merry Christmas, Sami. I got you a puppy, among other things."

"Dad! He's adorable, but…" She had almost spilled the beans that she wasn't sure she would be able to take a puppy with her when she went on the road with Jonah, but she bit her tongue.

He finished her sentence. "I checked with your apartment building in Georgetown and they said as long as he doesn't get over fifty pounds, he'll be allowed. I'll feel better with you having a guard dog with you in D.C. I don't like you living alone."

Their eyes met. "Dad. About that..."

Her confession to her father was cut off by her uncle walking their way from the great room. He had his signature fat cigar in his hand as he moved towards them pouring out smelly smoke he knew full well aggravated his niece's breathing.

"Samantha. You're home. I've been waiting for you," his aggravation at being kept waiting shone through in his tone.

After they'd exchanged their normal air kiss greetings, Samantha answered him. "Hello Uncle William. I see you're still ignoring Dad's request not to smoke in the house."

She had to fight to hold back her grin as her powerful uncle registered her censure of his actions with a scowl. People rarely dared cross the district judge. Not even his family members. She certainly never had before, and she hadn't planned to today, but in that moment, Samantha felt empowered. She'd had enough of being afraid; enough of being complacent. She had way too much to lose now and that meant she needed to speak her mind with confidence.

Her uncle wasn't impressed. "I see D.C. has changed you. I'm not sure I like it."

"D.C. did change me, but for the better. And yes, I'm pretty sure you're going to hate the new me."

The judge directed his dark warning glare her way. She'd witnessed it before, directed at others. She faltered briefly, but then took a deep, calming breath, staring right back. Her father tried to smooth things over.

"So what are you going to name this little guy?" Her dad had stepped closer, petting the puppy still wiggling in her arms. Their eyes met and she shivered, seeing he'd donned the icy cold mask he'd perfected when his brother was around.

"That's a great question. Maybe I should name him, Truth. It feels like we are in need of a bit more of that around here."

Samantha was playing with fire. She wasn't sure why she'd decided to declare war on her uncle the second she walked in the door. Maybe it was because she was tired of the games of hide and seek they'd played with the truth since the night of her senior prom. Maybe it was the anger she felt at seeing her father's fear in the car. More likely, it was her resentment that the men surrounding her were preventing her from being with Jonah and that was the only place she wanted to be.

Uncle William broke into an ugly grin. It was a warning to back down. Her father's hand slid to her lower back, trying to direct her forward to the great room. She finally moved her feet, allowing herself to be ushered forward, away from the foyer and deeper into the Stone mansion she'd lived in her entire life.

Funny, it didn't feel like coming home this time.

There were many topics to discuss, but Sam knew which one she needed to start with. She let herself be seated on the loveseat across from her uncle. Her father sat in the chair, half way between them, as if he wanted to play the role of the arbitrator between the two sides forming.

She didn't envy her father's job. She wouldn't be compromising. Not anymore.

Uncle William interjected, "I see your grades slipped a little bit at the end of the semester. You just squeaked out a B- in international law."

Samantha was furious. "I took the final less than twenty-four hours ago. How the hell would you have my grades already? In fact, how would you have my grades at all?"

"Don't be naive, Samantha. Thomas Horton is an old friend of mine from law school. Did you really think we'd let you go away to study with unknown professors?"

She was genuinely shocked that her uncle would go to such lengths to control her movement. She'd known he was controlling, but this exceeded anything he'd done in the past.

The irony that it had been her uncle's old friend who had auctioned off the ticket that got her reunited with Jonah brought a wide grin to her face. She wisely didn't share that little tidbit with the judge.

"You think this is funny, young lady?" She heard the cautionary tone in his voice.

"No, Uncle William, I don't think anything that's happened recently is funny." She stared him down, refusing to be outwardly intimidated, even though her heart was racing.

"We at least agree on one thing then," he glowered, taking a long drag from his cigar, blowing the smoke her direction as if to blatantly defy her request he stop.

Samantha buckled under his dark stare, turning to connect with her father instead. She was alarmed by the fear she saw in his every gesture. She took a deep, calming breath and then turned back to her uncle, recognizing her next announcement was for his benefit more than anyone else.

"Well then I'm glad I waited to share the news with Professor Horton." She took a deep breath, blowing it out slowly before continuing as confidently as she could muster. "I've decided to drop out of law school. I won't be returning to Georgetown after the new year."

She felt the weight of the world fall from her shoulders the second the words were in the open. She'd lacked the courage to say them the year before when she'd been accepted. She chickened out when she'd wanted to quit earlier that year as she'd moved across the country. Finally, the truth was out.

Her father tried to make light of her announcement, "Very funny, Samantha."

"No, Daddy, not really."

Uncle William almost spat out his objection in a poisonous rant, "You are a Stone. We have a legacy to uphold. You have responsibilities to carry on. We have very important... prestigious... *powerful* clients. They expect your participation. Your cooperation." He hesitated before adding, "Your *obedience*. The practice has made you a very rich young woman and now you will shut up, say thank you and do your duty."

"See that's where you're wrong. It's *my* life. *My* decision and I've decided I don't want to become a lawyer."

William turned on his brother, "I told you it was a fucking mistake to allow her to study away from Texas. You've lost control of her."

Her father sat stoic, while his brother berated him.

She glared back at her uncle who was now looking down at his expensive watch as if he were late for an appointment. The pressure of going up against her entire family was weighing on her. For a brief second, she resented Jonah putting her in this position. He should be here with her, fighting for their future alongside her.

She pushed down her resentment, trying to focus on the moment.

"Robert, turn on the television. There's a show I want Samantha to see. I'm pretty sure it will knock some sense into her."

Television? Since when did her uncle stop an argument to watch TV? Alarm bells were going off, but she didn't have enough information to put things together.

Her father moved slowly, but he did comply, using the remote to turn to the local news station. He was avoiding looking at her. Sam's stomach rolled with dread. The eleven a.m. local daily news program had come on and her heart almost beat out of her chest at the sight of the first story.

A grainy picture of Jonah being surrounded by pressing fans filled the screen. She'd been so focused on the picture, she'd missed some of the reporter's story at the start of the program.

"... Cash Carter, former resident of Texas, was ambushed by a crowd of pressing fans. WTNV's very own, Ashley Johnson, was there to catch the event. Ashley?"

They cut away to a close up of a reporter. "Thanks. Cash Carter has found himself in the news often lately. First for jumping off the stage into the crowd at a concert in Washington D.C. just a few weeks ago. Rumors after that event had him linked romantically with the unnamed young woman at that night's show, but I witnessed first-hand here in Denver last night that Mr. Carter is indeed reunited with Caroline Fleur, the actress who got her start starring in one of the Crushing Stone's music videos and has since gone on to play a starring role in Cash Carter's personal life."

Samantha's stomach was churning as the story droned on, the picture cutting away to a steamy kiss between Jonah and the actress who was more beautiful than Sam. More famous than Sam.

The anchor added intimate details Samantha didn't want to hear. "The celebrity couple will be turning heads at a Christmas charity event being held here in Denver this evening. Sorry, ladies, but the rumor mill has it on good authority that Cash Carter is about to be off the market. Sources close to the band indicate he's ready to pop the question to Caroline Fleur."

She had to swallow several times to stop the urge to throw up. Her ears were ringing. She needed fresh air. She pressed to her feet.

"Excuse me. I need..."

"Sit back down, Samantha." When she glanced at her uncle, he added a stern, "Now."

She collapsed to the loveseat, more out of defeat than the desire to acquiesce. Even as she internalized the pictures on the TV, a tiny part of Sam was screaming at her to wake up. On the surface, the story was so damning, but she reminded herself not to take anything on the surface ever again. Not since she'd learned the Stone men had secrets. Secrets she'd get to the bottom of or die trying.

Sam looked over to her father for support. There was a new

sadness in his eyes. She then turned to her uncle who looked equally victorious at her distress. It gave her courage.

"Why did you turn that program on?" she pressed her uncle.

His grin turned to an angry scowl. "Did you really think we didn't know you'd whored yourself out to that delinquent? We just wanted to show you his true colors."

His admission was as good as a confession to her. Her uncle never watched daytime TV. The fact that he'd turned the program on the very minute it was starting confirmed he'd made sure the story was planted.

Don't chicken out now. Go for broke.

"Jonah said you'd be desperate when you found out about us," she said calmly, refusing to let him see how terrified she was inside.

Her calm demeanor only angered the judge more. He pushed to his feet, yelling at her across the coffee table separating them. "Don't believe a word out of that hoodlum's mouth. He's been a pain in my ass for too long. He's damn near cost me a small fortune."

His words confused Sam, but she pressed forward with a guess. "Jonah never took a penny from you."

Her father surprised her by answering, "I'm afraid he did, Samantha. Like I told you back then, he took fifty-thousand dollars to stay away from you."

She knew she'd get nowhere with her uncle so she turned to her father for answers. "I know there's more to it. Daddy, what else did you do?"

"What I thought was best for you at the time," he said softly as if he were ashamed.

His brother broke in to scoff, "Come now, brother, tell the truth. You did what you thought was best for you. You still are which is why you'll shut the fuck up and just say thank you."

Sam turned on her uncle, "This is none of your business," she shouted.

"That's where you're wrong. Everything that happens in this family is my business. It's why you'll be going back to finish your law degree. It's why you'll never see Jonah Carter ever again. It's why you'll be marrying Antonio Munis next summer."

The man had truly lost his mind. She racked her memory, finding a vague memory of being introduced to her father's business associates at the country club a few times over the years. She had to be remembering him wrong.

"Are you talking about the businessman from Columbia? He has to be forty years old!"

"Forty-two. He needs an American wife to get his citizenship and he's ready to produce a few heirs. He had planned on letting you finish your law degree, but your fucking around has him nervous that we're going to renege on the deal we cut over seven years ago."

Samantha's breathing was becoming labored. Between the cigar smoke and the panic gripping her, she was becoming breathless. She had to be misunderstanding something.

"You're insane!" she managed to shout. She turned back to her father, "Daddy, tell him."

Her parent looked miserable. "It's too late, Samantha. The arrangements have all been made. You're a Stone. You need to pay our debts with the Munis family. This was destined long ago. The cartel allowed you to wait until you finished your schooling, understanding how valuable it would be to have you get your law degree, but they're getting nervous. They don't want to wait for the wedding any longer. In fact they're gonna be arriving tonight and you'll be introduced to your fiancé over dinner. There is no backing out, honey. There's too much riding on this deal."

"Well then you assholes have a bit of a problem then, don't you, since Samantha will be marrying me instead."

It was Jonah! He was there.

In her living room.

In Texas.

When she turned, she almost wept with relief to see him there. "Jonah?"

He smiled her direction. "Come here, baby." He held out his hand. It called to her.

Her father's shout warned her, "Samantha! Don't do it."

Her uncle was screaming, "You'd really go to him? After what you just saw with your own eyes? Are you a fool? He has another girlfriend on the side. He'll never be faithful to you."

The words echoed her insecurities. She stalled, surrounded by the men in her life.

Trust your gut, Samantha.

She rushed into Jonah's outstretched arms, almost collapsing with relief as he hugged her tight.

She could only choke out two words. "You came."

"Yeah, baby. I came."

Her uncle was still on his feet, looking ready to strangle someone.

Jonah called out, "Ryan, you can come in now,"

Things were happening so fast. Samantha turned to the entrance to see their old friend, Ryan, entering, dragging a reluctant Caroline Fleur behind him. Her first emotion at seeing the actress was anger, directed at Jonah.

Why would he bring her here knowing how it must hurt her?

Jonah answered her unspoken question. "I knew the second she showed up with cameras and reporters in tow that something was up. It took me a couple of minutes to put together that every single time something like that happens in my life, you bastards were behind it."

Her uncle's shouting startled Samantha. "You had one fucking job, you bitch. Seduce him. How hard could that be?"

Caroline ripped her arm out of Ryan's grip before she defended herself. "I'm not giving you back a dime. I held up my end of the bargain."

The truth was sinking in. Her uncle, and maybe even her

father, had paid the actress to seduce Jonah in hopes of driving a wedge between them. She had seen it all, or so she thought.

The judge had calmed down. A smug smile lit up his tanned face. "You know what, that's okay. This is going to work out just fine." He turned to face off with Jonah and Samantha huddled deeper into her lover's embrace. "You broke our deal. This time I'm gonna lock you up and throw away the key."

Jonah had to struggle to extricate himself from Samantha. She didn't want to release him, but he was insistent. The minute he was free, Jonah stalked forward to grab her uncle by the scruff of his dress shirt, pulling him forward until their angry faces were only inches apart.

"I'm not some scared eighteen year old kid with one-hundred bucks to my name anymore. You want a piece of me, come at me. I'll throw everything I have at you this time and it'll be you who ends up behind bars, not me."

She had no idea what was happening. She moved closer to Jonah, looking for answers.

"What are you talking about? When the hell were you behind bars?" she questioned.

Jonah directed his attention back to Samantha, then over to her father who stood by silently. She was surprised when he spoke to her father instead of her. "Are you going to tell her?"

She saw surprise in her father's eyes as he replied, "I would have thought you already would have."

"No. See, unlike you, Sami's happiness is what's most important to me. I know the truth will hurt her."

"Will somebody tell me what the hell is going on?" Samantha was impatient for answers.

It was Ryan who stepped up to fill in the details she'd been missing for almost seven years. "The night of our senior prom, your dad and uncle had Jonah arrested for statutory rape. You were only sixteen and he was eighteen. They held a circus of a trial in the middle of the night with your uncle on the bench. Even though the law protected Jonah, they made up lies about him doing drugs and other bullshit so they could throw him in the juvenile detention center."

"What?" She couldn't even believe what Ryan was saying. She looked at her father, desperate for him to deny the insane accusation, but saw only guilt there instead. "But he didn't rape me! We didn't even have sex!"

Her uncle's ugly words flung at her again. "Only because we got there and stopped it, you little whore. You almost blew the whole Munis deal that night by losing your virginity to this loser."

* * *

FOR THE FIRST time in his life, Jonah contemplated murder. If he thought for one minute he could get away with it, he was pretty sure he could kill the sonofabitch in front of him with his bare hands.

He pulled Judge Stone up by the shirt collar again, shouting in his face. "Don't you talk to Samantha again. Ever."

Behind him, Ryan was determined to finish filling in Samantha. "They blackmailed him, Sam. Jonah didn't have a chance. The judge ordered him held in solitary confinement. They didn't let Jonah see his mother, me, or even a real lawyer. In the end, they kept him there for almost five months before he broke. By then he would have signed anything they put in front of him to get the hell out there. He had to promise never to step foot back in Texas and to never try to contact you ever again."

Jonah saw the horror on Samantha's face as she listened to the story he'd hoped she'd never have to hear. It wasn't that he gave a shit about protecting the Stone men. They got what they deserved. But he knew it would kill Sam to find out what her family had done to him.

To them.

He needed to go to her. Comforting her was more important

than revenge against the man he held by the collar. Jonah pushed the judge away, but before he could reach Sami, the judge's accusations continued.

"Yeah, well the little shit did take the deal. He left you, Samantha. In the end, he took my fifty thousand dollar check as a payout and he left you behind."

Jonah could see the pain in Sami's eyes. It was bad enough both of the Stone men in her life had betrayed her, but she turned to him, confusion on her face. He couldn't stand it.

Jonah reached to his back pocket, pulling out his wallet. His hands trembled with emotion as he sorted through the many hundred dollar bills to finally pull out the raggedy old piece of paper he'd been carrying around with him like a badge for almost seven years. He turned back to the judge, throwing the scrap of paper in his face.

"Fuck you. I never took a damn dime from you. I've carried that check around with me all these years as a reminder. I have to thank you, really. Falsely arresting me. Forcing me to walk away from everything... everyone I loved. It did more to push me to succeed than your damn payoff money ever could have. I was determined to prove you wrong. Determined to show Samantha that she'd chosen the wrong men to trust. Only you cheated her too, didn't you? You spun the story to turn her against me. Well, wake up, asshole. Your story is falling apart now. She sees the truth."

"It's your word against ours. You have no proof." William Stone spoke bravely, but Jonah saw the perspiration gathering on the forehead of the portly judge. He was starting to realize how precarious the situation was that he was in.

"You know, I used to think the only way to crush you was legally. Financially. But I don't give a shit about that any more. All I want is Samantha. We're gonna leave here today and never come back."

He glanced at Sam and saw her tears. He prayed he wasn't delusional when he thought she'd come with him.

Samantha's father had been silent. Jonah hadn't expected that. He didn't know what that meant. He was even more confused when her father rushed to Sam and started to pull her away from all the commotion in the room.

"Please, Samantha. You have to believe me. I didn't know about all of what had happened until it was too late."

Jonah could see Samantha fighting to stay behind with Jonah as her father pulled on her arm harder. Her eyes searched for him. He could see the panic on her face that they might be separated again.

Jonah rushed to close the distance, holding Sami from behind and stopping her father's forward progress as the two men who loved her most physically fought over her. Jonah saw the desperation on the mayor's face as his brother taunted him.

"I'd be careful, brother. I'd sure hate to have to stop paying your gambling debts if you turn on me. You know damn well, the only way to see yourself clear is to marry her off to Antonio Munis."

Renewed fury consumed Jonah at the thought of the men using Samantha as some kind of pawn—payment for some back-door deal they'd made. That her uncle would sell her out was bad enough, but it was unacceptable to Jonah that her father would go along with such a bullshit deal.

Before he could think through the consequences, Jonah balled his hand into a fist and shot out to connect with the mayor's nose, sending the older man sprawling to the floor.

Samantha's scream filled the space seconds before the deafening crack of a gunshot scared them all out of their wits.

Jonah spun to see the smoking revolver in the hands of the judge. The warning shot had gone through the ceiling, but the barrel of the gun was now pointed squarely at Jonah's chest. It was clear the judge was done talking.

It was a good thing Jonah had brought his own backup as well. As if they'd choreographed the entire scene, the same local news crew who the judge had hired to go to Denver to get the dirt on Jonah came through the French doors to the great room.

He'd had the foresight to know that having witnesses to his little reunion with the Stone men might be a good idea. For awhile, he wasn't sure it would pan out, but by the looks of the cameraman and reporter, they'd heard the entire saga.

"It's over now, Judge. Put the gun down," he warned.

"Like hell. If I'm going down, you're going down with me," the judge rationalized.

The sound of the gun being cocked filled the otherwise quiet room. Jonah caught the flash of movement in his peripheral view just in time to see Sam moving as if to put herself between the gun and Jonah. "Sami, stay back, baby!" Relief flooded him when she obeyed.

He looked back at her uncle, nervously. He could see the man had gone mad. It was there in his eyes. He was going to pull the trigger.

Samantha cried out to her uncle. "Stop it! Enough! I love him!" When her uncle's trembling finger started to pull the trigger, she added, "He's going to be the father of my baby!"

Her words stunned the entire room. Jonah froze, but her uncle didn't.

The gunshot rang out simultaneously with Jonah being tackled to the ground by a running Mayor Stone. Time stood still until Jonah felt the warm wetness spilling down his neck. He reached up, afraid he'd been shot, but finding Sam's father collapsed on him, a gunshot to the shoulder instead.

"Daddy!" Sam rushed to their side and knelt beside her father as Jonah fought to be free. Not knowing what the judge might do next, Jonah lunged forward when he was free, curling in around Sam to protect her until he heard Ryan and the reporter jumping in to disarm the judge. Out of the corner of his eye, he saw the cameraman still filming the entire encounter.

Only when the scene had been secured and the police called did Jonah relax even a little. Only then did he let Sam's words truly sink in.

He's going to be the father of my baby!

"Daddy, hold on. We called an ambulance," she tried to reassure her parent as she knelt beside him, pressing a cloth towel against his wound to stem the bleeding.

Jonah knelt on the other side of Samantha's father and took over holding the towel for Sam who was trembling with emotion. Samantha leaned in to hug her father.

Jonah had never really known his own father. All of his memories were nightmares, really. Snippets of abuse he'd tried to block out. But he'd known the love of his mother. She'd been gone over four years now and there wasn't a day he didn't think about her. Miss her.

The look of love on Mayor Stone's face as he held his daughter was the first time he'd witnessed parental love and sacrifice since he'd lost his mom. The man had loved his daughter so much, that he'd risked his life to save the man she loved. For whatever other bullshit sins he'd committed in his life, in that one moment, Jonah had no doubts that while her uncle was a greedy sonofabitch, at least her father had done what he did out of his own sick sense of love.

"I'm sorry. I was wrong." Her father hugged Samantha, but he spoke to Jonah, his words shaky with emotion. "Whatever happens, I'm begging you, please take care of her."

"I will. I swear it," Jonah pledged. "I always would have."

The man lying on the ground nodded. "I see that now. You were just a kid then, but... you scared me. I didn't want you to take her away from me. She's all I have."

He'd dreamed of seeing this man rot in a jail for the rest of his days, but as he listened to Sami crying between them, Jonah couldn't rouse his blinding anger. While he couldn't forgive him, he felt pity for the broken man.

When Samantha turned towards him with love in her eyes, nothing else mattered. Well almost nothing else.

He got up the nerve to ask her, "Did you mean what I think you meant?"

Seconds dragged like minutes as he held his breath for her answer. Her shy smile betrayed how nervous she was. "I went to get birth control pills at the campus clinic yesterday. They did a routine pregnancy test first before they'd give me a prescription." Samantha paused. "Please, tell me you aren't angry."

Angry? How the fuck could he be angry? A plethora of emotions flooded him, but anger wasn't one of them.

He was going to be a father. More importantly, Samantha was going to be a mother.

That meant only one thing.

"Be my wife, Sami. Today."

"Jonah…"

The ambulance had finally arrived. The room was filling up with police and other support personnel. It was a crazy place to propose. He held his breath waiting for her answer.

He was surprised to get support from the bleeding man on the floor. "Say yes, Samantha. You've loved him since you were eight years old. No one else will ever make you happy like he does. I see that now. Hurry and then get as far away from here as you can."

She looked down at her father as the paramedics moved in to take over his care. Jonah could see the older man was pale from the blood loss, but he remained alert, determined to ensure he had things settled for his daughter.

Jonah cleared his throat before speaking up. "Mr. Stone, if you would be so kind, sir, as to give us your blessing. I'd like the honor of marrying your daughter."

Her father had tears in his eyes as he acknowledged the courtesy Jonah had just paid him. A courtesy he surely didn't deserve.

"Take care of her," the older man begged softly.

"I will. I promise. That asshole over there can rot in hell." Jonah motioned towards the judge who was being interviewed by the Sheriff's Deputy who'd arrived on the scene. Jonah looked back down at her father before finishing his promise. "But, Samantha loves you. So if it's all the same to you, we'll be keeping in touch."

Sam was overwhelmed. She leaned over her father to hug Jonah with all her might.

The pale man on the floor was visibly shaking, whether from blood loss or emotion wasn't clear. His voice was fading as he answered Jonah. "I don't deserve that."

Jonah acknowledged, "Maybe you do, maybe you don't. I won't lie. I look forward to seeing your brother rot in prison for the rest of his life, but... well let's you and I play it by ear."

Samantha pulled out of their hug, looking back and forth between the two men in her life. He could see confusion. She was overwhelmed. She was in shock.

The EMT who'd been trying to get close enough to the gunshot victim on the floor finally spoke up. "I really need to get in here, Mr. Carter."

Jonah pushed to his feet, pulling Samantha away from her father with him to let him get the medical attention he needed.

EPILOGUE

"*J*onah, please. No more."

Samantha begged, even though she knew it wouldn't do any good. By her estimation, she was only one month along in her pregnancy. At the current trajectory, she would weigh two hundred pounds by the time she delivered eight months later.

"You aren't eating enough. You're eating for two, after all," her husband countered.

Her husband.

They'd gotten married six days before on Christmas Day. They'd flown into Vegas, expecting to just go to the first chapel they came to, but had been met by Frank at the airport instead. When they saw him waiting, Jonah had worried he'd come to convince Jonah to make sure Sam signed a prenup. They'd been pleasantly surprised, instead, that he had made arrangements at the Bellagio for them to be married in the penthouse suite.

Samantha and Jonah had been blown away when they arrived at the hotel to find the room full of their closest friends who'd flown in at the last minute to witness the quickly planned yet years delayed wedding.

Of course the entire band was there after River had filled them in on all of the secrets the two men from Texas had kept from them over the years.

Megan and her boyfriend, Michael, had flown in from D.C. They had sat shell-shocked surrounded by all of the famous guests in attendance.

It had been Jaxson, Chase and Emma's arrival that had surprised Jonah and Samantha the most. The trio was supposed to be in Wisconsin with Emma's family, but had taken the time to fly west to witness their friend's nuptials. Even Spencer Cook, master of Black Light, had made it at the last minute.

The only person missing was her father. Robert Stone had still been in the hospital, but was on the mend. Her dad had a lot of legal problems in his future, but for that day, he'd at least been able to join the celebration via FaceTime.

So their ski trip to Vail had turned into their honeymoon. And Jonah, being overprotective, had forbidden Sam from skiing, sure she would hurt herself or the baby.

Samantha didn't want to tell him, but she was more than happy to stay snuggled together in their suite instead. They'd already spent more than enough time apart. Now was the time to be together. The non-stop sexcapades were awesome. The movie marathons and hours of naps were amazing. All-in-all, it was the best week of her life.

Samantha only had one complaint.

"I can't eat another bite. Please."

Her husband was determined to put more weight on her. "Just one more bite, and then you'll get your reward."

They'd played this game before. She loved her rewards.

Sam leaned in to take the last bite of the lasagna from the fork he held to her lips. As soon as she swallowed, she clapped her hands.

But instead of starting their next sexy marathon, Jonah got

serious instead, pulling a small, wrapped box from under his nearby pillow before holding it out to her.

"Jonah, I thought we agreed no more gifts. Christmas is over! It's almost the new year."

"I know, baby, but I just had to get you one more thing. Open it."

If she didn't know better, she'd swear he looked nervous. That intrigued her.

She tore the wrapping away to expose a jewelry box. She glanced up, nervously, at Jonah. What had he done? He'd already showered her with a replacement locket that was pure gold to replace the knock off one he'd given her as a kid.

Sam opened the hinged box slowly. The dancing light from the nearby fireplace caught the huge solitaire diamond just right, sending reflections around the room from the stunningly beautiful wedding set in the small box.

"Jonah! It's too much! I already have the ring you bought me in Vegas."

"Yeah, well that wasn't good enough. You deserve the best."

The solitaire was surrounded by dozens of baguettes that reflected the light like crazy. It was gorgeous, but she felt guilty accepting something so expensive when she already had a ring that was perfectly beautiful. Jonah sensed her reluctance and grinned .

"I knew you'd feel like this, you know," he gloated. Reminding her that he really did know her better than she knew herself sometimes.

"Oh really, and yet you did it anyway."

"Yep, because I have a plan."

He slipped the ring she'd worn for only six days off her finger, replacing it with the new stunningly beautiful diamond that fit her perfectly. Only then did he reach under his pillow a second time, coming out with another small box. This time he opened it and pulled out a man's wedding band that matched her set perfectly.

Their eyes met as he placed the ring into her palm and he grinned. They'd had a bit of a tiff in Vegas when Jonah had elected not to get a wedding ring. She'd thought it was because he didn't want to wear a band that would tell his rabid fans that the great Cash Carter was off the market.

"I just didn't want to spend money on a band I knew would be temporary," he confirmed for her.

Jonah held out his left hand to her. She saw him tremble just a bit as she silently held the band to his finger and slowly slid it down until it rested where it belonged.

Sam leaned down, pressing a kiss to her husband's ring finger. The lump in her throat was hard to swallow as emotions threatened to overcome her. The last month had been a whirlwind of ups and downs. Sometimes she had to pinch herself to believe Jonah was really there with her.

When she looked up into his eyes, she saw him fighting back his emotions as well.

"You know what this means, don't you?" she prompted.

"Naw, what?" His eyes were so intense.

"I went to your concert looking for closure." She paused, his eyes widened at the mention of the night they'd been reunited. He'd apologized a hundred times for losing control that night. She knew he still carried guilt; guilt she was determined to help him exorcize.

Samantha grinned, leaning in for a quick kiss before teasing him. "You know what this means, don't you? It means we've sealed our fates together. You're stuck with me forever now."

She loved his sexy grin. "I hate to tell you, baby, but that happened a long time ago. We just took a little detour there for a few years is all."

"Well, no more detours. Not unless we're taking them together."

Jonah reached out and pulled her into his lap as he answered seriously. "I think this whole parenthood thing is going to be a bit of a detour, don't you?" Like he'd done many times since finding out the news that he was going to be a daddy, Jonah's hand covered her flat stomach, trying to make an invisible connection to his tiny baby.

Sam leaned back until she could see those intense eyes she loved so much. "I wouldn't call having a baby a detour. It feels more like we're moving in the fast lane now."

Her words spurred him on. His hand inched lower, moving to cup her wet sex as he leaned in to latch his mouth onto her neck. She was always wet for him these days. How could she not be?

He eventually came up for air, promising her breathlessly, "I can't wait to show you how awesome I drive in the fast lane."

The End.

Did you enjoy Jonah and Samantha's story? It doesn't end here. Coming in January 2017, the next full-length book in the **Black Light** series will be released by the uber talented Jennifer Bene. Please enjoy the following excerpt from book two in the series: **Black Light: Exposed**.

* * *

She swore she'd do anything for a story.
He's the perfect temptation.
Will she lose her chance at love to achieve her dreams?

Maddie had been at the club for over an hour, but every time she wandered towards the rear hallway the security guard at the backstage curtain was standing with his arms crossed like a formidable wall.

Damn him.

Curving her path as if she'd meant to, she headed into the bathroom and dropped onto the little love seat in the lounge area, staring at the door that separated her from her mop of destiny. Here she was well-rested, in her sexiest little black dress, her nicest heels, with her hair and make-up done... and it looked like tonight was going to be another bust.

No way she had enough money in all of her accounts combined to bribe the asshole into letting her past.

As she glared through the wall at her nemesis, a group of loud-mouthed Georgetown co-eds burst into the bathroom from the dance floor entrance, letting in the pounding beat of the music for a moment before it was muffled again as the door closed.

They all went into stalls, still talking to each other.

"Can you believe Amanda showed up?"

"And with Riley? I mean, fuck *off*, right?"

"You know she only came with Riley because she was hoping to piss off Clarissa."

"Well, I already texted Clarissa and she said she doesn't give a shit. Riley cheated on her, and she's already going out with Mark on Tuesday."

"Why didn't she come out tonight? It would have been perfect for her to snag some hottie and dance with him right in front of fake-ass Amanda."

Maddie groaned and pulled out her phone to check the time. Barely after eleven, which meant if she couldn't get back to the mop and into that secret door she'd be listening to idiots like this all night. Laughter echoed off the tile as toilets flushed and several of the girls gathered together at the mirror to wash their hands and check their make-up.

"Natalie! Are you coming or not?"

"One second!"

"Okay, we'll be on the dance floor." The larger group of girls left and then the last girl wandered out of her stall to wash her hands. Maddie was deep in thought as she heard the clicking of heels coming towards her, and that was when she saw the one called Natalie tugging at the hot pink crop-top as she stared at herself in one of the floor-length mirrors in the sitting area. She looked like every other college girl that was trying too hard and would probably end up puking in one of these stalls before the end of the night. One too many shots later.

And *that* gave Maddie an idea.

"Hey, Natalie, right?"

Her voice made the girl jump, and she looked at Maddie a little nervously. "Uh, yeah... why?"

"I wanted to know if you could do me a favor?"

"Like what?" The girl looked even more freaked out as Maddie dug in her tiny purse for the twenty bucks she had tucked inside.

"It's not a big deal, I just need you to distract someone for me." She held up the twenty and the girl looked slightly less nervous.

"What exactly do you want me to do?"

A few minutes later she had her arm around Natalie's shoulders as they stepped into the back hallway. The girl suddenly lurched to the side and Maddie almost fell trying to hold onto her.

"I think I'm going to be sick," Natalie moaned in fake agony, bending at the waist to brace one hand on the wall.

"You'll be okay! We just need to get you some water!" Maddie raised her voice, glancing through her hair to see if the security guy had budged.

No such luck. Come on Natalie, play it up.

"No, I'm totally going to throw up." Some Oscar-worthy gagging noises came from the girl, and the security guy took a few steps forward.

Just a little more. "Oh shit! No, just stand up. You'll feel better if you stand up!" Pretending to try and lean the girl back up only brought an even more dramatic round of fake moaning and pre-vomit noises.

"HEY!" Security guy finally walked towards them. "Go back in the bathroom, do *not* throw up back here!"

"I can't *move*, I'll be sick if I move!" Natalie was playing her part beyond perfection, probably based on experience, while Maddie played the panicked friend.

"Shit, shit, I'll get you some water, and I'll grab Tiffany! Just wait!" Stepping away from Natalie, the girl started to slide to her knees, the fake retching increasing in volume. Security guy tried to grab her arm and lift her as Maddie took a few steps back, but Natalie just shouted that she was going to be sick.

"I've got a code four in the back hall by the women's room." He was speaking into something on his shirt, and he glanced over at her as she moved towards the doorway back to Runway's dance floor, but as soon as he turned to face Natalie's groaning form again she ran and darted under the curtain. With her heart pounding in her ears, Maddie steadied the fabric and then stepped away so he wouldn't see her heels under the edge.

She could still hear the soap opera style acting on the other side of the curtain, but the rush in her own veins was more powerful. It took a moment for her eyes to adjust to the dim lighting in the backstage space, but then she saw the door to the small closet to her right ajar. Success! She'd made it to the mop.

Thank you, Natalie.

Maddie couldn't stifle her smile as she wrapped her hand around it and pulled the mop towards her just like the security guy had. There was a distinct click of some kind of mechanism underneath it. Pushing it forward she felt another click, and with a slight movement to the left she heard the snap of a lock as the edges of a door were revealed.

Bathed in pale purple light.

She stepped inside fast, pulling the door closed behind her so he wouldn't see it open if he returned. It was a stairwell, brightly lit in a pale purple glow from recessed lighting in the ceiling that led all the way down. Swallowing, Maddie walked down carefully, trying to get a peek of what awaited, but there was only another door.

"This is it," she whispered to herself, grabbing the handle. Preparing herself for whatever lay beyond she pushed it open and almost tripped as she stumbled into a large room. There were small lockers lining one wall from floor to ceiling, and another heavily muscled security guy sitting behind a tall desk.

Oh. Fuck.

Smiling with that *I'm-supposed-to-be-here* confidence, Maddie walked forward. The guy glanced up at her and arched an eyebrow. "Member or guest?"

"Guest," she answered smoothly, but inside new questions were firing to life.

"Of?"

"Hmm?" She asked as she fiddled with her purse to pull out her phone, trying to buy time.

"Whose guest are you?"

Shit, shit, shit. Her eyes roamed over the room, trying to memorize every inch of it, but there wasn't much to see. There was a glass window on the left wall, just beyond some more lockers, that looked like a ticket window for a movie theater – and then there was yet another door. On the right wall was another door tucked by some lockers. The whole room seemed to glow with the same pale purple light of the stairwell, but there was nothing helpful. How the fuck was she supposed to get past this guy?

"Miss?"

The twin cameras aimed at her from the corners of the ceiling only made her heart pound harder as she struggled to think of an answer. There was so much security, whatever they were hiding underneath Runway *had* to be something huge. She had to get inside, had to come up with something that would make the guy let her through that door. He was looking agitated, her brain was whirling with possibilities, and then the stupidest possible response fell out of her mouth, "Jaxson."

"Mr. Davidson invited you." The blatant doubt in the man's voice made a chill rush down her spine, but she flashed her brightest smile and nodded.

"Of course."

"What's your name?" Security guy lifted a tablet and started tapping away at it, and then she heard the door behind her open and shut.

Oh please don't be the other security –

"Evening, Daniel." The silken voice was most definitely not the security guy from outside, this was someone *much* higher on the income scale. As she turned to look at him Maddie had to swallow hard, because this guy was incredibly good looking. He had the aristocratic smile and tailored suit of someone that came from money, and his warm brown hair was trimmed to perfection.

"It's Danny, Mr. Hathaway, and good evening." Desk security guy, Danny, gave a brief smile, momentarily distracted from her trespass. "Get lost? You don't usually come in from Runway."

There's another entrance to this place? As she made a mental note of Mr. Sexy's last name, the man laughed warmly and gave her a once-over that sent a thrum of heat across her skin. "I had the urge to people watch for a bit tonight, my coat is at the front. Now who's this?"

"Madeline." She answered before Danny Security could speak and moved over to him, only to realize he towered over her by at least six inches. With a kind of old world elegance, he took her hand and leaned down to kiss her knuckles.

"I'm Thomas, and I'm very glad to meet you, Madeline." His voice did something funny to her inside, and she couldn't tell if it was the slight growl he seemed to add to her name, or if it was the intensity of his hazel eyes. Either way for a brief moment the rest of the room seemed to fall away – that is, until security asshole interrupted them again.

"She says she's a guest, but I don't have a Madeline on the list."

There was a spark of something behind Thomas' gaze when he glanced back at her. "Why do you want to go inside?"

With a delicate shrug, she decided to play flirtatiously coy, which was not difficult as gorgeous as he was in his dark gray suit and pale blue button-down looking like he might be one of Jaxson Davidson's old modeling friends. "Curiosity."

"Just curious, or do you want to play?" His lips ticked up at the edge, a slight smile teasing his mouth, and she couldn't help but grin back.

Play? Holy shit, could it be illegal gambling? Jackpot!

"Oh, I definitely want to play, Thomas." Keeping the flirty confidence in her voice, she reveled in the brief flash of desire on his face.

He laughed, squeezing her hand before he released it to pull his wallet and phone out of his pocket. "Are you planning to play with someone else, or are you looking to have someone play with you?"

"Are you offering?"

For a moment Maddie thought he was going to back down, or that she'd overstepped, and then she'd have no hope of getting inside, but then he shrugged. "I don't have any other plans tonight, so I guess I am."

"She's not on the list, Mr. Hathaway," Daniel 'Danny' the security asshole chimed in and she wanted to throw something at him.

"That's fine, I'll have her as my guest for the night." Thomas walked the few steps over to the glass partition in the wall and pressed a button that resembled a doorbell beside it.

"Of course, Mr. Hathaway." The security guy gave her a long look, but she ignored him and stepped up beside her tall, gorgeous savior.

A young woman approached on the other side of the glass and slid the window aside. "Good evening, are you a member?"

"Yes," Thomas replied and opened his wallet.

Maddie couldn't stop smiling, because not only had she *actually* discovered a secret within Runway, she had *also* managed to get passage inside. The headline floated behind her eyes: *Illegal Gambling beneath Runway.* Which of the DC elite would she find caught in the act? The reporter inside her was positively salivating, but as a thank you to her white knight she'd leave him out of the article she'd write – as soon as she found out who exactly Thomas Hathaway was anyway. Trust fund aristo? Politician? Lobbyist?

He handed over a plain white card, and for a moment nothing was visible on it, and then the lighting in the room changed. All of the normal lights went out, and the purple glow was all that was left, revealing a logo and text on the card.

No way.

'BLACK LIGHT' was written in bold, all caps across the middle of the card, and underneath that was smaller text which simply showed 'Member ID' and then a series of numbers that she couldn't memorize before the lights came back to the normal pale purple. A combination of the black lights tucked around the room with the recessed lighting.

The girl tapped away at the tablet in front of her, and she

smiled as she returned the card to him. "Mr. Hathaway, so nice to have you back. I see you have a guest this evening?"

"I do, this is Madeline…"

"O'Neill," she filled in and blushed when she heard his quiet laugh.

"A beautiful name for a beautiful girl." He winked at her and then turned back to the woman inside the window. "A one-night guest pass, please."

"Of course." The girl gathered some pages together and attached them to a clipboard before offering them with a pen. "Madeline, please fill this out while I process the payment."

"Right." She took it and stared down at the dense legal speak, swallowing as she recognized what seemed to be a pretty serious non-disclosure agreement. The Post would surely defend her if they took the story. That's what they did when reporters exposed illegal activities, right?

"You'll just initial each page and sign the last one. Can I have your ID?" The woman was still looking at her, and now Thomas was too. Fumbling with the clasp on her little purse she tried to juggle the pen and clipboard, but he reached over and took them from her with a slight smirk.

"Sorry," she whispered as she pulled out her license.

"No need to apologize, beautiful."

The blush further heated her cheeks as she passed the woman her ID, but Thomas just smiled wider as he returned the clipboard to her waiting hands. She'd barely glanced down to start reading it when the woman spoke, "That's one-hundred and fifty for the pass, Mr. Hathaway."

"Sure." He didn't even bat an eye, but Maddie almost choked on her next breath of air.

Was that the buy-in for the gambling? Shit, that's a lot.

Quickly, she initialed the three pages and then signed the last one, clapping the pen on top to slide it back across the short counter. Thomas signed his receipt and then the woman handed everything back to them. "Alright, Madeline I'll just need to give you a stamp."

Maddie offered her left hand and the woman turned it over and pressed the stamp onto her wrist, where it was almost invisible to the eye. The barest shimmer of it showed, even more black light ink.

This place is bordering ridiculous with their security.

"Danny, can you open locker thirty-four?"

"Got it," the security guy replied to the girl and she heard the metallic clunk of it popping open.

"Please remember, there is no technology allowed inside. This includes phones, wearable devices, recording devices, and anything mechanical that is not medical in nature."

Guess they were serious about stopping cheating, which meant there had to be some major money being exchanged behind that door.

Ka-ching, ka-ching.

"Thank you." Thomas nodded before turning that intense gaze on her again as he tucked his wallet away and pulled out his phone. "So, we're sharing a locker since you're my guest, but I want to make it clear that if you want to leave all you have to do is tell me. I'll bring you back out here to get your things immediately. Alright?"

"That works for me!" She followed him over to the locker that had its door ajar, and pulled her phone out of her purse. Thomas had already laid his phone inside and was removing an Apple watch while he looked her up and down.

"We'll talk more once we're inside and have a seat, but I just don't want you to feel like you owe me anything. I bought the guest pass because I want to get to know you better, and while I'd love to play with you, it's not an obligation."

Maddie rolled her eyes before she thought about it. "I promise, I'm fine."

Did this guy think she'd never played poker before? Did she really look that sheltered?

Thomas laughed low as his eyes roamed slowly over her curves. "Wonderful. No more technology under that nice dress?"

"No. Why, do you want to check?" Looking up at him she knew her cheeks were burning bright from the situation, the flirtation, and the fact that her offer wasn't an innocent one. He was hot, and it had been way too long since she'd even had a date, if he wanted to pat her down she'd let him in a heartbeat.

"Maybe in a bit." He answered softly and then offered her his hand and she took it, the next door popping open as they approached. There was low, wordless music coming from the room beyond, with soft, warm lighting – and then Thomas pulled the door wide and Maddie realized the error she'd made.

It was most definitely, unequivocally *not* gambling hiding underneath Runway.

What the fuck had she just gotten herself into?

Black Light: Exposed, Coming January 2017

But wait! There's more!

Black Light: Valentine Roulette will be released February 10th, 2017. Six award winning authors will join Jennifer Bene and me to bring you an epic boxed set filled with eight naughty Valentine stories set in Black Light. Check out this line-up!

USA Today Bestselling Author, Maren Smith
USA Today Bestselling Author, Renee Rose
USA Today Bestselling Author, Lee Savino
Amazon Bestselling Author, Jennifer Bene
Amazon Bestselling Author, Addison Cain
Amazon Bestselling Author, Sophie Kisker
Amazon Bestselling Author, Measha Stone
And yours truly, Livia Grant

ABOUT THE AUTHOR

USA Today bestselling author Livia Grant lives in Chicago with her husband and two sons... one a teenager, the other a furry rescue dog named Max. She is blessed to have traveled extensively and as much as she loves to visit places around the globe, the Midwest and its changing seasons will always be home. Livia started writing when she felt like she finally had the life experience to write a riveting story that she hopes her readers won't be able to put down. Livia's fans appreciate her deep character driven plots, often rooted in an ensemble cast where the friendships are as important as the romance... well, almost. She writes one hell of an erotic romance.

* * *

Connect with Livia!

www.liviagrant.com
lb.grant@yahoo.com

Passion Series Books 1 - 3

Twist

The More the Merrier Two

A Lovely Meal

Sting of Lust

Hero to Obey

Stand Alone Books

Blessed Betrayal

Don't miss Livia's next book!

Sign-up for Livia's Newsletter

Follow Livia on Amazon

Follow Livia on BookBub

THANK YOU FROM LIVIA

Like most authors, I love to hear from my readers. The art of writing can be a lonely activity at times. Authors sit alone, pouring our hearts into our stories, hoping readers will connect with our words and fall in love with our characters. It's easy to get discouraged at times.

And that's where you come in.

I'd sure appreciate it if you'd take a few minutes to drop me a line or better yet, leave a review to let me know what you thought of the book you just finished. Reader feedback, good and bad, is what helps me continue to grow stronger as an author.

Happy reading!

Livia

Printed in Great Britain
by Amazon